THE JOURNALS OF SARAB AFFAN

Middle East Literature in Translation

Michael Beard *and* Adnan Haydar, *Series Editors*

Other titles in Middle East Literature in Translation

A Child from the Village
Sayyid Qutb; John Calvert and William Shepard, ed. and trans.

Disciples of Passion
Hoda Barakat; Marilyn Booth, trans.

Lebanon: Poems of Love and War
Nadia Tuéni; Christophe Ippolito, ed.; Samuel Hazo and Paul B. Kelley, trans.

Nightingales and Pleasure Gardens: Turkish Love Poems
Talat S. Halman, trans. and ed.

The Night of the First Billion: A Novel
Ghada Samman; Nancy N. Roberts, trans.

Return to Dar al-Basha: A Novel
Hassan Nasr; William Maynard Hutchins, trans.

Seasons of the Word: Selected Poems
Hilmi Yavuz; Walter G. Andrews, trans.

Sleeping in the Forest: Stories and Poems
Sait Faik; Talat S. Halman and Jayne L. Warner, ed.

Thieves in Retirement: A Novel
Hamdi Abu Golayyel; Marilyn Booth, trans.

A Time Between Ashes and Roses: Poems
Adonis; Shawkat M. Toorawa, trans.

THE JOURNALS OF
Sarab Affan

A NOVEL

Jabra Ibrahim Jabra

Translated from the Arabic by Ghassan Nasr

Syracuse University Press

First Edition 2007
07 08 09 10 11 12   6 5 4 3 2 1

Originally published in Arabic as *Yawmiyyat Sarab 'Affan:
Riwaya* (Beirut: Dar al-Adab, 1992).

The paper used in this publication meets the minimum requirements of
American National Standard for Information Sciences—Permanence of Paper
for Printed Library Materials, ANSI Z39.48–1984.∞™

For a listing of books published and distributed by Syracuse University Press,
visit our Web site at SyracuseUniversityPress.syr.edu.

ISBN-13: 978-0-8156-0883-7
ISBN-10: 0-8156-0883-7

Library of Congress Cataloging-in-Publication Data
Jabra, Jabra Ibrahim.
[Yawmiyat Sarab 'Affan. English]
The journals of Sarab Affan : a novel / Jabra Ibrahim Jabra ;
translated from the Arabic by Ghassan Nasr.—1st ed.
p. cm.—(Middle East literature in translation)
ISBN-13: 978–0–8156–0883–7 (cloth : alk. paper)
ISBN-10: 0–8156–0883–7 (cloth : alk. paper)
I. Nasr, Ghassan. II. Title.
PJ7840.A322Y3913 2007
892.7'36—dc22   2006036293

The mind is its own place, and in itself
Can make a heaven of Hell, a hell of Heaven.
. . . .
. . . Here at least
We shall be free . . .

—John Milton

Jabra Ibrahim Jabra (1920–1994), poet, novelist, translator, and literary critic, was born in Bethlehem, in what was then Palestine. He studied literature and the arts at Cambridge and Harvard. Among other works of English literature, he translated William Faulkner's novel *The Sound and the Fury* and William Shakespeare's *The Tempest* into Arabic. After moving to Baghdad, Iraq, in 1948, Jabra published several novels and short story collections, including *The Ship* and *In Search of Walid Masoud*, the latter published by Syracuse University Press. A memoir, *Princesses' Street*, was published in English in 2005.

Ghassan Nasr is a freelance literary translator, writer, and book editor. He resides with his wife Myriem in New York City.

CONTENTS

THE JOURNALS OF SARAB AFFAN

1

SARAB AFFAN

Somehow she had to be saved. The siege was tightening.

Salvation comes in many forms, and it comes, if it does, in one of several ways. To escape is one; to confront is another.

Confrontation is all that counts. When the thing confronted is defined, it may be faced head-on, and then struck.

But when it is not defined, and, like the air all around us everywhere, usually it is not, there is no other recourse but trickery, disguise, and circumvention, no other recourse but to follow the rule of "hit and run," dodge, only to hit again.

Confrontation may well require cunning, until salvation is realized, by realizing oneself against the will of the other.

Some are saved by trying to forget. There are those who drink to forget, and those who bury their heads in the sand, on purpose, to forget.

And there are some who try to forget by exploiting the senses or by giving in to love, to debauchery, to prayer even, or to Valium . . .

All these thoughts went through Randa al-Jouzy's head as she wrote, as though she were sampling items in a store before she picked out what suited her best. Lately at the office she pondered at least one thought every morning, or maybe several, or all, at the same time, and she wrote when she felt inspired.

And perhaps her writing was another way of forgetting or another form of evasion. She would sit at the typewriter and strike the keys, with no other preparation than her state of mind. When she had no more work to do and that tyrannical chaos again crowded her head, she would start pounding away, letting the words come as they might . . .

After I typed these lines, I paused, read them again, and said, "Poor Randa al-Jouzy, my other self. I burden her with my daily problems. You, Randa, are my tragic mask, my comic mask. Why haven't you turned against me yet?"

I went on typing.

From here to the farthest reaches of China, in every valley and on every mountain top, the eyes of neighbor and stranger alike explode with darkness, misery, and desire—with oppression also, and perhaps with madness, passion, and self-sacrifice.

Again I read what I had typed, and my fingers resumed their tapping. *Those running through plains, gliding among rocks, and those crammed inside noontime buses—all suffer from the same ordeal . . .*

The word "ordeal" caught my attention. Which ordeal, alas? The ordeal of being besieged, or, more precisely, of being confined, of refusing to accept one's situation and hoping for refuge in some existence where an inexplicable yet desirable freedom is to be found, whatever it may be. Freedom from immediate pressures and psychological pressures—freedom, that is, from the miserable state of the world. Freedom, whatever it may be.

My fingers resumed their tapping. *There's always a death that's deferred. In this pervasive darkness, the self stumbles in its search for that glimmer that might offer an escape to a place without people or sounds except for the sounds of cicadas on a hot day, and perhaps the sudden rush of the wind on a cold evening.*

A panorama of the countryside flashed before my eyes—terraced green slopes rolling down before vanishing into foggy depths. In the sun-drenched silence, the trees appear to have grown by some accident of nature. Loneliness prevails. Even the birds have abandoned the neglected fields, and the rocks look like mythical animals that petrified, victims of a sudden, unexpected death in the midday heat. Randa is there. She is there alone. She does not know why she is there. How did she reach this place, and where did she come from?

My fingers tapped again at the typewriter. *But before the wind blows there is the calm, and there is the wide blue sky, the shimmering silence. Has the earth become deaf? Mute? Or is nature staging a game to amuse herself until a* volcano erupts, sending shudders through the limbs of mountain and valley? Or is nature waiting for that secret waterfall to burst from the mountain peak, its waters plunging down with a tumultuous roar to the depths of a valley black with the thick green of trees?

I read what I had typed, still unable to keep up with the images that hovered above the pages out of my control. But I could hear the sound of the "secret" waterfall suddenly filling my head with sweet vertigo. I wondered, "Secret? Why secret?" Quickly I started tapping the keys again.

Ah, it is the waterfall that brought her forth among these rocks, not as a shepherdess carrying a stick and running after her wandering goats, nor as a villager in her red, blue, and yellow clothes gathering thyme and chamomile leaves—but as a modern city woman in blue jeans and a half-open denim shirt, wishing to be away from people, alone with the sounds of the waterfall, anticipating the wind that blows before sunset after basking in the sun's radiance and glitter. She embraces the radiance and glitter, gathering them in the palms of her hands and tucking them into her shirt between her breasts, feeling the warmth tingling inside her. The waterfall persists in its din until the din is all that prevails, like silence at death, a temporary death amid the continuous drone. The city is but a stone's throw away. The secret city, the naked city, the city from which she runs, but which follows her wherever she goes, the city with its congested streets and car horns screeching as though they were trying to drown the sounds of the cicadas and the waters plunging into the deep valley.

I stopped typing, pulled the page out of the typewriter, and inserted a blank one. I stared at the mute machine, a strange impulse filling my heart. Without reading what I had typed this time, I began a new paragraph.

Why do I keep clinging to all this? Why do I withdraw from myself and insist on my withdrawal, my stupor? No, I am not really withdrawing. I am merely retreating to that unknown region inside me, not knowing whether it is what makes me want to escape or whether it is the thing I seek in my escape but don't know how to reach. Perhaps I am running in circles that end where they begin and begin where they end. When work suddenly calls me back, I take off like a rocket launched toward a nebula spinning with planets and meteors of which the earth knows nothing.

I laughed at the words that came out on the page, and I typed.

What rocket, woman? And what planets and meteors, when I am among people but seem not to be of them? I hear them and don't understand them, I talk to them and they don't understand me, and moving among them is like walking endlessly in gluey mud. How then is salvation possible? Most likely there is no salvation. Are you listening, Randa?

I pulled the sheet from the typewriter and, without rereading what I had typed, put the two pages together in a plastic folder, tossed it aside, and went back to my work—three letters to which my boss had asked me to write the standard replies. He was confident in my abilities to word the proper responses, use "correct" language, and express myself well, even if most of the letters I wrote on his behalf were similar in style and content and rarely required special talent.

•   ◆   •

The next day I was by myself again at the office, still overwhelmed by the strange desire to explode in some unknown direction. I did not know what to do, so I fixed the usual cup of coffee and sat at my typewriter with the cup to my right, sipping from it and cherishing every drop. I slipped a blank page into the typewriter, and my fingers worked away at the keys.

I am here once again, for the hundredth time, or the thousandth time. The walls recede to a distance, and the room expands, but then the walls come back, creeping one toward the other, crawling and drawing near, and Randa, between them, is caught like a fish in a fisherman's net. The four deaf walls close in on her finally, almost touching her—one at her right elbow and one at her left elbow, so close that she would knock her head if she tilted it forward, or backward. But despite the small space between them, the walls are high, extremely high, rising, rising to infinity, appearing to touch the sky, which becomes a distant blue ceiling, bright and narrow, but letting in sweet breezes and lulling, seductive voices. Do the angels sing even when caged in a small sky from which there is no escape?

I stopped typing and drank the rest of my coffee. A thought that went through my mind made me laugh inside. I decided that it was time for Randa to leave, only for a while, and that I would speak, without her mask, about myself. I resumed typing.

I wonder, what is the meaning of these tempting voices? What do the angels say in their song, having folded their wings on their ethereal bodies, on their impossible dreams? Do they say that I should fall in love, maybe? And why not fall in love? But then who should I fall in love with, or who will make me cross the wilderness barefoot to see his face, hear his whispers? I shall fall in love! I shall declare to myself that I have fallen to a love whose path is unknown to me! I shall say that I am in love! But this love will distract me if it is salvation that I am looking for, or confrontation, or escape. It would be as though I were escaping from the one I love so that I might reach the one I love—another paradox whose essence and magic I will come to understand. Am I the woman trapped between these four walls reaching up to the clouds, as though, being high and lofty, they would make up for my confinement and defeat? So be it! I will sample all the men I know, even those I know by face and name only, to find, perhaps, the one who will carry me beyond these smooth, towering walls to God's promised heaven. . . . But oh! No! No! What kind of movie is this that spins out of my control, hurling all these faces at me! I know all these faces one by one, but none tempts me. I am not tempted by the wearisomely familiar. I want to see a face I have never known, hear a voice that will send a shiver through my body at the very first utterance. I must invent him! I must create from nothingness the man I love. But only nothingness can come from nothingness, unless God wills otherwise. And who am I to play God?

I stopped pounding out the letters as I reached the bottom of the page. I pulled it out, fed another one in, and before the images could slip away like water through my fingers, I went on typing.

Indeed, who am I? Let's see.

Randa, my dear, allow me to remove the mask once more, if only for a while.

I am a young woman, a woman, who has turned twenty-six, spent four years pursuing a college education, who now finds her degree useless. She has a job working at a company that in no way relates to her interests. And what does all this have to do with the question of my identity? Nothing.

Should I say that my identity is in my name? My name is Sarab Affan. Then what? My identity is that I sometimes want to explode into shrapnel because I can no longer bear the kind of life I live.

My identity is that my father loves me and is afraid of me and for me but does not understand me. An ordinary matter no doubt. So I am just like other women my age, but I know that I am different from them and that my identity is in my difference. Sometimes I am honest to the point of rudeness, innocent to the point of naïveté, and sometimes I demand my shares of the spiritual and material worlds with a violence that verges on insanity. My imaginings seem so far beyond my reach, and yet they are lodged inside me, inflicting suffering on my spirit and body until I lose control over both, sometimes. Otherwise, why wasn't I satisfied with Suhail al-Radi as a "sweetheart" during my school days, and why did I break my engagement with my cousin Wissam Affan after that? By now, wouldn't I have had a child crawling about my feet?

I felt that the words could not keep up with the tumult inside my head and chest. The storm is so powerful that it breaks away altogether from the realm of time. Time is necessary for putting the storm into words, but it also limits me to a superficial understanding of the storm. The problem, perhaps, does not lie in time—measured in seconds and minutes—but in converting a mental absolute—as free-flowing as air or as scattered as flying shrapnel—converting it to words, to letters, to an aural and visual utterance that falls short of matching the absolute in its free flow. It is the age-old paradox, I said to myself, and I will have to make do with whatever I can express with words that, no matter how fast I type, will always remain hostage to time. . . . It's okay, let me get back.

I fed another page into the typewriter after placing the previous one inside the plastic folder.

Therefore help me, oh Goddess of Imagination. Torture me as you wish, but grant me what we both desire by making us forget or by hurling us into the flames of temptation that destroys and rebuilds, which until now has always deceived me. Sarab Affan, from this day, from this moment on, is in love, madly in love. She will also be a courageous fighter for her homeland, for freedom. She will love humanity, heal the wounds of people everywhere. But Sarab the honest, innocent, quarrelsome, loud in demanding her share of life in the here and now—Sarab is in love, passionately in love, knowing full well that love, once it takes possession of a woman, overcomes all barriers, demolishes every barri-

cade, acknowledges no obstacle or limitation. Sarab will not settle for a lesser kind of love. It is all or nothing.

I paused and repeated to myself, "It is all or nothing." I let out the familiar self-deriding laugh, as the words played on my lips: "From everything, nothing! A problem! And from nothing, everything! Another problem!" I will follow this thought to where the words might take me.

I had to answer the phone when it rang. Two auditors came in, and I received them with the proper formalities. I went into my boss's office. He was in a meeting with one of his partners. I handed him the parcel of incoming mail, which he opened and read, scribbling in the margins. He signed some documents for me to send off. Morning and afternoon flew by. When I left the office at the end of the day and entered the narrow elevator, carrying all the typed pages in my briefcase, I felt lighter than usual, so light that I was afraid the elevator would shoot up like an arrow and slam into the roof of the building! I made sure that I had pressed the ground-floor button, pressing it again before the door shut. I descended slowly, feeling the tremors of the old, undependable elevator.

I stepped out into the ground-floor shopping-mall area of the large building. Shoes, bags, women's and men's clothing attracting all sorts of people filled the storefronts on all sides of the vast indoor promenade. There were stores that sold music tapes, electrical appliances, and refrigerators. Squeezed in the middle was Abu Hatim's bookstore, which sold more stationery, notebooks, and pens than it did books. I went in to buy a magazine or two, and before leaving I glanced at the few book racks crammed with the same volumes I saw every time I came to the store, pressed together and rotting.

Not a single book would have interested me had Abu Hatim not pointed out copies of a new novel in a small stack on the desk in front of him. "Have you read this new novel by Nael Imran?" He held out a copy of *Entering the Mirrors*.

"Nael Imran? Ah, yes, Nael Imran. I have some of his novels. I didn't know he had a new one out."

"It came in this morning," said Abu Hatim.

I grabbed the book, checked the bottom of its back cover for the price, took money out of my handbag, and paid him.

As soon as I was out on the street, I felt the urge to rush to my car in the nearby parking garage. I settled into the car seat and sped away as though late for an appointment when actually I was only driving back home from work, as I did every day around two o'clock in the afternoon. I pressed my hands impatiently against the steering wheel, and my impatience only got worse every time I had to stop at a red light.

The novel by Nael Imran lay on top of the two magazines on the seat next to me. I glanced at its title, *Entering the Mirrors,* and suddenly realized that it had been the reason for my inexplicable haste and nervousness. I wanted to get home quickly and read it. I felt it contained some very important message, for me personally.

Entering the mirrors. Could this be another way to the salvation I am so concerned about and for which even my typewriter reprimands me? Entering the mirrors, like our friend Alice did in Wonderland? But here she enters into not one but many mirrors. And who will she find among the wonders inside them? Nael Imran, no doubt! An old trick, my dear author. Even your title is not entirely original. You are prodding me to walk into the mirrors, into your mirrors, your reflections, the wonders of your illusions. But no, not so easily. My dear Nael Imran, we live in the age of ordeals. We enter one inferno only to leave it for another. Sarab might be led into temptation by the glowing promises of an unknown delight, but she'd be quick to catch on to the deception and resist being tempted. Nael Imran, you are trying to deceive me with the title of your book, perhaps because you imagine that Sarab Affan has decided to become the grandest lover of all, in this age of ordeals. Anyway, what does all this have to do with you? No, I will not go faster than the usual sixty or seventy kilometers per hour! A hundred? A hundred and twenty? This is sheer madness!

But when I did slow down, I don't think I slowed down much.

I got back home before my sister and father. I greeted my mother and went straight to my bedroom and tossed down the two magazines, the purse, and my book. I threw off my clothes, hurried to the bathroom, and stood naked under the shower. But the water was not cold enough.

The water tank up on the roof was more like a hot water tank at that time of day when the temperature was at its highest. Still, it refreshed me with its powerful spray. I remembered the secret waterfall plunging down from the rocky heights into the heart of the deep valley, and I felt an inner joy. How soothing is the water! Yes, the water! Nael Imran, maker of illusions, instead of your mirrors, try walking into the waterfalls, the flooding rivers, the seas! Sarab Affan, you are the greatest maker of illusions. Your death will be by drowning—in the rising, swelling depths. . . . I will write these words in my journals if I remember them.

I came out of the bathroom in my robe and went to the kitchen. I was starving.

"What are you cooking?" I asked my mother as I lifted the lids off the pots on the stove.

"What good fortune brings," she replied, somewhat wearily.

I laughed to cheer her up, as though that would make up for the mundane kitchen routine that she had to endure every morning, afternoon, and evening, despite all the help and effort she got from Fathiyya, who was always happy to serve the family.

"Mom, I bought a novel. You can read it when I'm done."

I filled my plate with some rice, gravy, and a small piece of meat. I was on my way to my room when my mother asked, surprised, "Why don't you eat here in the kitchen or in the dining room?"

"My room's much cooler," I answered. "You must have had the air conditioner on all day."

I shut the door to my room and sat on the edge of my bed, with the plate on a side table in front of me. Fathiyya had arranged the bedcovers the way I liked them. I held the book open on my lap and started eating and reading hastily, at the same time devouring the contents of my plate and book. I finished eating in a few minutes and stretched out comfortably on my bed. Unfortunately, it would take me much longer to finish my book, no matter how fast I read. Today I would skip my afternoon nap. I would be awake all day and maybe all night.

I heard some commotion inside the house. My father and sister Shaza had arrived. I heard my mother saying, "Sarab is in her room, sleeping."

I smiled, saying to myself, "Me, sleeping? If only you knew, Mama!" I went on reading.

Suddenly I realized that I had read seventy-two of the three hundred and twenty pages of *Entering the Mirrors*. I leaned over, pulling out a letter pad from the drawer of the small side table and a pen from my bag, and I sat in a more comfortable position by propping up two pillows behind my back. I drew my knees toward my chest to support the pad and began writing, unleashing the playful demon inside me.

He was very surprised today when I called him. I said to him, "I have much to say to you. Are you ready?" He said, "Yes, I'm ready, with all my mental faculties." I said, "That's what counts. You do know that I like you for your mental faculties." He said, "Are you making fun of me? Who would like someone for his mental faculties?" I said, "I would, though I may not be a 100 percent honest." He said, "Say, about 2 percent?" I said, "No, more than that, a little more." He said, "Okay, lady, and what else?" I said, "Your presence." He said, "My presence? On the phone?" I said, "On the pages of the book." He said, "Which book?"

"Any of your books."

"You mean my gripping presence! I understand."

"Your physical presence."

"You're dangerous! Do I know you?"

"I don't think you do."

"Do you know me?"

"I know you well, very well."

"Terrific. As for me, I only know myself well, leave 'very' out of it."

"That's because you don't go back and read what you write."

"Where would I find the time? Time is the least thing I have."

"Never mind. I'll fill you in on everything."

"God forbid!"

"Do you know I'm inside the mirrors?"

"God help you."

"And you're in there, with me."

"I couldn't be any happier!"

"You ought to be!"

"I will be happy for a while, until you leave."

"I'll be leaving tonight or tomorrow."

"You're fooling yourself!"

"No, I will."

"Let me know when you do. You've walked into a trap without knowing it."

"A trap I've been looking for, and found?"

"Found, stumbled on, fell into."

"Or did it find me, stumble on me, fall into me?"

"Does the cage look for the bird?"

"It depends who's the cage and who's the bird."

"That is clear, young lady."

"Now you're the one fooling yourself. You really think you're the cage?"

"Of course, and you the bird."

"Laugh as you wish, until you learn the real truth."

"Is there something I should know?"

"Many things, but first things first."

"Yes ma'am, I'm listening."

"It seems that for personal, complicated reasons, difficult to explain now . . ."

"Yes?"

"I've decided . . ."

"Yes . . ."

"Ah . . ."

"What have you decided?"

I almost told him of my decision to become the grandest of all lovers, but I didn't dare push my game that far, so I said, "I've decided to tell you, master of the mirrors, that, although I know you very well, I'd like to know you better still."

"Why bother?"

"For intellectual, mental reasons . . ."

"You mean psychological, say it frankly."

"To some extent."

"And what next?"

"Other truths."

"Then this will be enough, for now."

At that point I felt that I had perhaps succeeded in my plan. He didn't seem to be resisting. He was following my lead, and it was up to me to keep him compliant. He had without a doubt succumbed to a kind of playfulness and, as far as he knew, was taking part in a game with a mystery woman. I would have to be cautious of any slip that might distract me, or him. I would have to remain extremely ambiguous and anonymous, or my game might turn into cheap flirtation, which I didn't want, and I believed he wouldn't either. "Thank God you're not asking me to explain more," I said.

"The results are what counts, the actions."

"Actions? What actions?"

His response surprised me. "Isn't all this a prelude to some kind of drama?"

"If we have to make this some kind of drama, then it might as well be a comedy," I said, feigning soft laughter.

"Meaning, there's no death in it for anyone? No killing, no suicide? None of the fury that annihilates the world?"

"No, no, nothing of that sort, Mr. Nael. Perhaps some provocation, some innocent teasing, some poking fun at the world, despite all its cruelty and harshness."

"Young lady, don't disappoint me. Tragedy and I are like twins or, as they used to say, like betting horses."

"That's why you should lighten up a bit. You're carrying the world on your shoulders and running with it. What are you trying to do, shatter the mirrors?"

At this Nael Imran laughed, a real laugh for the first time. I heard the chuckle in his throat, and I wished I could hold his face in my palms and quiet him by pressing my lips against his, and maybe he would infect me with his laughter. . . . Sarab Affan! Be careful, or you will bring about what he himself predicted. You'll become the bird insisting on being caged, surrendering its right to fly. Not so fast! Beware! You cage him first. Anyway, who really needs to lighten up? He or I? He or I?

♦　　♦　　♦

I stopped writing, arranged the five or six typed pages, read them again, and wondered: if I had actually called this writer, would we have had such a conversation? Wouldn't he have answered tersely, apologized for having to cut the conversation short, or snapped at me and hung up? Or would his wife—if he had one—have answered the phone and wanted to know who was calling and what "Madame" needed exactly from Mr. Nael Imran? And she would have asked, "Does he know you? Did he ask you to call him? How did you get his phone number?" And so forth, and so forth.

I smiled as a devilish thought entered my mind. Should I try? Should I call him and see what happens? Would I find his number listed?

I shook my head, dismissing the thought. I threw the pages on the floor, put the two pillows back in place and lay down flat on my bed, numb and exhausted. In less than two minutes, I sank into a sweet, deep slumber.

◆　　◆　　◆

A flood of incoming mail kept me busy the next day at the office. I had to translate some letters for my boss, who admitted his poor knowledge of English. He always compared my translations to the foreign text, hoping to learn the meaning of a new word or business term. *Entering the Mirrors* was on my desk next to the cup of coffee, and I was now waiting for the first opportunity to finish reading it as soon as my boss would leave on other business. It was already past twelve o'clock when I finished going through the mail and my boss had left. As soon as I opened the book to where I had left off the night before and read two or three lines, I felt that sweet, flowing sensation in my fingers again and ran to my typewriter before the feeling could leave me. I inserted a blank sheet and ran my fingers aimlessly over the keys.

This is foolish and insane, I know.

My father couldn't believe I came into this world alive because of the miscarriages my mother had had before I was born. That day he said, "Call her Sarab, 'Illusion,' because as soon as I arrive at the hospital ward, I'll find out that I've been deceived again."

He wasn't deceived that day, but he kept fearing that what he'd seen would one day turn out to be another hoax. The day I turned twenty—and by that time he had also been blessed with another daughter, my sister Shaza, born four years after me—he said, "Why didn't I give you a name more worthy of you? May, for example, or Rayya,[1] because you quench my thirst every day, my dear, and yet you are Sarab!" I said to him, "Isn't this the miracle you wished for?" He shook his head laughing, "Yes, contrary to what most people would wish for!" I didn't understand what he meant at the time. Perhaps he did not mean anything in particular, but later I came to understand much of what he had not—or could not have—expressed.

Why did I have to come into this world to quench someone else's thirst, even my father's? Did I really quench his thirst, as he claims? It was obvious that my father, with all his medical knowledge, was living in one world and I in another. In the last few years the divide separating us grew even wider. He no longer cared about the same things he cared about during the hard times a quarter-century ago. He hurled me into the world, a phantom, and I've been one ever since, a vision that reveals something other than itself. A tempting vision, maybe, but to whom? To my own eyes, haven't I always been a phantom, one that I keep chasing as it takes me farther and farther away, leaving me in an eternally arid wasteland? What brought me here, among mirrors that only lead to other mirrors? The illusions multiply. The lies multiply. I will become the grandest lover of all at the first chance I get. But where, in my stubborn, eternal desert, is the mighty flood into which I will throw myself?

I quickly pulled out the page, feeling that I had digressed too much, and I thought, "I am done with all these questions, so why do I keep coming back to them? I set out to play a word game with my typewriter or with my pen at home, so I'll go on with my game, and if what I'm writing is all lies, then let the lies multiply." I inserted another sheet into the typewriter as my imagination took a sharp, new turn. I went on typing.

(the continuation of what I wrote yesterday at home)

I called him this morning shortly after I arrived at the office. He sounded uneasy, suspicious of having to speak again to a woman he did not know. I was afraid he would end the conversation, so I had to sound convincing, natural, persuasive—all at the same time. "Did you sleep well after we talked yesterday?" I asked.

"Why wouldn't I?"

---

1. *May:* from Arabic *mayy,* water. *Rayya:* from Arabic *rayya,* succulent.

"Nothing I said troubled you?"

"Not at all. But I would like to know who I'm talking to."

I almost said I was Randa al-Jouzy, but I decided to keep her for a different game. "I'll tell you my first name. Sarab."

He laughed sarcastically. "Ha! Ha! Sarab! Now I've figured out the game you're playing, Miss—or should I say Mrs.?"

I said, laughing, "Miss or Mrs., it doesn't matter. What matters is that I'm real, despite my name."

"I'll need proof of that."

"In due course."

"Have you finished reading The Mirrors?"

"I'm halfway through. I must admit your trap is working."

"Ha! A phantom in a trap or, better still, the trap that catches phantoms . . ."

"Or a phantom inside the mirrors, or the phantom mirrors."

Suddenly he said, somewhat serious, "Listen. Can we get together?"

"Why not?" I said with my usual impulsiveness.

"When? Tomorrow? The day after tomorrow?"

"Why put it off? Today!"

"Today? This afternoon?"

"This morning!"

"No! You're joking."

"Of course not. Write down my address."

"No, no. These are old, familiar tricks. You'll have me waiting for you while you hide nearby with a friend, both of you dying of laughter watching a man running after a phantom. Sorry, I can't."

"Then tell me where you live, and I'll come to see you."

"This morning?"

"Yes."

"No, no way. Sorry, I can't."

"You're afraid because you're married. Right?"

I was hoping he would say, "I'm not married." But all he did was bluff, like me. "Married or not, it doesn't matter. What matters . . ." And he fell silent.

I waited, and then he said, suddenly, "What's your address and phone number?"

I gave him my work address and phone number and explained to him how *to get to the building and take the elevator to the fourth floor—if he were lucky enough to find it working—and then walk to the third door on the left, etc., etc.*

•   •   •

I stopped and read the two pages I had typed, delighting in the devilishness of a girl preparing for a plot of unknown outcome. I asked myself how likely it would be for this famous writer to come running after a phantom, to use his words. But, as a young woman trying to break out of her situation and amusing herself with innocent games, I imagined anything possible. But was anything really possible, that simply? I had to remedy the situation.

I inserted another blank page into the typewriter and continued tapping the keys.

Less than half an hour had gone by when the phone rang. "Hello."

"Miss, or Mrs., Sarab?"

"Yes. Mr. Nael?"

"You guessed?"

"Of course. I've been waiting."

"I wanted to make sure you didn't give me the wrong number."

"Are you satisfied now?"

"Yes, but I'm sorry I can't come."

"I'm sorry too. Was the timing bad for you?"

"The timing, the place, everything."

"I'm sorry, really sorry."

His tone of voice changed suddenly. "Are you . . . pretty?"

"You're embarrassing me, Mr. Nael. Would anyone say their own milk is sour?"

"Or their olive oil turbid?"

"Exactly."

"So you think, at worst, that you're pretty?"

"You'll have to find out for yourself. And anyway, who said that my looks have anything to do with this? I was hoping you would ask if I'm intelligent, cultured, or if I'm an artist, a poet, or something like that. You've really disappointed me!"

"All right, all right. I'll take my chance, but not this morning."

"This afternoon, maybe?"

"Sarab, I didn't think you'd be so persistent."

"Sorry, you're right, I do rush into things. Forget all I said. I'm going back to The Mirrors. *Bye."*

I hung up before he could say anything, and I laughed. I lit a cigarette and started smoking it with leisure. I didn't care what he thought. Before I finished my cigarette, the phone rang. I knew it had to be him.

I was right. He had fallen into my trap, and I would now watch him squirming inside it. Right away he said, "I wanted to tell you that I can usually judge people from their voices, but so far I haven't been able to do that with you."

"You mean, you don't like my voice?"

"No. I mean I didn't get to listen to it long enough."

"Would you like me to say more?"

"Yes."

"If talking yesterday, twice today, and now for the fourth time, is not enough for you, keeping in mind that all I wanted was to talk to you about your books, especially your last one, then you're probably not the kind of person I imagined you to be from your writing. Haven't you heard me long enough? Or would you like me to sing for you?"

"No, you don't need to do that. Hearing you talk is like listening to music."

"Really? You're not being sarcastic?"

"Your voice is pure song. Put me on record with this confession."

"Then I'll have to stop singing, right now. Bye."

Again, I hung up on him.

I stopped and read the pages I typed, and my fingers went right back to the keys.

(I open parentheses to make a confession. It occurs to me that what I wrote yesterday and today is nothing but a plot for a relationship that I wish would come true. And why wouldn't it, with a man like Nael Imran, the master creator of the many complex relationships between his men and women? But when he writes, he is satisfied with conveying his own hopes and dreams, or reconstructing his memories, and does not seek new forms for his writing, or even old ones. His games, and the pleasure he derives from them, are mostly intellectual. He dreams awake, weaving the possible and impossible, the probable and im-

probable, to his own liking, and he might live for a time inside the world he cre-
ates, just as he does inside his mirrors, but in the end he does not make any
friends or fall in love with a woman, nor does a killer lie in wait of him, nor does
he fulfill a dream in a foreign country, as he claims through his female narrator
in Entering the Mirrors. *I, on the other hand, am seeking something different.*
I know I'm not writing a story. I tried that more than once before. Rather, I'm
laying out a feasible plan, whether I do carry it out or not. But wouldn't it be
better to write a story and dream the dreams of storytellers, sparing myself the
uncertainties of dealing with real people? But then my writing becomes unnec-
essary, and all I'd have to do is daydream like any other girl, be normal like any
other girl, and, like any other girl, know nothing of pain or the taste of pleasure
except that which comes in passing, hardly noticed, every day, every minute.
And Sarab can go on struggling and be crushed under the weight of the present
and future pressures she has accepted for herself.

No! I will stick to my plan. I am not writing a story. I am laying out a plan,
and I will look for a way to carry it out. All I need is time and determination,
some perseverance, patience, and control over my impulses. And why shouldn't
I ask questions, like anyone in these times or, as Nael Imran says in his novel,
like anyone who sees history being shaped around him in a way he cannot keep
up with. What am I capable of knowing? What do I desire? What actions must
I take? Are there among these questions relationships I can identify and under-
stand as a young woman living in a certain society, at a certain time, under cer-
tain conditions? Knowledge—does it lead to desire? And do knowledge and
desire together lead to action? Knowledge-desire-action—is this a trinity of the
individual or of society? Does the individual "I" unite between knowledge, re-
gardless of its cost; and desire, regardless of how much pain it brings; and ac-
tion, as dangerous as it may be? Or will society be the one to organize these
relationships, making them so closely bound, and perhaps meshing them to-
gether in the end to give the impression of their oneness, while in actuality fad-
ing them into oblivion? I need only to phrase my questions in terms that apply
to society as a whole, in a language free of my own original concerns—knowl-
edge, empirical or otherwise; desire, which is the yearning for the essence in the
other; action, which is the vehicle that reveals the connection between my senses
and the rest of existence. . . . And here I close parentheses).

I became aware of myself sitting in front of the typewriter. The page hung loosely from the back of the typewriter with only some space left at its bottom. I typed a new line.

The connection between myself and the rest of existence.

I scrutinized the words. Had I stumbled upon an important discovery? I pulled out the page, put it in with the rest of the pages and placed them all in the blue plastic folder, which I shoved inside the drawer.

I reached for the business correspondence that I had gotten back from my boss, partially highlighted and with notes in the margins. I arranged the pages in a way that allowed me to focus on writing the appropriate replies in Arabic—rough drafts that my boss would look over, modify, and then return to me to put in their final form, and I would translate into English those that had to be sent to non-Arab countries.

◆　　◆　　◆

I finished reading *Entering the Mirrors* in two or three days. It left me haunted by thoughts I couldn't get rid of. I stopped writing for several days, unable to confront with words the thoughts that kept bolting past me like wild horses then disappearing in a storm of dust. Everything is dust. Everything surrounding me is dust. Everything inside me is dust. Can a single book be the cause of all this tumult inside me, of these endless whirlwinds that will not allow me to settle on meanings I can control?

One thing kept coming back, almost revealing itself and confirming its own presence, only to be swept away by the storm. It was the face of Nael Imran, his hands, or maybe his voice—words coming at me without any plan or order. Had I fallen victim to my own plan, which at first I meant only as a joke—at most a game—for myself alone?

◆　　◆　　◆

After one week I went back to the pages, and I read over my journals, the so-called scenario. "Anything is possible, anything conceivable" is what I had written. During that week, the feeling that I had just returned from seeing my friend or was about to go see him stayed with me wherever I went, like an endless dream, whether I was in the company of friends or visiting with relatives. At night I had dreams that had nothing to do with my experiences during the day. Some were frightening. I would enter underground passages ending in muddy water or would be driving up a mountain leading to another mountain leading to a valley, and then all of a sudden I would find myself in the busy markets of the city among people pushing me against a wall, pulling at my hair and snatching my bag. But during the day I thought about other things. I would enter into the mirrors and meet a man whose pictures I had seen in magazines and whose age I could not ascertain, and we would share an endless conversation, about the self, knowledge, desire, action, and perhaps about love. A conversation about being and existence. About the siege. About escape. Confrontation. Struggle. Then a return to knowledge—is knowledge empirical or mental? And desire—is it in the body, in the limbs, or is it in the heart, in the soul? And action—how does it start, and how and where does it go?

I decided to go back to my writing, but this time I would try to be more in control, letting prudence rule over my spontaneous thoughts and the events confronting me every day.

I decided that I should keep two journals. I would call one A and the other B. I thought about using the first letters of the words khayal, "imagination," and haqiqa, "reality," but because they looked too much alike I went back to A and B. The A journals would contain all that comes from the imagination, and B all my daily events worth recording.

Immediately I realized that A would contain much more and would be much more interesting—even more dangerous—than B. I should therefore avoid the trap of making them too different. Instead, I should mix the two sometimes, but with caution, or else what would be the use of differentiating one from the other in the first place? I have to avoid contriving my experiences. But would I really be able to say anything interesting about reality without resorting in part to the imagination, or produce anything in my imagination without somehow rooting it in reality? But I will not let myself be confused, having just begun. Starting is what matters.

I almost left my room to go sit with my father, whom I heard coming in at his usual time from work. As usual, my mother greeted him and talked to him about his dinner, which he usually ate sitting at the small table while watching television in the sitting room next to the large living room, with his beer, cold from the fridge and served in his special Bavarian glass—the only one he enjoyed drinking his beer from. Instead of joining him, I sat at the same white desk I'd had throughout my high school and college years, and I took out a stack of blank paper and started writing.

A:

I think about you every day. I think about you every night. And I worry about you. And sometimes I come close to crying—tears or no tears—because I don't know what lies ahead for you. And for some reason I'm afraid for you. Doubts and fears take hold of me. I watch you enduring pain and hardship, and I am the one crushed by their weight. I ask myself, while you contend with the unknown, confronting violence, hunger maybe, and exhaustion: will the love within protect you, if only a little? Will that love give you enough strength to save you when your other faculties fail you? Imagine, I was afraid that love would soften your will and lessen your strength, but with your magic you turned every emotion into a fire to rekindle your resolve and urge you forward . . .

Hastily and without reading what I had written, I slipped the last page in with the other pages and placed them inside the drawer, and I darted off to my parents while a song from the television blared all over the house. "Hi papa. Have you had dinner?" I asked.

"No, I've been waiting for you."

"Then you'll starve to death," I said laughing.

"I know. As usual, a tiny slice of cheese makes you full. I asked your mother to fry two steaks for us, with potatoes, tomatoes, and onions, a meal that starving, hard workers like us deserve, workers who don't need to worry about gaining weight. As for Shaza, we'll leave her to her moods."

"Papa, I never feel like eating at night."

"Oh come on, come on, Sarab. You can't fool your father. It's your figure you're worried about, and you'll keep worrying about it until you get married."

"And then, I'll take revenge, and keep eating, and eating . . ."

"God forbid!"

He stood up, laughing, and went to see my mother and Shaza, who were in the kitchen preparing his dinner.

I went back to my room, where I felt I still had some unfinished business waiting for me but not sure what it was. Again, I sat at the white desk, and I took out the pages with an uncontrollable nervous twitch. I began writing at the top of a new page.

B:

I think about him every day. I think about him every night. What is the meaning of all this worry? Sometimes I come close to crying—tears or no tears— because I do not know what is happening to him. And for some reason I am afraid for him. Or am I afraid of him? Fears take hold of me. I imagine him suffering, and that makes me suffer with him. I ask myself: does he know the kind of love he describes in his novels? Is there a love protecting him from within, where the secret to surviving in an age of pain lies? Or is he preoccupied with other thoughts that leave him no room for love? I hope so! I hope he will not entangle himself in any emotions, whether good or bad, with any woman, until my turn comes. I will think of him as an unfinished marble statue, and everything I've imagined about him from his writings will be the raw material that I alone will give final shape. I will set his heart beating, ignite the senses in his body, and with this I will have reversed the story of Pygmalion, who fell in love with the statue he himself chiseled.

Suddenly, I said to myself, "It's strange how similar this B of reality is to the A of imagination? So what's the use of distinguishing between both? This is all vain, vain—a sickness, no doubt. What would my father say if he knew that I no longer distinguished between the real and the imaginary? I must take A where B cannot go, but how I wish I could do the opposite, taking B to where A cannot go."

◆   ◆   ◆

The next morning at the office I was busy till noon reading and responding to correspondence and answering phone calls. When my boss, Mr. Sharif al-Turk, left the office with his partner, Mr. Abd al-Rahman al-Mawla (I addressed them with the same formality as I did my professors in the School of Fine Arts), the only work I had left was typing translations of two short letters. I finished them hastily and placed them in a folder on my boss's desk. I went back to my office, that cherished dominion where I felt at ease sharing my secrets with myself, with my pages, with my coffee, with no interruptions from anyone or anything except the telephone.

I had barely taken two sips of my coffee when I experienced the same eruption of feeling I had two weeks earlier, and I knew that I was about to begin a new adventure with words that would be lost forever unless I produced them on the page right away. I started typing.

At about eleven o'clock last night, tired of waiting for his call and upset by his silly refrains—even though I excused his behavior as shyness or reluctance to be accused of harassing a stranger he'd only spoken with once or twice on the phone—I called him anyway, again saying to myself, "Let him think what he may."

The phone rang for a while before he answered, panting. "Hello, yes?"

"Did you come running to the phone?" I asked, cheerfully.

He seemed surprised by my question. "Yes, I was in another room."

"Still, it took you too long."

"Actually, I wasn't going to pick up and hoped the ringing would stop. I changed my mind. You're Sarab, right?"

"Were you expecting someone else? Another woman?"

"Sometimes, when I'm absorbed in my writing, I don't hear the phone until it's been ringing for a while."

"So, you were writing?"

At that moment, even though we were miles apart, I felt that he was trying to take control of the situation before I could. "Yes, I was writing, and, should you want to know what about, I was writing about you, a young woman who claims her name is Sarab, has long hair that she lets down over her shoulders like the curtain of night that God lets down for twelve hours every day, but Sarab's is there always—morning, afternoon, and night. . . . What's the color of your hair? Black? Is it long and flowing across your shoulders and back, like willow branches pouring over riverbanks?"

"How wonderful! All that and you haven't met me yet."

"Because I haven't met you. Who's to say you're not an old, gray-haired woman with a Parisian wig? Are you laughing?"

"Of course I'm laughing, because I might very well turn out to be an old, gray-haired woman, and without the wig even! Just imagine!"

"So what should I do?"

"Seeing is believing."

"When? Don't say . . . this evening!"

"This evening? I wish! We have to be practical."

"Tomorrow morning?"

"Tomorrow morning, at my office. I've already told you how to get there. The elevator will only take you up to the fourth floor."

"Why there? What's there for me in such an office?"

"Don't worry. We'll think of something, like better distribution for your books."

"Fine! Tomorrow morning. At ten?"

"Make it twelve. I'll probably be the only one there."

"Are you a secretary, manager? What do you do there?"

"Does it matter? What counts is: am I an old, gray-haired woman, or a young woman who lets her hair down like night over her shoulders? Weren't those your words?"

"Almost."

"Then come tomorrow and see for yourself."

"We have a deal."

"What if you don't show up?"

"Only because of an emergency."

"Ha! Excuses already! I don't accept excuses, any excuses."

"It's settled then! Nothing will keep me from coming. Tomorrow at twelve o'clock. On one condition, that you'll be there alone."

"Don't you want me to bring some friends to witness the great event?"

Chuckling, he said, "You're amazing. You know that some of the greatest events are witnessed by only two people?"

"God! How wonderful! Then, you'll find me alone waiting for you. Not a soul will know about our meeting."

"Except God."

"Or the devil!"

Our laughter mingled, even if it was only over the phone. I hoped that one day our laughter would mix with our breaths. No, no, this can't be important. It simply can't.

・　　　・　　　・

At first I did not realize how dangerous my game would be. I thought of it only as a game of chess I was playing against myself, moving my imaginary opponent's pieces with all the skill I possessed, only to counter him with an even smarter move. I remembered a quote from Nael Imran's *Entering the Mirrors* where he paraphrases the real Alice: "Would you like to be the red king or the white king?" Being the only player, I would choose both and would also record the moves in case I discovered new possibilities for the game, inspired by Alice when she frightened her old governess by screaming suddenly into her ear, "Nurse! Do let's pretend that I'm a hungry hyena, and you're a bone."[2]

The next day at the office left me with a feeling I couldn't describe. By twelve o'clock it became clear to me that I was believing my own lie. I had waited, my heart beating faster, for Nael Imran to arrive, in keeping with the appointment we had made in the previous day's journal. I was frightened. What if he really walked into the office and said, "Are you Miss Sarab Affan?" and I were to say, "Yes, we have an appointment, don't we?" but inside would really be saying, "I'm a hungry hyena, and you're a bone. You came right on time."

I wished that someone would drop in on business or just a visit to dispel my fears. Mr. Sharif had gone out early, leaving me with a folder on my desk and saying he would be back shortly after twelve if he got done inspecting the poultry farm he had recently bought with two other partners. Did he say shortly after twelve? But twelve noon was the time of my appointment with the author of *Entering the Mirrors,* who would not come. I carried the book everywhere with me, and when my mother reminded me of my promise to lend it to her I pretended not to have finished reading it. I decided to go back to my typewriter, hoping to ease my worries, my fears, my terror. I took *Entering the Mirrors* out of my bag and turned to a page I had bookmarked for commenting. That page was not, according to the author, his own original writing. He claimed to have quoted it verbatim from a French writer who had fascinated her

2. From Lewis Carroll's *Through the Looking Glass.*

readers with memoirs—real or imaginary, it didn't matter—that she had attributed to the Roman emperor Hadrian. On reading it again, I felt it was saying things I wished I had said myself, fed up as I was from dealing with people.

> The future of the world no longer disturbs me; I do not try still to calculate, with anguish, how long or how short a time the Roman peace will endure; I leave that to the gods. Not that I have acquired more confidence in their justice, which is not our justice, or more faith in human wisdom; the contrary is true. Life is atrocious, we know. But precisely because I expect little of the human condition, man's periods of felicity, his partial progress, his efforts to begin over again and to continue, all seem to me like so many prodigies which nearly compensate for the monstrous mass of ills and defeats, of indifference and error. Catastrophe and ruin will come; disorder will triumph, but order will too, from time to time. Peace will again establish itself between two periods of war; the words *humanity, liberty,* and *justice* will here and there regain the meaning which we have tried to give them. Not all our books will perish, nor our statues, if broken, lie unrepaired; other domes and other pediments will arise from our domes and pediments; some few men will think and work and feel as we have done, and I venture to count upon such continuators, placed irregularly throughout the centuries, and upon this kind of intermittent immortality. . . . [3]

"Some few men will think and work and feel as we have done, and I venture to count upon such continuators." I repeated this sentence aloud, imagining, in my modest way, that I was perhaps one of those few continuators. I confronted my typewriter, ready to strike the first key that my fingers would find, when a woman walked in. "Excuse me, I knocked on the door first, but you looked caught up in your book. Are you Sarab?"

3. *"The future . . . intermittent immortality"*: from *Memoirs of Hadrian,* by Marguerite Yourcenar (1903–1987), trans. Grace Frick (New York: Farrar, Straus and Company, 1963), 293.

"Yes," I said, and then I asked her, still distracted, "What time is it please?"

"Twelve o'clock. Seven past twelve," she said. "Is Mr. Sharif in, please?"

I regained control of myself, closed the book, and studied her more closely, noticing her distinctive elegance. "No, Mr. Sharif is out. Do you have an appointment to see him?"

"I'm his wife," she said modestly.

Flustered, I sprang to my feet to greet her, still holding the book. "How nice to see you. You must be Mrs. Tala?"

"You know my name?"

"Of course. Mr. Sharif talks about you often, and I've called you several times before with messages from him."

"That's right."

"I've been working here about a year now, and I finally get to see you. Please, have a seat."

She sat in one of the two big chairs. "Sharif mentions you from time to time. He relies on you a lot."

"I hope I'll never disappoint him. Would you like coffee? As usual Ismail left for the poultry farm with Mr. al-Turk. Would you excuse me for a couple of minutes while I make coffee? Here, feel free to look at this while waiting."

I handed her *Entering the Mirrors* and rushed to the small kitchen.

When I returned with the coffee, Tala reached for her cup, holding the book in her other hand. "You asked for the time when I walked in. Are you expecting a client?"

I sat back down behind the desk, holding the cup of coffee. "Sort of. He called yesterday to make sure he had our correct address and said he'd be here today at twelve. Actually, I'm the one who suggested he come at that time. So, when I saw you coming in. . . . Oh, excuse me!"

I noticed that she still had the book on her lap, and I got up to take it from her.

"Do you like Nael Imran? I mean, his writing?" she asked, handing me the book.

"Yes, very much, especially this novel. I think it's one of his best. Have you read it?"

"Not yet, but I have a copy from him."

"You know him? Personally?"

She was silent for a moment while I sat back down in my chair. She sipped on her coffee then said, "He's a close family friend."

"Are you serious?" I cried out.

"Why wouldn't I be?"

"I mean, it's wonderful that you're friends with such a great writer."

"He's kept to himself a lot lately. We hardly see him anymore, on rare occasions only."

"Is he busy writing?"

"I don't know, but he's such a dear friend."

"Wonderful, wonderful."

My strong reaction had clearly surprised her. I studied her face again. She was approaching forty and had faint blue eye shadow and sharply defined liner around her eyes, making them appear large and penetrating. Her hair, a chestnut color, hung loose, not a hair out of place, as though she had just been to the hairdresser. She was wearing a peach-colored linen dress suit—the jacket over a green low-cut top—and two delicate gold necklaces, one with a miniature gold Quran and the other with the letter "T" inside a ring. Her hands were adorned with jewelry and her fingernails manicured a dark red. When she crossed her legs, I noticed her Italian-made, expensive shoes. She was a true "lady," with all the commanding presence and self-confidence of a company owner's wife. When she laughed—I noticed later—her thin rosy lips revealed her glittering teeth. "You seem infatuated with Mr. Nael. Have you met him?" she asked, with a beautiful, captivating smile.

"No, and I don't think I ever will."

I wished she would disagree, but she didn't. Instead she repeated, "Yes, he's been keeping to himself, but only in the last few years."

"Did he suffer an ordeal?" I ventured.

She frowned and shook her head. "Yes. An ordeal." She fell silent. Then she asked, changing the subject, "Do you expect Sharif to be back soon?"

"When he left he said he'd be back in an hour, if at all. Would you like to wait in his office?"

"Oh no, no. This was on my way, so I decided to drop in."

I stood up as she politely came over and shook hands with me, saying, "I'm so glad to have met you finally. You know I own a good share of the poultry farm. I'll probably need to come back here from time to time. We'll meet again."

"Wonderful, Mrs. Tala!" I said as I accompanied her to the door and out into the hallway. I kept noticing her large eyes, hoping to see in them some trace of Nael Imran. But she was extremely cautious, and equally polite, not giving me a hint of anything that had to do with him. We reached the nearby elevator, which I called up for her. "What do you think of these plants?" I asked her, pointing to the creepers in the white flowerpots in the hallway. "I drive Ismail crazy with having to water them and expose them to the sun every other day."

She gave me that sparkling smile again. "If it weren't for you, there wouldn't be a single green branch in this hallway."

"Thank you. Good-bye."

The elevator swallowed her in.

Before my excitement could go away, I rushed to my typewriter.

With all respect for the Emperor, the future of the world does worry me. It worries me greatly, more so than the poultry farm. The farm has those who worry about it—its owner, his wife, his partners. Profit is certain for them. But if we didn't—if I didn't—worry about the world, then who would? For us profit is not certain. But that's okay. You have your farm and its profits, and I have the world, its future, and its losses. Sarab! You're jealous of Mrs. Tala, of her figure, beauty, charm, her friendship with Nael Imran, her owning half of a big farm and thousands of chicks hatched like worms every day. The future of the world? Ponder it—worry about it—as much as you like, and it will slip through your fingers like these words spilling out onto the page.

"Life is atrocious, we know. But precisely because I expect little of the human condition, man's periods of felicity," is each exciting moment another tiny miracle compensating "for the monstrous mass of ills and defeats, of indifference and error." My visitor brought that kind of brief excitement with her. She radiated a kind of energy that I couldn't quite explain, but it clearly had to

do with the writer who had presented her with a copy of his novel, which she hadn't even read. Maybe she didn't read it because she knew the author too well—the way he thought, the way he spoke. Why wouldn't she talk to me about the ordeal that Nael Imran had suffered? Why was she holding back? To her, I am nothing but a stranger, of course, who has to remain outside her intimate circle. Am I jealous of her, or did she become jealous of me after sensing the excitement in my voice when I talked about him, as little as I had talked about him? So do I really expect much from "the human condition," from "man's periods of felicity"? What periods, and what felicity?

·   ◆   ·

I inserted another page into the typewriter and continued typing.

What I wrote yesterday made me worry that Nael Imran would really come to the office this morning in keeping with our appointment. I decided to postpone the meeting, the thought of which was weighing on me as though it were a matter of life or death. I've been exaggerating everything these days. So I called him around nine o'clock, but he wasn't there. I tried him again at eleven. I felt like saying to him, "I don't know what you really look like, despite all the pictures I've seen of you in newspapers and magazines. I'd be fatally disappointed—yes, fatally—if you turn out to be ugly, dull, or cold. I wouldn't want to see or hear from you again, and you would spoil all of our past telephone 'encounters,' which up until now have been pleasant, suggesting that man's felicity is indeed possible even if it only comes in brief periods, as you quoted from the memoirs of Hadrian. I beg you, then, not to show your face. I beg you to go on being a telephone voice and not to come to me 'incarnate.' By the way, you're the one who keeps using this word, 'incarnate,' as though you are always trying to transform the soul into flesh and blood, or chisel out of thin air a statue of stone . . ."

I had spent all evening preparing a speech of that sort, but I wasn't able to reach him. Anyway, I hadn't let my hair down over my shoulders as I had planned, so perhaps he wouldn't come.

At twelve o'clock exactly, he arrived.

No! I was not expecting to see a man so dignified, so composed! He was wearing a light-colored summer suit over a light blue shirt and navy-blue necktie. His hair was graying around the temples. I loathed him almost from the start, and at once I decided to complicate things for him.

I stood up to greet him. What else could I have done? His dignified manner left no choice but to stand up. "Mr. Nael Imran, right?" I asked, extending my hand to him. He reciprocated with a handshake. I felt my hand vanishing in his grip. "Yes. Miss Sarab?"

"Sorry, I'm Randa al-Jouzy."

"Doesn't Miss Sarab work here?"

"Sure, sure."

"May I see her?"

"I'm sorry, sir, she left on important business. She asked me to keep you company until she gets back."

I wondered, right then, whether he would guess from our telephone conversations that my voice was Sarab's? Of course he wouldn't. People's voices sound different over the phone than they do in person. Only when one gets used to hearing them both ways do the two voices become indistinguishable. I was more worried that he might not wait for Sarab. He was even more handsome than I had imagined. I wanted him to stay.

He said he was in a rush to get back to his car, that it was parked in a no-parking zone, and he'd be fined unless he returned right away. He would have stood up and left had I not corrected the situation by saying, "I'm sure Sarab will be back any minute now. Please, have a seat. Coffee? I'll have it ready in a minute! If you get a parking ticket, we'll make Sarab pay half of it."

"We'll make her pay all of it. But if she gets back shortly, I'll forgive her. Frankly . . . I parked in the garage."

"Then there's no problem. And now, coffee. I brought some in a thermos. Would you like some?"

"Sure."

Steam rose from the coffee as I poured it out in a cup for him. "Sarab tells me you're a writer. Are you giving up writing to go into business?" I asked contentiously.

He was taken aback. "What business?"

"Pardon me! But Sarab, as you know, owns a share in this company. She gave me the impression that you'd also like to buy some shares."

"God forbid! I don't need this kind of business."

"You might find it more practical than writing."

"Your practicality does not interest me at all, and I don't think I was ever cut out for it. As for the pleasure of writing . . ."

"Ah, you writers! Always putting pleasure ahead of everything else!"

"To make up for all the misfortunes that are certain to befall us, Miss Randa. Tell me, are you and Sarab friends? I see only one desk here."

"This is my office. Sarab's office is inside. You might say . . . I'm her secretary."

"Then she must be older."

"Oh no, no, not at all!" I blurted out, terrified. That was the last thing I wanted him to think, and so I added, "She's my age exactly, twenty-six. We were students together at the Institute, but she's smarter than me . . ." Then I added softly, as though confiding in him, "And she's wealthier, much wealthier. Haven't you heard of her father, al-Hajj Ali Affan?"

"No, I know nothing about the world of commerce and industry," he said, naïvely.

"Maybe you'd like to at least learn something about it since it affects our whole economy, so you could write about it?"

He laughed, moving his cup aside. "Frankly, this world of yours does not interest me at all. Neither I, nor it, have any need for each other. And I'm not interested in writing about it."

I asked him, even more contentiously than before, "Then what do you write about? Politics? Love? Crime? Sarab told me about you, but she never gave me any of your novels to read."

"You don't sound like someone who likes to read novels, so why bother?"

"Aren't you interested in gaining more readers?"

"That doesn't worry me anymore," he said firmly.

"If I were you, I'd be dying for more readers."

"If you were a writer like me, you wouldn't be dying for more readers but for a subject that excites you, excites your mind, your imagination, even your body."

"Exactly, Mr. Nael. The subject is all that counts. Less than an hour ago this morning something happened in this office which, if I were a writer, I would have written about and then embellished with imaginative twists that even you would approve of."

I noticed him stealing a glance at his watch, probably concerned about Sarab's lateness. But he also seemed amenable to more socializing and conversation. Ah, these men! Sarab, Randa, Tala. . . . What difference did it make as long as all these women possessed some quality that stimulated the mind, the imagination, the body? "So what's the incredible thing that happened?" he asked.

I was thoroughly enjoying my game with him. This kind of amusement had to be a sign of love! "I don't want to keep you waiting any longer. Sarab must have lost track of time. She'll probably be much later than I thought."

"That's okay. Tell me what happened this morning."

"Mrs. Tala Sharif al-Turk, you know her of course? She came to see her husband this morning, but he was out on business. So we sat down and started talking. Then your name came up, and she spoke very warmly about you. She said you were a dear friend."

He laughed, as if to make light of the situation, and said, "Yes, a friend—a dear friend—and a longtime friend. Is Sharif al-Turk also part owner in this company? Anyway, what's so exciting about that?"

"The love triangle—the husband, the wife, and the lover. All I need is a fourth player to get the story moving . . . Sarab."

"Sarab? How?" he asked, feigning ignorance.

"The other lover."

"Whose lover? The husband's?"

"No, the lover's lover. Here's how it goes. The husband, in order to spite his wife after discovering she loves his friend, tells her he loves a young woman half her age. The wife doesn't care of course since she has a lover herself, until she finds out that the young woman actually loves her own lover. Then things get more and more complicated, leading to murder possibly!"

"What a vivid imagination, Miss Randa, and so free!"

"Yes, but where would I find the talent to write, Mr. Nael? Plus, these stories are so uncommon in our society."

"Unusual events are the most interesting to write about, our first encounters in forbidden regions."

"I'm sorry, these are mysteries I can't understand."

"Neither can I, thank God. I'm sorry, but it's time for me to leave."

He came over to my desk to say good-bye. I walked with him to the door. "Sarab has been driving me crazy talking about you and your visit, and now that she finally had the chance to see you, look what happens! I hope that, in some way, I made up for her absence, Mr. Nael?"

"Randa! How about you as the fifth character in your story? Things have really started moving. Why don't you write all of this down?"

"As I said, where would I find the talent?"

When he held out his hand to say good-bye I almost fell into his arms. Here was a writer I really admired who had arrived promptly to see me, at my own insistence. So why was I acting clever and playing games with him? But I was also scared of exposing my game, so I controlled myself until I could find a way out of the trap I had set for myself. Reluctantly, I kept my composure, saying to him as we stood in the doorway, "Good-bye. I'll make sure to scold Sarab for being late. I'm sure she'll call you and apologize. I hope you'll visit us again, and maybe we'll help you take part in the big poultry farm project that we're expanding."

◆   ◆   ◆

Two or three days later I went back to my blue folder and read the last few pages. I laughed and thought about minor details that I might add here and there to secure the outcome of my game. I had been unfair to Nael, and to myself, for no good reason. At first he was very hesitant to come to the office, and when he did I denied him the pleasure of meeting the woman I had conjured up for him. I pushed him on a stranger instead, not even knowing if he was interested in meeting someone like her, someone as serious as her. Had that upset him? Had he made up his mind not to accept any more invitations? Had Randa shown him enough interest to elicit a response from him if she were to call him again, whatever that response might be? But more importantly, had he found in Randa, during their brief meeting, qualities that would stimulate his mind, imagination, and body, to use his own words? I must find out what his impressions were after he left the office. I must take control of the situation before it gets ruined from the start.

As soon as I'd gone through my paperwork and my bosses had left for their other office, I sat down at my typewriter to continue writing from where I had left off.

I waited about an hour for him to get back home and eat lunch. I took a deep breath, cleared my throat, and called him. In order to assure him—and myself—that I was now Sarab, and not Randa, I loosened my hair over my shoulders and back. As soon as I heard his voice at the other end, I said, "Mr. Nael, this is Sarab Affan. I just got back. I'm very disappointed with you."

The coldness in his voice was evident. "You disappointed? How about me?"

"Why didn't you wait for me? Couldn't Randa hold your attention for one more hour?"

"I came to see you, not your secretary."

"Very well then, I'll take the blame this time. In any case, you have a new admirer."

"One who does not like to read?"

"But with a great imagination."

"Yes, so it seems, and she's already gotten us all involved in a quintuple drama that she'll tell you about. But in the end, I'll be the only loser."

"You the loser? I am the loser!"

"Have you heard the story of the man who spent all his life pious and God-fearing, praying and fasting, not committing any sin and staying away from temptation . . . ?"

"Yes . . . ?"

"Never drank or smoked, never touched a woman . . ."

"Why? To please his God?" I asked.

"To secure a place in heaven for himself. And once there, he would indulge freely and make up for all that he had so obediently stayed away from in the world."

"So, did he go to heaven?"

"As death came nearer, he was overcome with a different kind of fear. He said to his family and friends at his bedside, 'Listen to me, people, I have no fear of death, but what scares me is what comes after death.' So one of them said, 'Listen man, you've denied yourself the pleasures of the world, so you've earned the right to the pleasures of the Hereafter.' "

"And then what happened?"

"He said, 'But what I'm worried about now, people, is discovering that there is nothing after death, no heaven, no hell. And then I will be the loser. My God, yes, I will be the biggest loser, people, the biggest loser . . . ' And with the strength he had left he went on beating his chest in regret, until he breathed his last."

"Ha, ha! In other words, you came expecting to find paradise and didn't find it?"

"Exactly. Now you see why I am the loser? And you're disappointed with me, on top of that!"

"I forgive you. But I have something to ask."

"What?"

"That you come tomorrow, same time."

"No, Sarab, try something else."

"I mean it."

"I mean it too."

"Should I ask Randa to persuade you? By the way, what did you think of her?"

"I thought she was nice."

"Nice? That's all?"

"Listen, Sarab, leave Randa out of this."

"Guess what she came up with moments ago? She said that if you were to ask her to marry you, she'd be willing to do it the next day, even though you're as old as her father! She's right here, standing next to me!"

"This is what they call a backhanded compliment. I'm sure she's just pulling your leg. And anyway, what have I got to do with marriage?"

"So you're coming tomorrow?"

"I was getting ready to eat lunch. I'm hungry. Let's talk later."

"I'll call you tonight. Maybe you're easier to convince then. Good-bye."

"Wait, wait . . ."

His tone changed, as though surprising himself with some new idea. "Tomorrow, at ten in the morning. I'll be alone at the house. I want you to come see me, here at home. We'll have coffee. What do you think?"

"Your place? You and me, alone?"

"You will come alone, of course."

"Since it's our first time alone together, may I bring Randa along?"

"That's fine, as long as you don't bring everyone from the office."

"At ten? What about work?"

"To hell with work."

"Very well, Mr. Nael. We'll drive my car."

"Then let me give you directions . . ."

"You don't need to. I know where you live. What do you think I've been up to the past three months?"

"Sarab! You scare me!"

"If I could only show you what I've gathered about you!"

"Tomorrow then?"

"Tomorrow at ten."

• ◆ •

How can I take Randa along with me? Why am I again coming up with these devilish ideas? When he sees me standing at his doorstep tomorrow, he will recognize me as Randa. So who would Sarab be? I can ask my sister Shaza to come along and pretend to be me, and this way I would give her a part in my little conspiracy. But Shaza can't talk to him the way I do. She knows nothing about him or his books except for what I mention to her every now and then. And anyway, I don't want anyone to know of my relationship to him, even Shaza. In time maybe, but not now.

I must watch out for the traps I seem to be setting for myself every time I get carried away with my imagination. All I have to do is rewrite the last page and correct the situation by telling him that I'll be coming alone. And when we meet, I'll tell him that what I did to him when he visited me at the office was only an innocent trick.

I read over what I typed. It was past two o'clock, so I gathered the pages I had written and rushed out of the office to the elevator, then to my car, and drove quickly back home.

After lunch I went to my room and slipped into my pajamas for an afternoon nap, but there was too much on my mind, and I couldn't fall asleep. So I took out some blank paper and began writing in bed.

It was exactly ten o'clock when I parked my car along the sidewalk in front of his house, which I had driven by many times in the past weeks hoping to see him coming out or sitting out on his balcony—in vain. He was there now, sitting out on the balcony alone and holding a magazine. He was waiting for me.

He saw me getting out of my car and rushed to the sidewalk to meet me in his khaki outfit. When he saw me shutting my car door, with my hair up the same way I had it when we met at the office, he exclaimed, "Randa? By yourself? Where is Sarab?"

Disappointment showed on his face. I said, lightheartedly, "Let me explain, Mr. Nael. Did you know I drove over here in Sarab's Toyota?"

"So what? It's Sarab I want to see."

"You'll see her later this morning."

As we entered the house, he said, somewhat irritated, "No, Randa. You're hiding a secret. She doesn't want me to see her. There's no other explanation."

He led me into a small room, its walls lined all around with bookshelves. "Is she so ashamed of her looks that she wouldn't want me to see her?" he added, and motioned for me to sit in a comfortable-looking chair, while he sat down close to me on the edge of a matching sofa. I said inwardly, "It serves you right, Sarab! Ashamed of your looks, huh? And what next?"

I faked a laugh. As I searched my purse for my cigarettes and lighter, he ran over to a desk stacked with books and papers and brought back a pack. I had already taken out one of my own cigarettes and explained to him that the brand he smoked irritated my throat. "Did you say ashamed of her looks?" I asked as he lit my cigarette. I took in a long drag of smoke then puffed it out slowly, and continued, "Poor Sarab. She was considered one of the prettiest women in college. It's funny that your imagination should bring you to strange conclusions, just because she didn't show up for an appointment yesterday and will be a little late today."

"What's her excuse today?"

"Lots of work and irksome responsibilities. Think what you like."

"So she lent you her car?"

"Yes, so I would get here on time. She gave me directions to your house, but I almost got lost twice."

"What's her number at the office? I'd like to talk to her myself."

He started dialing the number as I was giving it to him. I wondered secretly who would answer his call: Mr. Sharif, Mr. Abd al-Rahman, or our office helper Ismail?

"Miss Sarab Affan please," he said, speaking coldly into the receiver. Then he added, in response to the answer he got, "It's not important, thank you. I'll call later." He put down the receiver. "You see? She's away from the office on business. The man I spoke to wanted to know who I was. By the way, is she really a Miss?"

"You may say so, yes, even though many call her Mrs."

"Did you leave the office together?"

"Yes. I dropped her off for an appointment she couldn't miss. She asked me to go ahead of her and see you."

"Another appointment?"

"A business appointment. Aren't you going to make me coffee? Do you live here alone? If you show me to the kitchen, I can make the coffee."

I stood up, curious to discover at least part of the house I had constructed in my imagination for days on end. He didn't reject my offer to make coffee—my gracious, lazy host! He showed me into the kitchen, saying, "Here's the sugar, and here's the coffee, the spoons, cups. . . . Ah, and pot." Then he went back to his library.

I was laughing inwardly at the way I had angered—disappointed—him. But I too was disappointed at how little attention he had given me as a woman—a young woman who had come into his life, regardless of her reasons! Was he strong when faced with temptation, or was I not tempting enough for him? Was he being loyal to Sarab, whom he thought he hadn't met yet, and was afraid of showing even the slightest interest in her friend—her secretary—Randa? Had he passed his first test? No, not yet. First, coffee, and then we'll see.

I came back with the coffee, and we both took our cups off the tray. "I heard what Sarab told you on the phone," I said.

He had calmed down. "What did you hear her saying? She said many things."

"Whatever had to do with me . . . that I'd get married to you if you asked me, in spite of our age difference."

"But you didn't hear my response, that you were only giving me a back-handed compliment about my age."

"Oh no, I said it out of admiration, or should I say attraction?"

"Randa, you know nothing about me. Maybe you're just taken with what Sarab had to say about me. What you hear before seeing . . ."

"Maybe, but actually she hardly talks about you, although she wanted to know what you looked like when she got back an hour after you left—your height, your complexion, what you were wearing, the way you talked, whether you're serious or funny. So I described you with the one phrase that is sure to win the heart of any young woman—that you'd make an ideal husband."

"Hypothetically, of course."

"Of course. . . . Ah, how's your coffee?"

"Excellent, Randa. Are you a good cook too?"

"A good cook? No, I'm sorry. I can cook eggs if I really have to, but that's about it. See? I don't even pretend to make a good wife."

Prodded again by the playful demon inside me, I said, "Actually I've been divorced for three years."

I gave him the look of a woman who'd had a bad shake in life. "My marriage didn't even last a year. Seven months to be exact. I realized my awful mistake from the very first day. I even gave up my postnuptial dowry[4] to gain back my freedom."

"Do you really believe you got back your freedom?"

"Yes, as much of it as one could ask for in a rotten, confining society such as ours."

"Freedom, ultimately, is a personal matter, Randa. You create your own freedom, so don't blame society."

"Sometimes Sarab talks about her desire to unleash the freedom within her. She must have learned that from you. I, on the other hand, have looked in vain for the freedom you speak of. But tell me, Mr. Nael, about the ordeal that has made you, from what I understand, a recluse."

"Ordeal? Who gave you that idea?"

"Mrs. Tala al-Turk told us yesterday that you suffered an ordeal."

"Tala?"

---

4. *postnuptial dowry*: from Arabic *mu'akhkhar,* that part of a woman's dowry due to her after divorce.

"Yes."

"We all have things in our lives we keep private, things that affect our lives nonetheless, the positions we take, our opinions. Do you know of anyone who hasn't been through some sort of ordeal? I'm sure that even Tala has been through some ordeal she'd rather not share. It's always easier to talk about other people's ordeals."

"I disagree. We almost never care about the ordeals of others. It's easier to talk about one's own. As a writer, you know that best."

"Because I'm a writer, I think about the ordeals of others to forget my own. Anyway, what do you care about my ordeals?"

At that moment I felt I'd given Randa a bigger role than I should have. I, Sarab Affan, the grand lover writing her daily journals in truth and honesty, must save Randa, my other self, from a situation I never wished upon her. But who of the two of us is supposed to be the serious, rational one, and who the frivolous jester playing a game with a man she knows went through an ordeal that she is trying to make him forget? In any case, I have to intervene somehow, even if it requires my sudden, unannounced appearance.

I asked him, changing the subject, "Mr. Nael, may I trouble you for a glass of water?"

"Certainly," he said, and he ran off to the kitchen.

Right after he left I rushed out of the library into the entrance hall. I went through an open door that led into a large, elegantly furnished living room. It too had many bookshelves, but what really made it stand out were its large paintings and wooden and bronze sculptures. The curtains seemed to have been shut on purpose to keep out the bright morning sunlight, but their upper corners were lit by two lights pointing upward toward the ceiling. Ah, that was exactly how I had imagined his surroundings, the place where he received his friends, visitors, and others who sought him! But I must not waste any time in wonder! I quickly took off my short indigo jacket and threw it on one of the chairs, exposing the sleeveless orange shirt I was wearing underneath. I let my hair down over my shoulders and combed it with my fingers as best I could. Then I picked up my jacket and folded it on my arm, and I stood gazing at a wide, blue painting whose meanings I couldn't make out in my confusion. I heard him coming back to the library, calling, "Randa, Miss Randa! Randa!"

There was a brief silence. Perhaps he thought I was in the bathroom. I wandered around the room among the paintings and books, waiting for him to start looking for me again.

I heard him moving about the house. From the noises he made, I imagined him walking into the entrance hall and out onto the balcony to make sure my car was still there, and then coming back inside and slamming the door shut. "Randa!" he shouted out again. My eyes roamed the beautifully decorated living room, appreciating its furnishings, before settling back on the blue painting. My back was to the door. Finally, I heard his footsteps coming toward the living room. He cried out, "Oh, God! Who is this black-haired beauty?"

I didn't react. I kept motionless, on purpose, my eyes raised to the top of the wall painting. I sensed him approaching slowly from behind, as though on his toes, until he reached and held me, clasping my bare arms. He whispered, as his lips brushed against my hair and neck, "Woman, who are you?"

I leaned my head with its long locks of hair backward onto his chest. He was still holding my loose arms, and my jacket had fallen to the floor. I turned my head around, reaching for his lips. "I am Sarab Affan," I whispered.

Before he could utter one word of astonishment or disbelief, I released myself from his grip and stood facing him, looking into his eyes and almost touching his chest. Quietly he held my face in his palms and gave me a long, long kiss on my mouth . . .

◆   ◆   ◆

Overcome with fatigue, I threw the pages on the floor, straightened my pillow, and lay on my bed facedown like a corpse that had just been dropped from the roof of a forty-story building. I fell asleep right away. Perhaps I fell asleep in his arms . . . I couldn't remember! It was a deep slumber, dark and dreamless.

I woke up to Shaza's voice. "Why all this sleep? Come on, it's dark already! Dad called from his clinic to ask if we'd like to eat dinner with him at the club tonight. He said we should all start getting ready so we can be there by nine-thirty."

At first I wasn't sure where I was while Shaza spoke, but then I realized I was in my room and that it was already dark outside. "Dinner at the club? No, Shaza, I'm not in the mood for it tonight."

"Do you mind if mom and I take your car?"

"No, I don't."

"You dropped your papers on the floor."

"It's okay. I'm getting up soon. Leave them. I'll pick them up later."

Shaza left, and I rested my head on the pillow again and closed my eyes, surrendering to a stupor that was half sleep and half wakefulness. I tried to remember where I'd been a few moments earlier. Did I say moments? It was more like two hours . . . or more. Strange voices would get louder and then die out in my head. I wasn't at the office. I wasn't in my car. I wasn't at home. A genie inside me was playing tricks on me, and I was the one who knew that genie best. Even Randa al-Jouzy was the genie's invention. Unless I was careful, she too would join in on his tricks.

I remembered! I was in Nael's house, in his blue living room. I had finally told him that I was Sarab Affan. I was acting out a monodrama in which I played at least three different roles, speaking with three different voices, burying my head in the chest of a man I knew by name only. Every time I got closer to him, or he to me, Randa would come in between us. If she wasn't the invention of the wily genie inside my head, then she had to be someone I created in a moment of fear and caution, content with her as my other self. She was the rational, balanced, logical one, and Sarab was the one refusing to be rational, balanced, and logical. Some people brought out the Randa in me, and others Sarab. Nael Imran seemed to bring out both at once, preparing me for my journey inside the mirrors. With Nael I found myself alternating—quickly, incongruously—between Randa and Sarab . . .

I would go back to writing.

I reached with my hand to the floor while still lying on my bed, and with the tips of my fingers I felt the smooth, cool surfaces of the pages scattered on the floor. Why am I not writing about the real events of my life these days? But what events? What is there to write about that I haven't already, the same grind, the same disgust, day after day? And how about memory and imagination? How would the world be if they became one? I will let A stand for imagination and B for memory, as I have already decided. I will write about my life the way it is, and can be, making me the sum total of both, $A + B$. Or was I the product, $A * B$? I prefer the latter, since it is greater than the first. Therefore my equation will be: $S = A * B$, where S is not only an unknown, but Sarab herself.

$S = A * B$, the essence of everything that humanity has ever written, and will write.

In what I've written so far of my story with Nael, I feel that I'm the savvier, and perhaps the smarter, of the two protagonists. All the actions and words are because of me, and Nael is nothing but the "straw man." Why not? It is my story, after all. If Nael were the one writing it, he would have been the savvier, smarter one, and I the "straw woman." So let me revel in my powers, so long as I am the one with the pen.

Clearly, it won't be hard for me to explain to him the secret behind Randa becoming Sarab, the secretary becoming the boss, the friend becoming the lover. We will enter together into one of his mirrors, into a world of impossibilities such as he, the master of impossible dreams, never imagined. We will have candlelit dinners and go to extravagant parties attracting the city's most beautiful women and most famous men, and everyone will be whispering, "Who could this tall, slender lady be, with the flowing hair and enchanting laugh, holding onto his arm? What about his wife? Has he divorced her? Is this his new wife, or his lover? Is she another writer he's trying to promote?" We will travel together to Paris and London and attend plays and ballets every night, and on the way back we'll stop in Rome and we'll look for the ruins of Augustus and Hadrian, and we'll only stay in five-star hotels, so eat your hearts out all you bourgeois! In Cairo, the young, rebellious literati will gather around us, and among them there will be government infiltrators who will monitor all of our movements and outbursts because we, it is said, like to stir up trouble and are not content with normal tourist trips to Aswan and Luxor. In Baghdad, they will ask me to inaugurate a writer's club with a reading of one of my short stories, and after it they will insist on hearing one of my poems. And Nael will give a lecture that will air on television about the long experiences that he wrote or didn't write about. And I will talk in Amman about the Jerusalem I see and live through the accounts of my grandmother Khadija and through the works and novels of its writers, and we will see the distant hills of Jerusalem through clouds from the balconies of tall, white buildings. And many travels will follow, from the whitewashed cities of the Gulf, rich with sun, ocean and desert, to the cities of the Mediterranean, rich with sun, ocean and rocky shores. And if we have to go to Sanaa, despite the length of the journey, then we might as well go as far as Kayrawan, Wahran, Rabat, Tanja, and Tatwan. . . . Oh, how many are our cities, how beautiful their names, how splendid the emotions they evoke, if only we were free to travel among them and weren't shackled to our own neighborhoods, coming and going in our own alleys like rats. Nael Imran! Where are you? Why do you make me rave like this? Why do you unleash my fantasies and desires, letting them burst forth with such pleasure, cruelty? I swear to God I'll leave you if the day comes when you're no longer able to excite my fantasies and desires with such pleasure, but without the cruelty, I beg you, without the cruelty, or I will leave you alone with Randa al-Jouzy, with all her reason and logic, and I will run off with Sarab into the deep valleys and over the rugged mountains, to cloud-covered summits overlooking cities glittering among forests and rocks and on the banks of the roaring rivers. I am still firm in demanding freedom for myself, in seeking my liberty and salvation. I will not be another rat crawling down the endless alleys, full of the refuse of time.

Nael: today words, and tomorrow hellfire.

2

NAEL IMRAN

The day I started writing *Entering the Mirrors* I was in a state of hopeless grief that stifled me for months after the death of Siham. I had watched myself languishing in mud, unable to wade out no matter how I tried.

When the first words of *Entering the Mirrors* came to me, I felt as though I had been locked inside a dark room for months, but all of a sudden a crack opened up in the wall above, and a streak of light seeped in and I clung to it. Somehow the light lifted me to the crack, which widened to a small window through which I could make my escape into the open air again.

The more I wrote, the more the crack widened and the more light poured over me. Even my breathing became more regular, my vision more keenly focused. Perhaps I had also grown more forgetful, or maybe my memory was selectively pushing only the things it chose into my consciousness to lessen my pain, making me more indifferent and moving me closer to a pleasure I could not, or did not care to, describe.

When I entered the mirrors, I experienced real action, real movement, where shapes contended, broke apart, undulated, waned, and took form again—all to the rhythm that my words, in spite of me, created. And so the crack in the wall above widened, and day after day the adjacent parts crumbled away. I only had to step over the rubble and go forward. By then I had written most of my novel, and all I had to do was to write an ending somehow—an open ending, of course—in order to claim victory over the grief that had almost destroyed me and severed all my ties to people and things, as it had done once during a difficult period in my early youth.

I knew that *Entering the Mirrors,* as a story, was more like a daydream that a power hidden inside my consciousness had forced upon me. I realized I needed to forget my wife's death or accept it as an irreversible judgment. During those first gloomy months, it was as if I had been buried with her or had refused to go on living so I could remain worthy of her love until my death. Whereas some would have lost their will, I willed myself toward death, determined to deny life, because Siham had been deprived of the right to live past thirty-six, two years of which she had wasted in a hopeless fight with illness. I had watched as her face shriveled little by little and her radiance and consciousness waned before the eternal darkness.

Ghassan, seven years old at the time, did not understand what had happened despite his constant crying the first few days. I was at a loss whether to make him try to forget the tragedy of his mother's death or remind him of her love and tenderness, which he had lost by losing her. I thanked God that I had convinced Siham that one child, Ghassan, was enough. As an only child, he became my only joy and redemption from grief, but he was also my worry and concern whenever I thought about him growing up without a mother's care, which I wouldn't be able to make up for no matter how hard I tried. Perhaps my younger sister Salima, still single at forty, found a kind of fulfillment in taking care of him from the first moments after Siham's death. She did it with warmth, affection, and selflessness that added new meaning and excitement to her mundane existence. I saw her as she came to life taking care of him as though he were her own. During his school breaks, she would take him to stay with my brother Wael and his children in our old house while coping at the same time with her job as director in the Ministry of Education.

Especially during the first two years, my sister insisted on sparing me the responsibilities of Ghassan's daily routine, but she could not persuade me to move out of the house that Siham and I had finished building four years before she died. It wouldn't have been easy for me to move out of those rooms that we had designed together and furnished gradually to our unique taste—with little furniture and without those chairs, couches, tables, and closets that clutter most people's houses. I went on living with Siham inside the rooms as though she had never left, and never would.

I even kept our clothes together in the large bedroom wardrobe and kept her perfumes and powders on the vanity for months, despite what Salima saw as an undue attachment to Siham's memory and a refusal to accept the will of God, whose wisdom in deciding our fates was not for us to question. And yet I chose to be with Siham in my solitude. The large oil portrait my artist friend Diya Ismail had painted of her, which occupied much of the front part of the sitting room, was not enough for me, so I asked the sculptor Nizar Haydar to make a bust of her, relying on old photographs I gave him and on his own acquaintance with her since the early days of our marriage. He sculpted a beautiful bust out of white marble, slightly larger than life, and he gave her lips an expression like a smile, but one that seemed to be melting into mysterious sorrow. I placed the sculpture on a black marble pedestal directly facing my bed. Her face was the last thing I saw before turning off the lights at night and the first thing I saw when I woke up in the morning, when the sunlight would shine on it through the cracks in the curtains. I could almost feel Siham moving, coming closer, urging me to get up if I stayed in bed longer than I should. I felt that we were in a never-ending, evolving conversation, ebbing and flowing with voices inside my head, as though the marble might be secretly conspiring with me and strengthening my resistance against some malevolent power intent on destroying me. But sometimes I also suspected that in spite of its wistful smile the marble might be secretly conspiring against me. I often caught myself surrendering madly to the coldness of the marble between my palms, my burning lips trying to radiate some warmth into hers, hard and cold beneath mine.

Thus my journey into the mirrors had become inevitable, more than two years after my last novel had come out. My daily encounters with a piece of marble into which I wanted to breathe life, as a diversion perhaps, or out of sadness or joy—or whatever were those unsettled emotions and imaginings that kept on agitating inside my head—were pushing me far away, toward denying the daily realities constantly weighing on my chest, suffocating me. Was I longing for death, taking refuge in a dream that would take me beyond the life I knew to a life fashioned by my desires in a way that no one could imagine? Or was I retreating, defeated in the face of my recent tragedy, in the face of the people surrounding me all the time, as though I were carrying a shell I would withdraw into away from the noise, the demands, and the cruelty of people, and inside it I would reconstruct my existence with visions that my words would capture in a way all my own?

All of that came to me as I delved deeper into the mirrors. But as the days went by, I realized that when I wrote I was moving away from what I had imagined for myself at the outset. Each time I entered the world of reflections and refractions, of distortions and echoes, where the distant and the impossible are brought forth, I emerged from the miserable shell I had been forced into and met people face-to-face, with all their noise, demands, cruelty, and, should I also say, from time to time, their splendor? My legal practice, which I could not neglect no matter what I was experiencing personally, reminded me of those things every day. I realized that no matter what I did, thought, and wrote, whether I willed it or not, I had become part of an accursed history, accursed as much with its triumphs and joys as it was with its defeats and tragedies—a history whose achievements were realized in spite of itself, while its destruction was realized with its full consent and with the stubbornness of fools. I became convinced that no matter how much people knelt before God praying, "Lord, comfort us and ease our hardships," that their true guiding principle was the exact opposite: hardship, not comfort. There were moments even in which I would imagine the words "Lord, bring us hardship, not comfort" written at every street corner and above every city gate. I heard them repeated by our institutions, laws, rules, and customs, by our officials, workers—young and old—by everybody.

More and more I suspected that all those years—earning a doctorate in law, teaching it, working as a legal consultant, and finally practicing it—were wasted. I had done my share of excusing and even promoting evil. I had worked on the narrowest fringes of humanity, within a social order crammed with prohibitions, in order to save only the few from its crushing weight. You could see me as I passed my fiftieth year, another small wheel among the wheels of a history relentless in producing an age that bred nothing but crisis, catastrophe, and sorrow.

All the legal briefs I had written in between my five novels over a quarter-century, before writing *Entering the Mirrors,* were only attempts to understand that side of human behavior, either through my knowledge of history or through my own observations of present-day society or of how they both functioned together, inseparably. The death of my beloved Siham further increased my doubts about the worth of all I was doing. The place I had "earned" for myself in society was nothing but a pit of mud in which I was flailing about, a drowning man who wouldn't drown, a survivor who wouldn't survive—God, except for now, and by the grace of this new artistic creation. *Entering the Mirrors* came to me, as Siham's white marble bust went on gazing at me from the black pedestal, smiling at me, provoking me, urging me on with all her love, with her confusion, with her fear that I might lose myself inside my thoughts and fantasies.

I thought of how the emperors of the past erected magnificent monuments in memory of the loved ones they had lost, or named cities after them. But would I demand a magnificent monument in a city that has hardly enough space for its miserable graves, a city in which opposites contend—may God have pity on your soul, Abu al-Alaa![1]—or demand that a city be built on sands that could not possibly give birth to a single genius, sands that had become mere breeding grounds for hyenas? Or should I, like the ancient pharaohs, preserve the mummified corpse of my beloved in a dark cellar with a mask of gold over her shrouded face, immortalizing her beauty and death at the same time?

I had no gold, nor could I build monuments or cities. I had only

---

1. *Abu al-Alaa:* Abu al-'Ala' al-Ma'arri (973–1057) was an Arab poet-philosopher known for his pessimism. On his tombstone are written the words *hadha janahu 'abi 'alayya wa ma janaytu 'ala 'ahad,* "This is what my father has brought upon me and I haven't brought upon anyone." The miserable graves of a city in which opposites contend is a specific allusion from al-Ma'arri's *Elegy on Abu Hamza,* where the poet envisions the dead crowding together in graves that cover the earth.

words. So I would use words and write a book in memory of my beloved, a book without parallel, unique, like her, a book like no one ever wrote.

A book like no one ever wrote! What a wonderful thing, vanity! But vanity was necessary at first, so I could set a difficult goal before my eyes. I had to imagine possibilities far beyond anything I had conceived of in the past, whether out of resolve or vanity. I soon realized that I was again not facing up to my insufferable reality and that neither resolve nor vanity had anything to do with what was tossing about inside me every day, every hour. I would have to catch the flying shrapnel, no matter what. Entering the mirrors was like entering a place where real and imaginary images are immortalized together, images that get etched into the soul by a life of joy and suffering, with all the longings and disappointments of these accursed times.

With the first word I wrote, I wanted to see in Siham's death a return to a new beginning where the soul was safe from what it had to suffer hour after hour, to a place where it was liberated from all tyranny, hardship, and ugliness, a place where it became an unabashed beatitude, even though resurrection was within eye-reach, or even closer.

There she fell, and as she fell there was the faint chirping of far-away birds, the lapping of the gentle, foggy sea she had known years back. And there were laments drowning in her ears, unintelligible to the so-called politicians and untiring preachers. She fell, and she kept falling into a deep abyss that sucked her back into the depths of her love and dark memories, where she would feel the desire of eternal existence and discover the essence of her life again to make of it a new miracle. How sweet was such finality, where she would find a way to take her back to life, to the only place where miracles were possible. And she saw his hands, with their long, delicate fingers, moving through her mind, and his lips moving with all the beauty of words! But she continued to fall in a flowing, endless rhythm amid the sounds of people and nature. Oh God, who was beckoning her with all this music? She could not understand a word of what she was hearing, but she could pick out certain meanings, and she knew that there she would have a final meeting, final comfort, in the heart of the lover she could hear calling, and calling, as she fell through the abyss of years, back to life, life, life . . .

After writing about my experiences with the mirrors, I can see clearly today what I couldn't then see. I was not writing about Siham, in spite of all my love for her, as much as about some apparition I had to lay my hands on and give form to, capturing its essence. I wanted to dig my nails into its arms and bury my mouth in its hair. I wanted to see it metamorphose into a new form every day, provoking me as it submits and resists, turning into an angel sometimes and a devil at others. Its miracle would be in its ability to divide, multiply, and then become one again. It would get me past these accursed times, despite every injustice, cruelty, and ugliness. And through convex and concave mirrors, through deformed faces and rectangular, dwarfed bodies, this tangible apparition—its body unscathed, its face ever brimming with splendor—would steal away with me and guide me, finally, to those concoctions and pleasant visions that I could have never reached without it . . .

The man on his endless journey in the regions of night . . .

The sun had plunged into the horizon, spitefully, leaving me in the dark, without even a moment of twilight, as if some unknown power had turned off the lights in a room just as I was coming in, after it had made sure the room had no windows. I imagined one lock after another clicking shut inside my head.

But I knew I was sitting under a tree, and I could feel the dry leaves scattered around me and under my feet. Perhaps there were many trees around me. I could feel the leaves snapping and then drifting past me. When I held out my hand to feel if the thing next to me was a tree trunk, I felt as if I had stuck my hand out an open window into the cold air outside and dropped it feebly onto a heap of dry leaves. I imagined more locks clicking inside my head.

In the pitch darkness, there was a voice saying, "When you were a young man you sinned with virgins, and then you abandoned them or they abandoned you for the next caller. Some got married and had children and forgot about you. Some never got married and kept chasing the shadows of their desires until they wasted away and grew old, and some lived better than queens, trying every day to rid their bodies of your memory, only to fail. Do you remember her, and her, and her?"

One woman's image after another came out of the darkness and disappeared again. I wasn't sure if I knew them or had even seen them before, but each came toward me as though she knew me, and then her image blurred and disappeared, giving place to another.

A woman came forth—slender, slight, with flowing hair that made her look taller than she really was. Her eyes appeared out of the darkness, glowing with savage beauty, imploring, full of pain. She stood there a moment or two, her arms languid, and suddenly she started moving in a panic, like a fugitive surrounded by enemies, looking for an escape. She ran and disappeared.

There was nothing but darkness and dry leaves bristling with every movement of my hands and feet. The voice came again, whispering this time, "I have with me a little bird, you might say a nightingale. You heard him singing one day and you laughed. Yes, you laughed. Why? Because he was trying to express an emotion larger than himself, or so you thought, not knowing that he was speaking of none other than your fate, your sadness. But you thought he was singing about his own little sadness. Do you remember?"

"I don't remember," I said. "I don't remember."

And then a blue sky burst out of the darkness, full of screeching, cawing birds that crowded the air with their flocks, diving down like arrows above my head and then soaring up again in ever-rising circular formations to where their noises could barely be heard. But then they descended again, together, with great force and a roar like that of cymbals, and they put down on trees that bent under their weight until the branches touched the ground. Then they flew away and rose again, and the leaves poured down from the branches like rain.

The birds circled into the distance until they vanished, along with their voices. A heavy, deep silence fell upon the dark forest.

I wanted to hear a voice, to see something, but the silence and darkness were thick, deadly. I moved about randomly, shook my arms, squirmed, turned my head left and right. I heard panting, a choked, irregular breathing, which I thought was coming from my throat. I wanted it to stop. But then it seemed like it was not coming from me but from somewhere in the dark. It sounded familiar, very familiar, coming from a throat I knew well, one that in the past I used to rub my mouth against, feeling with my lips the vibrations of its soft moans of love, of passion.

My lips touched hers, and I knew that she had returned from the heart of darkness at last, at last. . . . I grabbed her shoulders and shook her violently. "You will not go away this time! You will not go away! Is this hell? Where are we?"

Her panting stopped for a moment, and she said, "We're in your room.

Can't you see the marble smiling at you? Can't you see the mirrors all around you? Can't you see me inside each one of them, beckoning to you?"

I really saw all of that.

We stood up together, and she led me to one of the mirrors. We stepped right into it as though stepping into empty space, and we saw a path paved with pebbles in front of us, winding along the green hills down to the sea.

We went down to the shore where the waves and foam were crashing against the rocks. In a cove there was a motor boat bobbing up and down in the churning water, about to sink from the water that had gathered inside it.

A tall, black man came out from a nearby cave, walking slowly, naked except for a piece of cloth around his waist. He pointed to the boat, saying, "If you're ready to go out to sea, I can have it ready in just half an hour."

◆　　◆　　◆

It was a winter day full of sunshine after a night of heavy rain. The showers had arrived with the magnificent, awesome ceremonies befitting long-awaited rains after weeks of drought, accompanied by thunder and lightning that shook the city. I was sure that in the morning, once the rain stopped, we would hear of men who were turned into charcoal figures by the fires of heaven as they roamed the haunted city.

The sun came up into clear skies, sending sparkles of light everywhere. The trees had shaken off their coats of dust to expose a glittering green. Even the old houses seemed to have recovered a lost beauty and become new again.

I came back home from my office around two in the afternoon feeling very hungry. I ate my lunch facing a window that looked out on my garden, which was known for its bittersweet oranges now glittering like golden lamps among the burnished leaves.

Just before four o'clock I went out to the street feeling unusually robust. I had the urge to walk for hours, even though I knew the sun would set in about an hour. I felt like embracing the air around me and drinking the bluish, shimmering light like champagne from a glass overflowing with bubbles. It was one of those rare moments that made me forget about everything past and present, except for the immediate, pleasurable glow that speaks of nothing but itself or speaks possibly of some reflection inside me that would liberate me not only from others, but from myself also.

The sky was clear, infinite, and the sun, dancing about on trees and rooftops, cast its waning reflections like little red sparkles across the puddles of rainwater that had gathered here and there along the road.

Cars passed me by, but they were not moving as fast as they usually did. There were young men and women rushing or walking slowly, calling out to each other. Something like laughter filled the air. Even the stray dog that passed by me appeared to be enjoying the sight of the world around him and had no reason to bark at anyone.

A car came from behind and pulled up next to me. I kept on walking, undistracted, but the driver honked softly. I turned around and saw a beautiful face I hadn't seen in a long time—a year or more—smiling at me from behind the glass window. I came closer to the side of the car, and the woman with the beautiful face quickly rolled down the window and cried, "Nael! Absent-minded as ever!"

I bent down to get a better view of her face and that of her husband, who was sitting next to her in the driver's seat. "And you, beautiful as ever!" I replied, as I would have to any woman stopping me on the street during a moment full of nature's intoxicating pleasures, especially if that woman was Tala al-Dahir.

"Come on, get in," said Sharif al-Turk from the other side, "We'll give you a ride."

"No, thanks. I came out for a walk. Who wants to be in a car on such a lovely day?"

"Sharif and I, as you can tell!" she said, laughing.

"Why don't you park your car and walk with me?"

I wished they would, but then Sharif said, "Sorry, we have to get to an appointment. How come we don't see you these days?"

"We seem to run into each other in all the wrong places!" I said.

Tala laughed again. "It's your fault. Call us, for once in your life."

"I will."

Sharif shouted, "Seven-seven, one-one, four, six, zero. Remember four-six-zero, and the rest is easy."

I gave a throaty laugh. "I'll remember! Of course I will!"

How could I not remember when I'd known her number even before she got married and also knew that Sharif had moved in with her and her family because he was poor at the time. Even the car had belonged to Tala. I remembered, reluctantly, much of what Sharif knew—or maybe didn't know—about Tala, Siham's life-long friend. As they drove off into the distance, I pictured Tala as a pigeon I had once held in my palms and had then lifted as far up as I could and set free, so I could get married to her friend and she could be free to make her own choices.

At that moment I noticed a man on the opposite sidewalk wearing a long, black coat, walking slowly with bent shoulders despite his erect body. I recognized him immediately as a former prime minister. Every time I came out for a walk at that time of day, I saw him walking slowly by himself along the row of pine trees, his eyes glued to the ground in front of him, almost completely oblivious to the people around him. I wondered what thoughts went through his head during those long walks, whether they were thoughts he chose to have or ones that came to him without his will. He was prime minister for only a year or less, but how many prime ministers like him managed to stay alive and take walks alone and unguarded in the long afternoons, reconstructing their past at their own leisure? Or was he not reconstructing any past but avoiding it like something that would bite his hand if he were to reach out to it? Or else he wouldn't have become a common sight for the people who saw him walking every afternoon, people with whom he had severed all ties; it was as though they had raised him to the highest offices only to drop him afterward into this strange isolation that might have tormented him for a while but had now become something he could no longer live without. Each time I saw him walking, still on his long journey and his shoulders getting more bent, I remembered some lines of a poem by an English poet (Was it Keats? Shelley?) that said something like: *What has become of the songs of yesterday? / Ah, what has become of them?*

The forgotten prime ministers and lost songs of yesterday mingled in my head with the memories of Tala and Siham, memories like flocks of birds that disappeared in winter only to return in the summer months with their many newborn to their nests in the soul.

I leaped over a puddle of rain, gazing at the long road ahead, the two rows of pine trees still glittering on both sides. The sky had turned red against a horizon scattered with sparse clouds whose edges blazed like embers with the last rays of the setting sun. Overwhelmed, I didn't at first notice a young man catching onto my arm. "Excuse me!" I said.

I noticed his red, teary eyes. He appeared very sad. "Don't you remember me, Dr. Nael?"

I recognized his face, but at that moment I couldn't remember his name. I used to see him once every two or three months, and we would greet each other from a distance and go on walking. "How can I not remember you? You're . . ."

"Hammad."

"Yes, of course! Are you okay?"

His voice choked on a sudden sob, and he quickly took out a handkerchief to wipe his tears. "My father . . ."

"What happened . . . ?"

"I just received news of his death."

"How? Where?"

"In Amman. I just picked up a telegram from Abu Hassan the shopkeeper. A heart attack. He dropped dead walking in the street."

He pulled the telegram out of his shirt pocket as though he were afraid I wouldn't believe him without proof. So I said to him, holding his hands, "I'm sorry, Hammad. We're all . . ."

He broke down in tears again. "Yes, yes," he said and walked away in the opposite direction.

Al-Saha building came into my view, about half a kilometer away. I decided on a sudden impulse to visit Talal Salih in his office at the top floor. He was usually there working in the evening. More than two weeks had passed since I had last seen him. I was ready for a cup of Turkish coffee from the expert hands of his office helper Abbas.

To the unsuspecting eye, what happened next would have seemed no more than a simple sequence of random events. If there had really been an eye watching me from some point in space, it wouldn't have been at all surprised by what it saw and would have thought nothing of the matter beyond the ordinary urges that make people do what they do: a man walking hastily down a street, as though rushing to a nearby appointment, and from a distance a woman sees him as she comes out of a store where she had wanted to buy a dress but had changed her mind. The woman is taken aback when she sees him, even though he is a good distance away. The man keeps walking. The woman follows hastily behind. He is completely unaware of her presence. But her high heels prevent her from walking fast enough to cut the distance that separates them by less than a minute's walk. The man enters a seven-story building. He will probably disappear into a room inside one of its many floors, the woman thinks in a flash. So she runs. She runs in spite of her high heels, before the man can disappear from her sight. She reaches the building entrance and finds him waiting for the elevator. When the elevator arrives, the door opens and the man walks in. But before the door shuts, the woman dashes to the elevator and pushes the door open as the man reaches for one of the buttons. She is panting, her face red, her mouth open, her chest heaving noticeably. The man shows utmost courtesy, as he would to any woman about to fall flat on her face from being in such a hurry. "What floor?" he asks.

"The same one you're going to!" she answers.

"Seven?" he asks, making sure.

"Seven," she says, nodding.

The man presses on seven. The door shuts, and the elevator starts moving up. The woman looks at her elevator partner, her eyes wide open and still breathing heavily, not saying a word. The man is embarrassed by her stares and looks away toward the elevator door, waiting for it to open on the seventh floor. When the elevator stops and the door opens, the man steps aside for the woman to go out first. She does and then waits for him by the door. He comes out and walks to the left toward Talal Salih's office, expecting the woman to go the other way, but instead he finds her walking by his side.

"You too are going to Mr. Salih's office?" he asks.

"No, no. I'm just crazy!"

"Excuse me?"

"I'm crazy, crazy, Mr. Nael."

"You . . . know me?"

"Oh yes, very well, very well . . ."

•   •   •

This is how it all began, exactly the way the eye that was following both me and her recorded it, like a hidden camera that could see through walls and closed doors but not into people's minds and souls.

Or so I imagined the incident when I recalled it later.

I didn't know exactly how to react at that moment, but I did my best to stay polite with this stranger. The idea crossed my mind that she might really be crazy, as she herself had said, but only a sane person would say such a thing about herself.

"I think it's wonderful that you know me, and to know me very well," I said, being formal. "May I help you?"

"No, no, not at all. I just wanted to talk to you."

"So, you're not coming to see anyone on this floor?"

"Not on this or any other floor. I ran like a madwoman to catch up with you. You sure walk fast."

"You should have called out to me on the street."

"What would you have thought of a woman, a stranger, calling out to you in the middle of the street, in front of everyone?"

"I would have thought I was just imagining, or that I was the crazy one."

"For now, one crazy person's enough," she said, in a more serious vein.

"When the sun shines with such splendor after the rain," I said laughing, "we're all entitled to some craziness. That's how I felt on my way here today."

I realized that we were still standing in the corridor outside my friend's office.

"Strange!" she said. "This afternoon I came out of my apartment to enjoy the sun. But it seems like some other impulse, more powerful and mysterious, was urging me to come out."

"To see me?"

"To see you, maybe."

"You're serious?"

"Dead serious."

"Destiny, don't you think?"

"What destiny, Mr. Nael? Insanity is more like it. Did you leave home with the feeling that you would meet a woman you didn't know?"

"To be honest with you, I used to get that feeling every time I went out for a walk. But with time I came to realize what a false, deceptive feeling it is. How about coming in with me to see my friend?"

"I don't want to spoil your plans."

"There are no plans. I just decided to drop in for coffee."

"No wonder! You had an impulse much like mine."

"Okay, my lady, let's say it was fated. How about a cup of coffee at Talal's?"

I started leading the way to my friend's office, still not knowing her name, but then she grabbed my arm and stopped me, looking straight into my eyes. "How about going some place for coffee . . . where no one knows us?"

I hesitated, again surprised. What did this young woman want from me?

"Do you want to talk to me about something?" I asked.

"Many things," she replied with desperation in her voice. "Many things!"

I studied her face more closely, noticing her hair tied in the back and her succulent lips. "What's your name?" I asked.

She laughed, sounding more playful. "Are you interrogating me?"

"I would like to know your name, that's all."

She answered tersely. "Sarab."

"What?"

"My name is Sarab. Sarab Affan."

I smiled and held her arm as we turned the other way.

"How can I resist having coffee with a woman named Sarab, even if I know she'll keep me thirsty?"

"I'm sure she will!"

We walked to the elevator, but then I stopped. "I really should see Talal since I came all this way, even if it's for a few minutes."

She seemed at a loss. "Whatever you like," she said, somewhat disappointed. "Should I wait for you here?"

"Wait for me? You're coming in to meet him. He's a really nice man, and we might find him busy writing another poem."

Without hesitating—I don't know how I got the courage—I grabbed her arm and hurried with her to his office and rang the bell. Abbas opened the door.

"Good evening, Abbas," I said. "Is Mr. Talal in?"

He said yes, and I walked straight in to Talal's office with Sarab almost stumbling at my side. Talal jumped to his feet and raced out from behind his big desk, greeting me and looking curiously at my companion.

I introduced them to each other, without the formalities. "Mr. Talal Salih, attorney. Miss Sarab Affan."

I could tell from Talal's look that he thought I was bringing him a client I didn't have time to represent. They exchanged greetings, and he motioned for us to sit down in his ritual formality.

"Thank you, Mr. Salih." She looked at me, confused, not sure if she should sit down.

"Talal, we're in a hurry," I said. "I thought I'd drop in and say a quick hello then come back for a longer visit another day."

"But . . ."

He did not understand, so I said, "No, really, we're in a hurry."

"A cup of coffee at least. Abbas . . ."

"No, no. Coffee means we'll have to sit down, and Miss Sarab has another appointment."

Sarab nodded in agreement. "Yes, an appointment," she said, and as she got ready to leave I stopped her again politely and asked Talal, "Have you written a new poem?"

He laughed. "When you're in such a hurry? Poetry calls for a longer visit, and lots of coffee and time."

"A lawyer who writes poetry?" asked Sarab with genuine surprise.

"Don't you know that three out of every four lawyers write poetry?" said Talal.

"How else would they pass all their spare time at the office?" I added.

"Ask him, he'd be the one to know," said Talal. "Mr. Nael doesn't only write poetry. He writes novels too. Long ones."

Sarab smiled. "I know. Six of them. I read them all."

"Ha! You're one of his many admirers!"

"Sort of. . . . It was nice meeting you, sir." Then she added, as she held out her hand to say good-bye, "I hope to hear one of your poems, sometime."

"Sometime?" I interjected. "It sounds to me like a date. Is it?"

"I'll be expecting your visit," said Talal as we shook hands. "Soon, I hope."

As we walked out of the building, I said, "And now, coffee. Where shall we go?"

She gave me a confused look. "I don't know. I don't come here often."

"Are you driving?"

"I left my car at home and took a taxi so I can walk around and shop. How about you?"

"Me too. I left it at home. Walking is my only exercise. Do you see that hotel? It has a nice restaurant. What do you think?"

The Ansam was less than a couple of hundred meters away. Its proximity to my house made its restaurant and café convenient, especially when visitors dropped in on me unexpectedly and I needed to take them out to eat. I was afraid that she might not want to go with me to a public place, especially on a winter day when it got dark early. But hadn't she herself suggested drinking coffee in a place where no one would recognize us? Perhaps a waiter or two might recognize me at the café, but I didn't care.

We walked fast. I didn't know where to begin my conversation with this stranger even though she claimed to know me and to have read all my novels. It occurred to me suddenly that she could be a reporter wanting to interview me for her newspaper or magazine. In the last two or three years, I had become used to being asked for interviews. I was impressed by the growing number of female journalists, most of whom were young, recent university graduates with a special interest in poetry since they, it appeared, wrote poetry themselves and hoped to take a short-cut to the path of miracles by hearing its "secrets" from the mouths of famous writers.

My guess was right. As soon as we sat down at a table near the big window, I asked her, "What magazine do you write for?"

"*The Weekly.* Do you read it?"

"Rarely. Is it the one that comes out of Paris?"

"Yes."

"So you interview writers?"

"Writers, thinkers, actors, artists . . . anyone," she said laughing.

"So, where's your tape recorder?" I asked.

My question took her by surprise. "Tape recorder? Um . . . you mean for the interview? I prefer taking notes, and I had no idea that I'd end up meeting you today, all of a sudden like this, without warning."

The waiter came, and we ordered Turkish coffee with little sugar.

"In any case, let's not make this a formal interview," I said. "Just coffee, and a . . ."

I couldn't think of the right words, but she rescued me. "And a chance to get acquainted," she said. "Are these the words you were looking for?"

"I was hoping for something more intimate, something with a bit more warmth to it than 'get acquainted,' " I replied jokingly.

At that moment her transparent cheeks seemed to turn red. She parted her wide lips as though gasping for air. I noticed her large eyes and long lashes. She had a fair complexion. Her high, prominent cheekbones accentuated the wideness and depth of her eyes and the fullness of her lips. Her hair was pulled back, exposing her ears—adorned with two simple gold earrings—and her slender neck, which she seemed to be showing off on purpose. I pictured her wearing a necklace hanging down over her green, woolen sweater, and better still if the necklace had large red or black beads.

During our brief silence, as I observed her face and her light makeup, I imagined her pleading with me about some matter that I knew nothing about and couldn't help her with. But right away I said, taking a pack of cigarettes out of my pocket, "Then let's start getting acquainted. Do you smoke?"

"Yes, sometimes," she answered politely. We lit our cigarettes, and I placed the box and lighter between us on the table as if to suggest that our coffee social could go on as long as we needed it to.

"Are you surprised that I've read all your novels?" she said, puffing on her cigarette.

"Yes, somewhat. I'm used to people telling me they've read this or that novel, or maybe two, and that they preferred one over the other. And usually the conversation ends with them asking me for a copy of one of my earlier or later novels, as a gift, of course."

"And then, what do you say?"

"I say, 'Of course, it's my pleasure.' But most of the time I have to apologize since I rarely keep extra copies."

She chuckled as the waiter brought our coffee. "So I guess I won't ask you for a copy of *Entering the Mirrors*?"

"Didn't you say you read it?"

"Yes, but I don't have a signed copy."

"Sarab, you're trying to get a copy because you really haven't read it."

"Oh, no. You'll see how well I'm able to discuss it when we have our interview. Wasn't it your last novel?"

"The last one I published."

"So, you're working on something new?"

"I'm always working on something new. But that's beside the point. What I really want to know is who you are exactly."

"I already told you. I'm Sarab Affan, and I'm crazy."

"No, no, I think you're perfectly sane."

"Okay, so I'm perfectly sane, but sometimes I get crazy." She laughed and said, correcting herself, "Or should I say I'm crazy, and sometimes sane?"

"Right now, what are you?"

"Both."

She put out her cigarette nervously, still laughing softly. I did not know how to deal with her, although I had become accustomed to strangers who imagined they could invade my privacy with their questions, while I warded off their attempts by giving short answers to their questions and keeping a distance in both mind and spirit, by feigning ig-norance and being evasive and playful.

She looked up at me suddenly, daunting me with a desperation in her eyes that betrayed the faint smile on her lips. At that moment I re-membered Siham patiently fighting illness and trying to hide her pain. I remembered her marble face as it gazed at me early every morning, smil-ing and crying at the same time. Sarab's eyes had penetrated me against my will, and I was refusing to give in to one of her fancies, or one of mine. She was no doubt a spoiled young woman who had now been given the chance to play a game—albeit an innocent one—with an older man about whom she knew much both from his own writings and writings about him. So she was acting out for him the role of a woman at once crazy and sane, at once happy and desperate, as though she might qualify as a char-acter for one of his novels. I was sure that she would soon start telling me about some emotional difficulty, some terrible crisis that was driving her to contemplate suicide: "Can't you see how I'm suffering, how miserable I am. Would I fit, dear writer, as a character in one of your stories?"

I had to resort to my time-tested method in handling such situa-tions, so I asked her, still being lighthearted, "Are you really that sad, desperate. Are you contemplating such horrible thoughts?"

Her answer betrayed the look in her eyes, still brimming with that mysterious misery of hers. "Not at all, Mr. Nael, not at all. Do I look sad and desperate? It's just that for several months I've been hoping to meet you, and I'll be honest in saying that at the beginning I expected to meet you as an admirer, not as a reporter. Yes, an admirer, as your friend Talal guessed. I never thought I'd meet you, I mean, sit and talk to you like this, one on one. You see what belated adolescence can do?"

"Ha, ha! So you never meant to interview me for *The Weekly*?"

"At first, no, but later it occurred to me that I could call you for an in-terview as part of my work, that's all."

"But you didn't."

"Well, you know. Procrastination. You tell yourself that the person you want will be there, that he's not going anywhere, that in due time you'll call him as planned."

She was still gazing into my eyes with that same intensity, in a way that contradicted her words. She reached for the cigarettes and asked me if she could have one. As I lit one for her, there seemed to be a slight tremble in her hand, but I pretended not to have noticed and went on with the same playfulness, "So you might say . . . it's too late to mend?"

"Mend what, Mr. Nael! Tell me, who was your father? Where were you born? Why did you study law? What makes you want to write? Do you have brothers or sisters? Who were your childhood influences? Why didn't you publish anything during the five years between *Salamander Island* and *Entering the Mirrors*? How many times have you been married?"

"Sarab, have pity on me, please," I interrupted, "and spare me your long list of journalistic questions. Didn't we agree this would only be a coffee social?"

"And a chance to get acquainted."

"Okay, get acquainted, but without all those life details where one can't sort truth from fiction. Anyway, I too would like to know something about you. Didn't you say that you knew me well, very well? Likewise, allow me to get to know you, if only a little, just a little. It's my turn to ask. Who is your father? Where were you born, and when? What did you study? Why do you read my novels, one after the other, and why do you ask me to account for the wasted years?"

"The wasted years! The most wonderful of years? Or the most horrible? Look! It's raining again, pouring!"

I hadn't been paying attention to the rain beating against the glass window next to us. The lights from street lamps and neon storefronts and signs added a colorful glitter to the falling rain. "A festival of rain!" I said.

"Yes, but look how the raindrops trickle down aimlessly," she said, then added softly, "Like tears."

Before I could respond, she raised her hand toward the glass window with an expressive gesture, gazing at it and saying, "Little streams here and there. Raindrops stopping halfway on their paths, some pushing slowly and merging with other drops."

My eyes wandered between the streams, the drops, the gestures of her hand. "Are you able to see things I cannot see? Like a coffee-cup reader?"

"Precisely."

"Lines and shapes inside a cup tell the drinker's fortune, but whose fortune is told by lines and shapes on a coffee shop window?"

"You don't know? That of the two people sitting next to it."

"You and me?"

"Of course."

"Then go ahead, tell us our fortune."

With the feigned seriousness of someone pretending to know what she's talking about, she traced with her long, bare fingers the paths of the raindrops as they merged with one another and said, "What an incredible map of intricate paths that no person can possibly follow to the end. You see? The paths either get blocked, or fall toward some abyss. But . . ."

I interrupted her in the same tone, half serious, half joking. I was starting to enjoy watching her hands move in graceful, harmonious gestures resembling a montage of close-ups in a film shot by a brilliant cinematographer. "Is there hope left?"

She pointed to a section of the glass where colorful reflections from the neon lights of the shops outside had converged. "Yes, I see a small lake, a paradise fencing in those inside it."

I had hardly focused my eyes on this "fenced-in paradise" when a gush of rain washed over it, and Sarab cried, "Oh no, no! Even this tiny paradise is drowned by the flood!"

"So, will the flood drown us too?"

"I'm afraid so."

"Please, don't have us doomed so quickly. Maybe somewhere in this great expanse there's a small lake to give us refuge?"

"Where?"

With more of her lighthearted seriousness, she raised her head and pulled closer to the window for a better view of the glass. She stood up to give herself a view of the far corners as I watched her being playful, at once delighted and amazed by her ability to so quickly and easily erase all formality between us. When she stood up to look at the window, I took pleasure in noticing her small, swelling breasts under the long, green sweater, and her slender waist and the wide, black belt strapped around a sweater that covered part of her kilt.

She sat back down in her chair, shaking her head left and right, her lips pursed. "Not a single lake to protect us. The flood is everywhere, Mr. Nael."

"You know, you're something, you're really something," I found myself saying.

"Really? Have you discovered in me some new quality worth mentioning?" she asked with delightful sarcasm.

"A first-rate fortuneteller!" I said, laughing. "But I wish you'd found us another 'fenced-in paradise,' as small as it may be."

"The next rain, God willing!" she said, laughing.

"Who says we're to meet again?"

"I say so, and all these streams of rain back me up."

"First, tell me . . . how will you get back home in this rain?"

She looked at her watch. "Oh, I'm late, really late," she cried out. "And I forgot that I didn't bring my car."

"Neither did I."

"What should we do?"

"Take a taxi."

"Of course, then there's no problem."

"You know? Ten years ago everybody was always complaining about everything being a problem. A problem if they got bad service at a restaurant. A problem if they didn't have a car to get them around. A problem if it rained, or if it didn't rain. But these days nothing is a problem anymore. If the water gets cut off at home, no problem. And if we can't get our car to start on a cold morning, no problem. And now that we're standing out in the rain . . ."

"No problem," she interrupted. "But it will be if I'm not home by eight. And many more problems will come after that! You see, Mr. Nael, the real problem is that it always takes one problem to fix another. Now you'll start explaining to me how this is Hegel's dialectic, and make me forget what I'm in."

"I've already forgotten what *I* am in."

"Good. So we've both forgotten what we are in."

At that moment I felt madly attracted to that cheerful stranger who had come to me with the setting sun on a rainy, winter day. I leaned forward toward her as closely as I could without drawing the attention of other customers in the café. "Who are you exactly? Are you really a *sarab*?"[2]

She raised her cup and sipped the remaining drops of coffee mixed in with the residue, licking its brown traces off her lips. "I am a *sarab*, but sometimes I wish I were a lake. Actually, I wish I were a sea. But . . . no . . . seas are salty. I wish I were a lake."

She was silent as I studied her face and wide lips. Then she added, laughing, "And of all the lakes of the world, I wish I were Lake Tiberias. Can you imagine?"

"Lake Tiberias? They say it's beautiful, amazing."

"I like its name."

"One minute it is as peaceful and calm as a dove, and then, suddenly, it goes into an insane rage. There's no lake like it."

"Really? Does this remind you of how I described myself at the beginning?"

"Sarab, you're not *a* problem, you're a whole lot of problems!"

We went outside when the rain subsided to a tolerable drizzle, and we stood under the portico waiting for a taxi. When one arrived, I offered to ride along with her to make sure she got home safely, but she declined. I held the taxi door open for her and closed it after she got in. As the taxi drove off, I remembered that we hadn't exchanged phone numbers.

I waited in the wet glitter of the street and hailed another taxi. A sudden feeling of loneliness came over me when I got into the car. I wished that the beautiful reporter had gone back with me. I thought of her laughter, the smell of her perfume suddenly wafting from her hair when I opened the car door for her. I tried recalling the name of the lake I had seen before, in a movie perhaps, and wondered if I had given her the right description of Lake Tiberias.

2. *sarab:* mist or thin cloud.

Around midnight—as I was about to turn off the lights in my office and go to my bedroom after Salima had put Ghassan to bed and was herself about to do the same—the phone rang. Someone calling so late, I thought, must have an urgent matter that can't wait till morning.

"Hello."

"Mr. Nael? I'm sorry to call so late."

"Who is it, please?"

"Sarab Affan."

"The beautiful reporter."

"I bet you're used to beautiful reporters flocking around you!"

"And not-so-beautiful ones. Good news, I hope?" And before she could respond, I added, "I remembered after you left that you hadn't asked for my phone number, as reporters usually do. And I didn't get yours."

"It doesn't matter if you got mine or not. I've had your number for a long time."

"So you made it home okay?"

"Yes, and I remembered that we hadn't set up a time for our interview."

"Maybe you lost interest, after getting to know me over coffee?"

"On the contrary. I left feeling certain that I'd see you again tomorrow. I don't know why!"

"The streams of rain must have told you that. Did you say tomorrow?"

"Yes, tomorrow."

"What time?"

"It's up to you."

"I'm busy most of the time, especially mornings."

"As soon as I got back home, I made sure my tape recorder was working and that I had one or two blank tapes. I would like a long interview, an hour or two if possible. I know your mornings at the office are busy. Are there many people working with you?"

"Three or four, your typical law firm."

"And in the evening?"

"I prefer not to go to the office at night, although we're open for business."

"Will you make an exception, tomorrow?"

"No, no. I don't like meeting with reporters in my office. How about meeting at the same café as today?"

"Excellent. Six o'clock?"

"Six o'clock."

In the past few years, whenever someone asked to meet with me I would purposely schedule the appointment two or three days later. And here I was tonight, breaking this and perhaps other rules at the suggestion of this young woman. For the first time in years I was looking forward to an appointment with excitement and anticipation. And for the first time I had planned to meet the person in public, worried—though she was the one seeking after me—that she might not show up on time, or not show up at all.

The next day, I arrived at Ansam at six o'clock or a few minutes later. I started worrying that my beautiful reporter might have arrived earlier, waited, and then left. I grabbed the same table as the night before and sat right by the window, hoping to see her arriving among the passersby on the dimly lit street, while periodically looking to see if she was coming in through the inside entrance. When she arrived a few minutes later, I might not have recognized her had she not walked straight toward me. She looked tall and slender, with long hair flowing over her shoulders and large eyes that seemed to contain the world inside them. As reserved as I tried to appear, I greeted her in a way that could only be described as "ceremonious," contrary to what might be expected of a meeting between a writer and reporter.

"What beautiful hair!"

Those were my first words. As we shook hands and I studied her eyes and smiling lips, I was jolted by the feeling that she was perhaps sending me a mysterious signal from her cold hand into mine. She was wearing a long, unbuttoned, olive-green coat, which she kept on after sitting down opposite me, pulling her arms out of its sleeves and letting it hang loose over her shoulders, her hair ruffled about the collar. A jade necklace hung over the top of her beige woolen dress. Siham often criticized me for not paying enough attention to the way women dressed, and I always agreed with her but would add that I quietly appreciated what *she* wore—the cut, the tailoring, the colors. "I don't believe you!" she would say.

And now, after meeting Sarab for the second time only, here I was carefully observing the colors of her dress and coat just as I had yesterday the colors of her sweater and skirt. I said, looking into her eyes, "Are your eyes black or green? Are they black with some green, or green with some black?"

She shook her head, laughing. "I'm not telling you, and it won't help you to stare at them like that."

"In this dim light, they take on the color of your coat combined with the darkness of the place. Where's the tape recorder?"

Before she could answer, the waiter came. We ordered coffee with little sugar, as we had the day before.

I repeated my question. "Where's the tape recorder?"

She pursed her lips. "I'm sorry, Mr. Nael, I forgot to bring it."

"You forgot? Does a soldier go to the battlefield without his weapons?"

"Yes, I'm an unarmed soldier." She opened her large handbag and took out a book. "But, I did bring one of your weapons, *Entering the Mirrors*. Would you sign it for me, a gift from you to me?"

"A gift, when you bought it?"

I opened the book to the first blank page, hesitating with what I should write. Should I write something that might reveal my spontaneous feelings? Of course not. Only part of what I am feeling, maybe. So I wrote: *To Sarab, who shines brighter than the mirrors.* Then I signed.

She took the book from me impatiently. "Oh my God!" she exclaimed. She brought the book to her lips, closed her eyes, and kissed it.

I felt very embarrassed. Did she love me that much—that she would kiss the page where I had signed my name? Or was she just acting? But what reason did she have to act? When she looked up at me, still holding the book to her lips, there was a strange, imploring look in her eyes, but perhaps it was the same desperation I had noticed in them the night before. "What am I getting myself into with this stranger?" I thought.

Fortunately at that moment the waiter arrived with the coffee, dissipating the heavy feeling that had unexpectedly charged the atmosphere. Raising my cup, I said, "I still think you have a tape recorder in your bag."

"Here, see for yourself."

She held her bag open. I apologized. "Then, you've done well," I said.

Before taking a sip from her coffee, she raised her hand to her chest and fondled her green necklace as though connecting with some special power. "I have a confession to make, Mr. Nael."

"Why, have you sinned since yesterday?" I asked jestingly.

She nodded. "Yes, but I hope you won't think of it as a deadly sin."

"It depends how serious it is."

"It's deadly."

I was still enjoying her half-serious jest. "Then confess and get it off your conscience . . . at least for now," I said.

She sipped on her coffee. "Mr. Nael," she said, hesitating, "I lied to you." She paused for a moment then looked straight into my eyes, making sure that she was being unambiguous and serious this time. "I'm not a reporter."

"And you don't write for *The Weekly*?"

"No, and I don't interview writers."

"Not even artists, actors, and so on?"

"No, and the tape recorder I have at home is the bigger kind. I use it to listen to music."

"In that case, Sarab, you've made me happy."

"Really?"

"Of course, because now I know that all you wanted was to get to know me, for who I am."

"I wanted to hear your voice, to look at you while you talked."

"This scares me. Hearing about someone is one thing, seeing him another."

"This is what my friend Randa al-Jouzy said. More than once she warned me against meeting you. Do you know her?"

"No. Who is she?"

"An unknown writer, like me. She shows me her writings, and I show her mine, but neither approves of the other. You know what she said about you? She said you ruined me."

"Ruined you, when I didn't even know who you were until yesterday?"

"You ruined me with your last novel. As soon as I finished reading it, I tore up the manuscript of a novel I had almost finished writing, while Randa watched on and giggled. She too had read your novel. 'Nael Imran,' she said, 'has terrified you! Ruined you! I dare you to write from this day on!' "

"Nonsense. You'll keep on writing in spite of Nael Imran, and I wish I could say, because of Nael Imran. Tell your friend—what's her name?—that these are Nael's words."

"What makes you think my writing is so good when you haven't read any of it? Or did yesterday's streams of rain tell you that?"

"Of course they did. Look at how clear the glass looks right now."

"All I see is darkness."

"Don't be so pessimistic. What you see is darkness disfigured by light."

"Is darkness a body for it to be disfigured?"

"Darkness is the soul and light the body."

"I'm not sure I agree. I imagine darkness as the body, and the soul, if it exists, as the light that disfigures it, or, at least, rearranges and illuminates it."

"You might be right, but unlike most people I think of the body as the light, which, if afflicted with a dark soul, gets extinguished. And once the body is extinguished, it becomes lifeless matter. But the body can also give light to the soul and ignite it, that they may both shine together."

"I think we agree, essentially."

"And why not disagree?"

"Then let's disagree."

"What's the color of your eyes?"

Without thinking, I reached across the table and held her hand. She turned her hand over and squeezed my palm with her soft fingers for a few seconds. Then she pulled it away and took another sip of coffee.

Can this really be happening? Can love be coming back like light- ning? Or have I lost all resistance, giving in to the first temptation? I re- membered Rasha Mansur in Beirut more than ten years back, before the tragedy that destroyed her. I remembered the night I held her in my arms, when she was a student at the university and we had met for the first time after a lecture I gave at the American University. Suddenly that night everything ceased to have meaning except her face, which seemed to have come to life out of some painting by Botticelli, making me relive feelings I had long forgotten. The following evening I was a guest at the dinner table of an older, respectable lady. "Is it possible for a twenty- one-year-old woman to fall in love with a forty-five-year-old man?" I asked her. She laughed, giving me the look of someone experienced in such matters. "When a woman loves a man, she does not ask his age." I'm not sure her answer satisfied me, but I didn't ask her further, re- minding myself that I was the best judge of my own situation. The day I spent with Rasha was like a trance. We went from one café to another and gazed at the sea from the rocky shores of al-Rawsha while talking about the suicide of lovers. I'd been thunderstruck by a love I thought I would never again experience, one that only happened to people in their early twenties, the same kind of unruly love that had led to my marriage with Siham Khayr al-Din and caused us both painful compli- cations with our parents. I'd been married to Siham seven years and not once had anyone or anything come in between us—not even for a day— except for Tala al-Dahir, who during the early days of our marriage hov- ered around us like a specter that might attack at any moment, until she finally got married to Sharif al-Turk and left us alone once and for all. The first week I spent with Rasha in Beirut, Brummana, and Jounieh was like a week outside of time. Each hour seemed an eternity full of ex- citement and vigor. When I went back to Siham, I discovered that I still loved her, perhaps even more than I had before, and that my desire to hold on to her had grown stronger despite my attachment to Rasha. I lived this rending yet pleasurable contradiction hour after hour. The next few months of me writing to Rasha and her writing back left me in a state of Sufi ecstasy. I returned to Beirut every five or six weeks pre- tending to be involved in a court case for which I had to be present in person, and on each trip I experienced more of that mad ecstasy. This went on until Rasha finished writing and defending her master's thesis on Jalal al-Din al-Rumi and Saint Teresa, after which she moved back to Ramallah in the West Bank, making it impossible for me to go see her under the constant threat of Israeli guns.

Is lightning again ripping through the dark of night? Am I again being struck by thunderbolts? As Sarab went on talking about the body and spirit, I had enough sense left in me to ask myself, "Can I once again be experiencing the ecstasy of dervishes? Is it the touch of her hand? The color of her eyes? Her smile?" Here is this playful, charming woman who came out of the void between yesterday and tonight, hiding satanic visions in her flowing hair.

Sarab asked me, noticing my morose expression as I listened quietly, "Did you hear what I said?"

"Not a word, yet I understood everything."

"Or did you hear everything and understand nothing?" she giggled.

"Do you remember how the thunder and lightning kept on and on two nights ago?" I asked in a more serious vein.

"Thunder scares me. I couldn't sleep all night, afraid that the sky might collapse over my head and crush me. When I opened the curtains I saw the incredible light flashing as though it were the one producing the roaring sounds threatening the universe with destruction."

"Sarab, I love lightning. And it seems I've been thunderstruck."

"God forbid, Dr. Nael! If that were true, you'd be a block of charcoal by now."

"I *am* a block of charcoal, and a smoldering one at that. Sarab, who are you? Why won't you tell me? Where did you come from? Who sent you? Why didn't you listen to your friend, what's her name?"

"Randa al-Jouzy?"

"Yes, Randa. She has a beautiful name. I'm sure she's smart too."

"She's very smart. And like me she's dead scared of thunder and likes to watch the lightning. We watched it together two nights ago."

"Too bad I wasn't the one there, with you."

"Why, to protect me?"

"To be thunderstruck, with you!"

I squeezed my palm into hers, our fingers mingling and carrying on their own conversation, or so it seemed. For about a minute neither of us felt the need for words. Then suddenly she looked around, scared that someone in the café—crowded by now—might be watching. She pulled her hand away and raised her cup, empty except for the thick residue at the bottom, and held it close to her lips without touching them, gazing at me with her green-black eyes.

I kept silent, observing her face. I offered her a cigarette. As I lit it for her I noticed her lips and nose, bright under the flame of the lighter. I remembered Siham's marble face. Here too was a smooth, chiseled marble surface in need of caressing. After putting the lighter on the table, I was tempted to feel her lips and nose to make sure her marble face responded to the touch. Perhaps she knew what I was thinking because she raised her head and tilted it sideways slightly while puffing out on her cigarette as though wanting me to take my fill looking at her.

"Your profile is like a Greek sculpture," I said. "The bridge of your nose, your forehead. I've seen your face among the statues of the gods at the Acropolis."

"What a wonderful compliment. Women like being flattered."

"I am only describing something I see."

"*Something*, Dr. Nael?"

"Something among the greatest of human creations. A presence, an incredible, splendid presence."

"Only my face? The bridge of my nose?"

"Everything about you, everything. Sarab, how is it you're not married, no one has made off with you yet?"

"I was married once. It was a short and bitter experience, and very difficult to get out of."

"Tell me about it."

"Right now? While bathing in the pure water of your springs?"

"On such a cold day?"

"On such a beautiful, cold day, pierced by thunder."

"Sarab, in a few words you painted a picture, an unusual picture. I can almost see the god of thunder—Jupiter, I think—throwing his fireballs around the water nymph who, consumed with love, was out bathing in the waters gathered among the rocks on a spring day. Jupiter, the cunning lover, wooing the nymph in a way all his own."

Sarab burst out laughing, her hair swaying left and right. She leaned forward as close to me as she could. "You know? You remind me of my classical drama studies at the School of Fine Arts. I haven't told you yet that I studied theater. Our teacher, Munzir Fadil, who was educated in France, loved Corneille and Racine and would have us practice by acting out scenes from their tragedies, in the manner of the old Comédie Française. So we had to learn all the allusions to Greek and Roman mythology."

"Drama is so foreign to what I studied," I said.

"I'll make another confession. Despite what I've read of your writing, I was afraid that when we met you might start using the jargon of penal code, corporate by-laws, the amendments to misdemeanor laws, the amendments to the amendments, and conflicting laws."

"I studied international law in Geneva but later ended up in a general practice. For me it's just a living, not my real interest."

"Which would you choose if you had to, bread or love?"

"My dear lady, I'm a practical man. I would choose the bread."

"What a pity! I'd say give me love and I'll survive on water."

Confronted with her big eyes and lips, which looked like they'd been sculpted from rose-red marble, I felt an urge to reach across the table past the leftover coffee and cigarette butts and hold her cheeks and kiss her. "Ah . . . and on a little wine!" I said, with a muffled cry.

The smile froze on her face. Was it that same desperation suddenly coming back? She leaned forward, bringing her face closer to me. "Didn't I tell you I'm crazy?" she whispered.

Sadness overcame me as I gazed into her eyes and whispered, "I'm the crazy one."

"Do you realize what time it is? It's past eight, and I've had my share of the evening. Cinderella must leave in a hurry."

"Then why not have my share of the evening? It's all yours. Please stay."

"I wish! I have to be home before my father gets back from his clinic."

"Then I have no more to say!"

"Shall we go?" she asked, shoving *Entering the Mirrors* inside her bag.

"Let's go. Are you driving? I'll walk you to your car."

We had parked on the same narrow, dimly lit side street, two cars apart. She opened her car door and held out her hand to say good-bye. I brought her hand to my lips and kissed it. Then, without looking around to see if there were any passersby, I held her face in my palms and kissed her lips—a delectable kiss that we had to cut short, afraid of being seen. Despite the dim light, I could see the terrible pain and desperation in her eyes and on her lips, which she offered to me again in earnest and I took in my mouth hungrily as though I hadn't kissed a woman in ten years. "Oh, Nael," she said, breathing on my cheek.

"Tomorrow?" I asked, as she settled into her car seat. Then I added, "Oh, but I'm invited to dinner tomorrow . . ."

She started the engine and said, "We'll talk later tonight."

When I got back home, Salima had already fixed dinner for Ghassan and herself. She brought out another plate, explaining that she hadn't been sure when I'd be coming back. After I ate dinner, Ghassan showed me his math, science, and reading comprehension notebooks and the homework assignments he had finished. When his aunt and I took him to bed, he resisted, asking for our permission to stay up longer and watch television, and so we explained the importance of sleeping early so he could wake up feeling strong and outdo his classmates in work and play . . .

At midnight I went to my bedroom and placed one of the two telephones on the side table next to my bed. I had a strong feeling Sarab would call before I fell asleep. I tried reading in bed but couldn't concentrate. I answered the phone at the first ring. She spoke in a whisper, as though afraid someone might hear her.

"Haven't you gone to sleep yet?"

"You promised to call. How could I sleep?"

"I'm incredibly tired. I feel like sleeping right now!"

"What makes you so tired?"

"Writing my journals."

"Journals?"

"For some time now I've been recording the things that happen to me every day—and things that don't."

"Things that don't happen to you?"

"Yes, in a way."

"So today you wrote about what really happened, our meeting last night."

"Yes, page after page."

"Passionately?"

"And deeply."

"Will you let me read them?"

"No way! And reveal my secrets?"

"Would that be a shame?"

"A great shame. Did you say you're invited to dinner tomorrow?"

"Unfortunately, yes, with Talal Salih and other friends I haven't seen in a while. Remember Talal?"

"How can I forget him? He promised us a poem. We'll have to take him up on it."

"I'll remind him. And after tomorrow . . ."

"Nael! I can't think that far ahead."

"Okay, we'll talk later."

"Good night," she said, then added, "Wait. If I can't fall asleep, may I call and wake you up, to talk? Would I be disturbing anyone?"

"You may call anytime you like. But what if your father hears you talking on the phone at three in the morning?"

"He'd kill me. But why worry? My father's a heavy sleeper. Ah, I feel like sleeping now. I'll talk to you soon. Good night."

◆　　◆　　◆

I was happy to see my old friend Abdullah al-Rami after a long absence. I hadn't seen him since the early seventies, after that conversation-filled summer we spent mostly in Souk al-Gharb in Lebanon. His political activities since the mid-seventies required him to be extremely secretive in his movements, and he was most likely traveling under one or more pseudonyms. As far as I knew, he conducted most of his *fedayee*[3] activities in West European countries. I was surprised to see him, a man close to fifty, looking as if all those years hadn't touched him: black-haired, with a resonant laugh and fiery eyes, walking erect as if the world's ordeals—and God knows he had experienced many in the last fifteen years—could not bend his shoulders.

He asked me right away about Siham. He hadn't forgotten how fond she'd been of his writings for one of the Lebanese journals, how she never missed a chance to join us in our gatherings and conversations, and her clear admiration for his passionate convictions, which he always balanced with lightheartedness and a sense of humor.

I didn't expect him to be as shocked as he was when I told him she had died. "She was one of the most wonderful ladies I've ever met," he said, shaken with sadness. Later on he talked to us about his Danish wife, whom he'd left behind in Copenhagen, telling us in his endearing frankness how his love for her "started out political, then became sexual, and now is somewhere in between."

Our group met at the Holiday Inn. Talal, also an old friend of his, was in the usual poetic mood that followed his second glass of whiskey. Also present was Salman Abu Awf, who referred to himself as "the intellectual who had taken the vow of silence," despite his fame throughout the seventies for his weekly column in *Al-Raqib* newspaper and two novels that had gained widespread attention both here and in several other Arab countries, after which he decided that after all he'd been saying for the past twenty years there was "no longer anything left that is worth saying." Once in a while he would say, teasingly, "Look at Nael. Despite all his success in exploiting the contradictions of our laws and statutes, he never quits making his voice heard in one novel after another. I swear, if I were King Shahriyar I would have ordered Masrur to behead Shahrazad before the break of dawn, so she would quit telling her tales!" Amid our laughter, al-Tayyib al-Hadi commented that Shahrazad would have frozen Masrur's hand in midair as he got ready

---

3. *fedayee:* from Arabic *fida'i,* someone who sacrifices himself for a cause.

to strike with the sword by saying to him seductively, "It hath reached me, my auspicious executioner . . ." And how much more powerful are words when compared with swords?

Al-Tayyib al-Hadi, also an old friend of mine, was here on a rare visit researching an article for a magazine in Paris. He'd been residing between Paris and Rabat ever since leaving Beirut with all the Palestinian fighters forced to evacuate aboard the ship that took them to Tunis in the early eighties. He was one of those few Moroccan writers who had settled in Beirut in the seventies, where he worked as a journalist. At first, he was marginally involved in Palestinian activities, but later he devoted all his writing—his entire being—to the Revolution, making a name among the extraordinary group of men and women who, based in Beirut, went on to change the face of Arab journalism everywhere and, starting from the realities of the Palestinian struggle, participated in changing the future course of poetry, fiction, and literary criticism in the entire Arab world.

I loved al-Tayyib very much. He was there during the magical times I spent with Rasha Mansur. The three of us often met and stayed up till dawn in Beirut cafés and restaurants. In addition to his intellectual courage, he always impressed me with his exquisite memory. His ability to recite Quranic verses was amazing. Whenever an argument arose about a particular Quranic verse, al-Tayyib would point out the exact *sura* it came from and explain its context. Anything he read and liked got permanently imprinted in his memory! He loved poetry so much that both the old and new mingled freely on his tongue, from the poems of Imru al-Qays to those of Ahmad Shawqi and Ibrahim Tuqan, not to mention those poets who were his friends and contemporaries.

And so it was a wonderful evening for all of us. Our conversations spanned many topics, from the intimate and personal, to shared memories and current issues in the Arab world and outside it. Al-Tayyib had recently discovered the Norwegian writer Knut Hamsun, whom he had read in French. He had perceived in his Nietzschean influence the kinds of impulses that caused solitary heroes to arise among peoples who, in al-Tayyib's words, were, unfortunately for them, in need of heroes. And so they would give rise to heroes who brought misery not only upon themselves but also upon those people over whom they ruled, thus triggering endless chains of tragedies and massacres! Then he quoted one of Hamsun's important characters, Kareno, the hero of his trilogy, who had said something like, "I believe that certain types of people are born to be leaders, tyrants created by nature itself, master-leaders, not men appointed by others, but men who appoint themselves as rulers over the masses. I believe in one thing only, and I hope to see it happen: the return of the great terrorist, the living embodiment of human power, the Caesar . . ."[4]

Al-Tayyib asked, "Had Hamsun prophesied eighty or more years ago what the Arabs and other Third World nations were moving toward, in search of the great terrorist, the Caesar who would achieve the exact opposite of what Nietzsche envisioned? Two months ago I wrote an article about this same hero of Knut Hamsun in an attempt to explore the likelihood of such a leader emerging in the Arab world of today. Guess what happened? The journal issue in which my article appeared was banned in most Arab countries! That was the third time the journal had gotten banned because of something I wrote. The editor-in-chief reprimanded me, 'For God's sake, Abu Muhammad, I have nothing but respect for your views, but please don't get my magazine banned every other week all over the Arab world. I'm only trying to put bread on our tables.' From that day on Abu Hassan made sure he always read my articles before they got published!"

Throughout our conversations, Sarab didn't leave my thoughts for a minute. I consoled myself with the thought that our meeting would

---

4. *"I believe in . . . the Caesar"*: from Knut Hamsun's *Kareno Trilogy*, presumably from the French translation: "Je crois au seigneur-né, le despote naturel, l'autocrate, pas l'élu mais celui qui se dresse seul pour devenir chef des hordes de la terre. J'espère et je crois en une chose, le retour du grand terroriste, de l'homme essentiel, de César" (*Aux Portes du Royaume; Le Jeu de la Vie; Crépuscule*, trans. Catherine d'At and Karin Meland [Paris: Actes Sud, 2001], 87). Robert Ferguson, Hamsun's biographer, has translated the same passage directly from Norwegian with a slightly different emphasis: "I believe in the born leader, the natural despot, the master, not the man who is chosen but the man who elects himself to be ruler over the masses. I believe in and I hope for one thing, and that is the return of the great terrorist, the living essence of human power, the Caesar." (*Enigma: The Life of Knut Hamsun* [New York: Farrar, Straus and Giroux, 1987], 164).

likely come to an end around midnight and I'd still be able to call her before going to bed. But an evening that had brought us together after all those long years would not end that soon. It lasted till after one o'clock in the morning.

When I got back home, I found my sister in the library with a pen in hand and looking over some papers. "Salima! You're still up?"

She took off her glasses, looking ill. "I have to turn in our annual report to my boss tomorrow. I only finished it an hour ago. I'm going over it for final corrections. How was your evening?"

"Wonderful. Did anyone call?"

"Yes. A woman called twice, probably to consult you on a case."

"Did she leave her name?"

"I wrote it down, right here."

She handed me a piece of paper. "Randa al-Jouzy? Are you sure?" I asked, surprised.

"Yes. Why do you let your clients call you at home? You should only give them your office number."

"I didn't give her any of my numbers. I haven't even met her. Didn't she leave a message, a phone number?"

"No. She called a little after ten, and again at midnight. I don't understand how someone can call so late! When I told her you're not in, she said she'd call you tomorrow at the office."

"She must be calling about an important case. Come on, dear, go to bed. Is Ghassan sleeping?"

"He stayed up a bit late, but I talked him into going to bed."

"Okay. Good night."

As I walked to my room, I wondered, "What could Sarab's friend want to talk to me about, and so urgently? I hope nothing bad has happened to Sarab." I stood in front of Siham's bust, looking long and hard into her eyes, at her nose, her lips. What are you thinking about, my dear? Are you sad? Angry? Are you being sarcastic? I got closer to her, feeling her cool face and forehead, running my fingers across her lips, her neck. Yes, Siham, I can almost hear you asking me, "You're at it again, aren't you?"

The next afternoon I was revising the Arabic and English texts of

Mr. Abd al-Khaliq Shuayb's contract when Razzuqi asked me on my private line, "A lady by the name of Randa al-Jouzy wants to talk to you. Do you want to take it?" I said yes.

As soon as she said hello I felt that in spite of my curiosity I had to be careful in anything I said about Sarab. But who other than Sarab would she want to talk about?

"First of all," she began, without any introductions, "I hope you'll excuse my persistence. I had to call you at home yesterday, and when your wife answered . . ."

"The woman you spoke with is not my wife," I interrupted. "She's my sister. How did you get my phone number?"

"From my friend Sarab. Actually, I need to talk to you about Sarab."

"I guessed that much."

"We spent most of the day together yesterday, and we talked much about you. I'm not sure why I always bother listening to her endless stories when she hardly ever listens to my advice, and even when she listens to it she never takes it."

"What did you call me about last night, at midnight?"

"I promised Sarab to give you a message from her after she found out yesterday afternoon that her phone was out of order. She asked me to call you from our house, hoping that by then you'd be back from your dinner party, to tell you that she was waiting to hear from you about your meeting with her earlier in the day. That's why I called you again at midnight."

"Thank you, Miss Randa, for your concern."

"What should I tell her when we meet for lunch an hour from now?"

"Tell her same place, same time."

"Ansam, at six?"

"You know the details?"

"All of them. I worry about her. I worry that she might be overdoing it."

"Excuse me?"

"Pardon my saying it, but she talked about you as if she'd never seen a man before. I told her frankly that she should keep a level head and avoid any trouble."

"I don't see any trouble. All she wanted was to interview me for her magazine. And even though she denied it later on, I still think all she cares about is the article she's writing."

"Don't you think you might be oversimplifying matters, Mr. Nael?"

"Do you have any other way of interpreting what she said? Even when she gets on to other subjects, I feel that her mind is still going over the same interview questions she prepared beforehand."

"No, no. Her ravings yesterday had nothing to do with magazine articles. . . . Anyway, I hope to meet you some day. There's much to talk about."

I responded, diplomatically, "I'm always ready, my lady. Until then, or until six this evening, give her my regards."

What a strange friendship those two women have, I thought. How openly they tell each other everything! Randa seems more like the logical one, but maybe it is her jealousy of Sarab that makes her act in this way. Even the way she speaks reminds me of Sarab. I would have to warn Sarab not to be so open about her personal life. People are harsh and full of hypocrisy, and a woman must protect herself even from those closest to her, if she means to stay out of trouble, that is. But Sarab has no intention of staying out of trouble. I will talk to her about all of this today, at six. But how far away it seems! Nael Imran has become "man-of-wisdom" Nael, always stating the obvious and giving empty advice. If Sarab chooses to share personal matters with Randa or anyone else, what business is it of mine? Sarab, you're wonderful, no matter what you do or say. Every day that goes by without seeing you is another day lost in a life full of losses. And I should be thankful to Randa for so faithfully passing on my message to you.

But I realized that Randa, like Sarab, had not given me her phone number.

Not important. Not at all.

◆   ◆   ◆

When I entered Ansam, I found it hard to believe that I had only met Sarab twice, and that this was only the third time. Impossible. It seemed as though I'd known this young woman for months, for years, from the time I was a child. But I didn't know anything real about her. It was as though she were a creation of my venerable mirrors. She could be seen and heard but not touched, without physical form. And there she was, sitting at the same table, next to the same window, waiting for me. I hastened toward her, extending one hand to greet her and holding her shoulder with the other. She was still wearing her coat. "I was just thinking to myself that you might be only an illusion!" I said.

"Am I a ghost to you?" she said laughing. "Have I disappointed you?"

"No you haven't, you've only proven me wrong, fortunately. I hope you'll always prove me wrong. You got here early! It's not even six yet."

"I was in the area shopping and finished sooner than I thought. I couldn't find anything worth buying."

We sat down and ordered coffee, and she asked me about my dinner the night before. I filled her in then said, "I reminded Talal Salih of his promise."

"What did he say?"

"He wants us to visit him at the office tonight. A bit later."

"And the poem?"

"The poem is ready. He wants to read it to us in his office. I asked him to give me a copy and save us a trip over there, but he insisted on reading it to you himself, of course. How often does he come upon a beautiful woman like you, who'd pay him a special visit and listen to his poetry?"

"We'll be tough judges."

"Do you write poetry too?"

"Do I look like a poet?"

"Very much."

"Strange."

"The look in your eyes, the desperation. Your rebelliousness. The ring in your laughter. Your flowing hair. Your smooth hands. Your fingertips . . ."

"Mr. Nael, now you're the one attempting poetry!"

"And all that comes to me is prose. I wait for Sarab to call, but I hear from Randa. What can I do?"

She giggled and made a marvelous gesture with her hands, raising them to cover her face as though, jokingly, she were hiding her embarrassment. Then she said, peaking at me from between her fingers, "I'm sorry, I'm sorry. Our phone was out of order yesterday. I had to reach you somehow. Today I felt jealous of Randa talking to you. Of course, I won't encourage her to call you again, unless it's absolutely necessary. I'm worried about her, and you."

"Do you look alike? She reminds me of you, her voice, her intonations, something about the way she talks. Is she as beautiful as you?"

"Sometimes I find her very beautiful."

"And at other times?"

"She can look like a demon, when she gets angry or frowns. You remember the demon you described in *Entering the Mirrors*? She's a lot like him. She told me today that you're not married."

"My wife Siham passed away four years ago. She was only thirty-six."

She was taken aback. Her face became sullen and her abundant hair fell over her face. Silently, she reached across the table past my coffee cup and held my hand. She spoke softly, her whispers coming out like tears. "Nael! I'm so sorry!"

Damn her! She moved me with her act, with her terrifying beauty. I had to rid myself of the obsession she had stirred up inside me. "Sarab, your sadness is fantastic! Is this the Stanislavski method, internalizing the emotion to the point of making it your own?"

She pulled her hand away angrily. "Why? Can't I be saddened by your sadness? I want to be sad and happy with you. This, even Stanislavski wouldn't have understood."

I felt as though the veins inside my head were bursting. "I love you," I whispered.

She moved her face closer, her hair almost covering her lips, and whispered back, "I don't love you. I'm crazy about you! Crazy!"

I stood up. "Come on, let's go and see Talal. The time flew by so quickly!"

We walked the short distance to the tall building that housed Talal's office on the seventh floor. As soon as the elevator door shut, I took her in my arms and kissed her passionately, feverishly, fiercely. I pressed the button to the seventh floor as she clung to my chest, and we went back to our passionate, feverish, fierce kissing, but only for the few seconds it took us to reach the top floor! The elevator door opened and closed again as Sarab pressed a button sending us back to the ground level. We went back to our insane kissing as the elevator started moving. When the door opened on the ground floor, Sarab pressed on seven again, and back we went to our hasty, delicious game. This time the elevator stopped on the fifth floor. We drew away from each other in a flash when a man walked in, giving us his back and pressing on seven. As he exited the elevator—our loathsome intruder and destroyer of pleasures—we were forced to leave quietly behind him, suppressing our laughter. He walked to one end of the hallway and we walked the opposite way to Talal's office.

Abbas opened the door, and Talal came running out of his office and led the way inside, showering us with greetings. As was his habit when not receiving clients, he sat next to me on the couch rather than at his desk, while Sarab sat in the chair next to me. I helped her with her coat as she stood up again, and Talal was about to take and hang it for her on a nearby hanger, but she preferred keeping it on her chair. I noticed my friend devouring her with his eyes as she moved about until she finally settled into her chair and we all sat down. We exchanged the usual formalities and lit our cigarettes. Abbas brought us coffee promptly and left the room.

Sarab and I were still in the warm glow of that brief, impassioned moment. I hoped Talal would not notice. Sarab's face seemed redder than usual and her lips fuller and more enticing from the mild swelling that comes from kissing. She kept her composure, smiling or speaking when necessary, and left me in control of the situation, except for her brief admission to Talal that she was the one who reminded me of his promise to write us a poem.

"My God! What beautiful roses!" she blurted out, turning my attention to the tall, thin vase on Talal's desk, which he had perhaps placed there for the first time in years. It had a rectangular neck and five freshly picked red roses with long stems.

Talal said laughing, clearly overjoyed, "Just for the occasion, just for the occasion."

I had known my friend to be very timid with women when he first met them unless they were clients coming to see him about legal matters. He usually needed a drink or two before he could get rid of what he called "the accursed fetters." He told us that if he had known that he really would be writing a poem each time he promised one to a woman, he would have showered his promises left and right, and maybe then the knot in his tongue would loosen up on its own.

At that point I couldn't help saying, "But would *any* woman you promise with a poem be able to loosen up your precious knot like Sarab?"

I hoped he would understand that I was only trying to be nice to Sarab and not providing him with some "incriminating evidence" for a "love crime" that he would try proving to me.

He walked over to his desk, took two pages of foolscap paper out of a drawer, and came back and sat down. "I just finished writing it this evening. It probably still needs a lot of revising."

"Read it as it is, man," I said.

He looked intently at the first page, then he laughed. "The title of the poem is 'Do You Love My Eyes?' I hope, Miss Sarab, that you'll grant me poetic license in making this a love poem."

"A love poem?" she asked, acting surprised.

"What else can we expect," I interjected, "from a man who has to deal with counterfeiters, crooks, and murderers every day, shuttling back and forth between courtrooms and legal offices? God help us Talal!"

"And anyway, let's leave puritanical poetry to its practitioners," added Talal.

He cleared his throat, took a sip from his coffee, and in a soft voice that lacked neither strength nor that theatrical intonation acquired perhaps from his experience arguing cases in the courtroom, he began reading slowly, giving me, then Sarab, a quick glance every now and then to stress certain words:

She said, "Do you love my eyes?"
I said, "I love your cheeks,
those two fruits,
and your lips,
those two live embers,
crackling with laughter."

She said, "My eyes, do you love them?"

I said, "I love your breasts,
playful, defiant."

She said, "I asked about my eyes,
Do you love them?"

I said, "I love your body,
supple as a willow."
So she said, exasperated, "But my eyes?"

I said, "I love your legs,
slender as sabers,
your ankles gleaming,
as your feet flutter
like two doves."

So she said, "And my eyes?
Don't you love my eyes?"

So I sighed, "Ah, your eyes?
Can I ward off the sun?
Imagine two suns, not one?"

She said, "Who did I kohl them for?"

I said, "For the world, to shine,
even in the dark of night."

She said, "How you exaggerate,
how you connive, deceive."

I said, "For your love only,
do I connive, deceive."

She said, "Then stay with me,
connive, deceive me."

I said, "Do you believe me?"

She said, "What do I care,
as long as you love me today?"

So I said, "Today, and every day!"

She said, "Hush, do not exaggerate!
Enough that you love me today,
What tomorrow or the day after brings
I do not care.
But tell me . . .
Do you love my eyes?"

He finished reading. During the silence that followed, he got up and placed the two pages on his desk and sat in his chair without looking at us, as though worried about what we might say.

"What do you think?" I asked Sarab.

"Wonderful. It deserves the five roses in the vase."

"My gift to you," said Talal.

"The roses or the poem?"

"The roses and the poem."

"I accept!" she blurted out with joy, picking up the pages of the poem from the desk.

"Each time you come here to visit with Nael, you have a rose from me," added Talal.

"Wonderful! And if not a rose, a poem will be enough."

"A humble gift for a most deserving person!" said Talal laughing. "Fine with me!"

Smiling devilishly, Sarab turned around and fixed her eyes on me. "Do you love my eyes?"

I snatched the two pages from her and read, "Can I ward off the sun? Imagine two suns, not one?"

•　　•　　•

We walked back, Sarab holding the five roses in her hand. I asked her if she had brought her car. She said she had lent it to her sister Shaza for the afternoon. Shaza, a fifth-year medical student, relied on Sarab for rides, and so Sarab found it easier sometimes to lend her her car. Their father, Dr. Ali Affan, rarely gave out his car and needed to have it handy at all times in case of medical emergencies.

"I'll give you a ride," I said.

"Never mind, I'll take a taxi."

"No way!"

"I live pretty far."

"Where? The South Pole?"

"No, a bit closer."

I held her arm and led her to the side street where my car was parked, the same street we had parked on two nights before. She resisted mildly as I brushed my mouth against her hair, inhaling its fresh perfume in the cool, humid night.

In the car, with the engine running, we resumed the fierce, breathless kissing that we'd broken off in the elevator. I don't remember how Sarab, amid all our excitement, was able to direct me to her house, which we reached around nine o'clock. I had no idea where I was when I started driving back home. I got lost on highways with no familiar landmarks that I could recognize in the dark night. More than once I had to stop and get directions from a pedestrian walking along a sidewalk, until I finally reached Janeen turn and from it drove straight to my house, relieved finally and feeling like I had just returned from a Sufi trance, where one is satiated to the point of eruption, outside time and space, only to return to a wakefulness of silence, and the emptiness of time and space.

With what detail can I talk about my return to that same intoxicated state day after day with Sarab, whether I saw her or not? Each hour was one of satiation and eruption, with Sarab next to me and in my eyes, we the eternal dancers in this trance that I was losing myself inside once again, for the last time, outside space and time.

3

SARAB AFFAN

Whenever I came back home after spending two or three hours with Nael, everything around me seemed boring, faint, dull—but only until I'd return to my journals or start feeling the urge to see him again. And how quickly that urge would come back to me! Only time stood between my pages and our next meeting, unwanted time that ought to be cast out of eternity.

◆　　◆　　◆

I have only to write about him and me—and no one else—in my journals. What does not relate to him means nothing to me. All my plans can wait. When I am sober and my mind is clear, I realize that I want to get on with trying to break out of my old siege. It is as though my soul were a fenced-in city surrounded by enemies, and breaking the siege means getting away to other cities, other horizons, other desires. I must act on the thoughts that have occupied my mind for the last few years. But right here, right now, all that I'm able to do is go after this sensuous dream, no longer a dream, an experience I segregate every day from all my other experiences and those of my family, because mine do not belong to theirs. Dream and experience, together they are the jewel whose glitter gets me through this everyday darkness I refuse to accept.

I remember copying in my journals a quote from a French writer who describes some of what I am now experiencing. "Love," he writes, "is the pleasure you get when someone loves you, the pleasure of touching them, hearing them, feeling them with all your senses, with your innermost being, with the faculties closest to your body and soul."[1]

The need to explain and justify ends here. I am capable of all the explaining and justifying I want, but seeing him, hearing his voice, is enough for my emotions to wander off with me, and all the explaining and justifying can come later, should I need them.

* * *

From the moment I left him tonight, I cried. I cried for a long time. I started crying in my car. At home I locked myself inside my bedroom and cried, without a reason that I could identify or reflect on. I told myself I would ask him and perhaps he would have the answer, he the experienced, understanding one. Or did I have the answer but like any woman was bluffing and pretending not to? Were my desires just as strong as his, and had I tried to show him the opposite? Was I scared of myself, knowing that inside me there was a woman capable of things beyond his imagination or mine? Had I sought that predicament for myself? Was I destined to live my life torn between those endless contradictions? Must I forever revolve between two selves: the seductress wanting to be seduced but afraid of going all the way, and the woman searching for love who wants it all to the last drop? I am torn because I know that the agony awaiting me will torment me in ways I can't even begin to imagine—that agony of having to constantly reassure myself of how and where a relationship I'm in is going. Ah, Nael, how and where? Tell me.

1. *"Love . . . body and soul"*: a paraphrase from Stendhal's *De l'Amour:* "Aimer, c'est avoir du plaisir à voir, toucher, sentir par tous les sens, et d'aussi près que possible un objet aimable et qui nous aime" (*De l'Amour* [Paris: Garnier-Flammarion, 1965], 34). In the English translation by Gilbert and Suzanne Sale: "To love is to derive pleasure from seeing, touching and feeling through all one's senses and as closely as possible, a lovable person who loves us" (*On Love* [New York: Liveright Publishing Corporation, 1947], 5).

You lured me with your compassion, that compassion that became so much more evident to me after our telephone conversation last night, when you got onto personal matters that I persuaded you to talk about with my unending desire to hear you speak. Your accounts of your childhood, of your sister, of Siham, of your friend Jasim who died drunk in your arms—all put the finishing strokes and colors on a painting that none of our past days together could have. I needed to see you more clearly than I did from reading all your novels. I kept doubting as long as some strokes and colors were still missing, until you yourself filled them in, and in a way all your own. That was the beginning of all beginnings for me. And here I am, once again, entering your magical world with renewed resolve. But this time I enter fear-stricken, intoxicated, full of desire, with no arms to raise against you. On your journeys you always have all you need, but with nothing except my unruly fantasies, I worry that you might keep shaping or reshaping me the way you like so that I'll no longer know who I am except through you. But why not, why not, why not? . . .

That was the first page of a letter I gave him two days later at our usual meeting place at the Holiday Inn bar. After reading it to himself, he asked me to read it aloud "so the words would come to life with the tremors of your voice." I began reading slowly, afraid at first that someone might hear me, but I quickly dropped all my worries. Was I not, after all, the passionate lover who had vowed to announce her love from the rooftops of the city? When I finished, I asked him to write a response, at least twice as long as mine!

"I will," he said.

"Tonight, so I can read it tomorrow."

He folded the letter and put it in his pocket, looking into my eyes. "Tonight, so you can read it tomorrow. Right here."

• ◆ •

Our meeting at the Holiday Inn today was short. It lasted an hour or less. But what a wonderful hour it was. It seemed like two weeks at least. Or should I say two months, two years? He brought his letter with him. As I read it silently, I felt as though I were losing my senses! When

I finished I asked him to read it to me, slowly. Wasn't it my right to ask?

Can you imagine how hard it is writing to you? You got me so used to talking, to being taunted and provoked, my words pouring forth spontaneously with yours. But now that I've promised to write, look at me! A hundred thoughts come to me at once, leaving me scattered and lost, and not a single one to hold onto.

Again I read the two wonderful, troubling pages you wrote. I ask myself whether I am really capable of what you describe, of having this power over your emotions, to the point of causing you tears and anger, longing and desire. How sweet are the tears, sometimes, and how beautiful they are! And how pretty your smile among them! I am the one suffering the pain of seeing. I suffer in a different way each time I see the look in your eyes, approaching me, then turning away, then attacking—the look of an elated tigress proud in her beauty, becoming that of an anguished angel lost between earth and sky.

All of that took me by surprise. I wasn't prepared for such a confrontation, both gentle and harsh, where neither player knows if he is the one winning or not. But you always make it seem as though each of us is both a winner and a loser at the same time, and with that you put off the confrontation from one hour to the next, from day to night, from night to day. And every morning you wake me up to your whispers, ending my nighttime dreams and ushering in my daydreams with the cunning of a lover and cleverness of a hunter. But there's nothing I love or fear as much as that cunning and cleverness. Again, I find myself asking: Am I or are you the cunning and clever one? Am I the lover, or are you? Am I the hunter or the game? But I realize finally that each of us is both at the same time, and please God keep it this way so my questions would be answered, at last!

I must also say that I won't try to shape you the way I like, as you thought I would, because I want you just as you are, as much as I might picture myself sometimes—or you might picture me—as Pygmalion busy hammering away at the tempting marble. Actually, I worry about Pygmalion despite his skill at what he does. As I told you once, I worry that the sculpture might turn against its sculptor, that the maker might become the very thing he is making, that love might come wearing a mask no one expected. As you probably know, I came to you an innocent man, pouring out words and hoping to see them change from *illusion to reality, from voice to body, as anyone would who idealizes beauty above everything else. Ah, that bittersweet coffee one drinks on a night of pouring rain that draws destiny's impossible lines on a glass window.*

The obsession lingers, each moment putting on a different guise, and imagination plays with me the game I like, but sometimes the game is so difficult and bitter that I want it to end, and imagination keeps contending with me and the obsession prods me on for no reason except to keep me busy with things whose shape and course I cannot define.

From this sort of chaos words are born—blurred shapes on wayward paths. They are like flocks of spring birds flying toward you and not knowing where they will set down. What's the harm in that, as long as the words grow wings and soar in the sky, and go crazy even, while you look on as they search for refuge in your skies? Let them be, then, your unexpected blessing from the skies . . .

◆　　◆　　◆

I saw his house at last, on the inside!

He had no idea how many times I had driven by his house, back when I was still gathering information about him and he didn't even know of me. The black iron gate, the wide balcony at the front of the house, the marble fountain visible through the iron fence—all were familiar to me. But I hadn't once seen the fountain spraying its water into the space above, not even a little to moisten the dry basin. I didn't know he had turned off the water after Siham's death. I knew nothing about her at the time. I had purposely driven several times unto the street he lived on after discovering that the Janeen turn led all the way there. I would slow down near the iron gate, hoping to see him, but I saw him only twice during the afternoon, sitting out on the balcony by himself and reading, not noticing me.

He suggested a few days ago that I go home with him, but I declined. I was afraid. I was happy with the mental picture I had of the inside of his house, which I have described in one of my journals. But as soon as I got into his car at our usual meeting place today, he said, "Let's go drink coffee at my place."

"In your castle? With Salima and Ghassan?"

"Unfortunately, no. Salima and Ghassan are staying with my brother Wael. The only one there is Umm Hadi."

Umm Hadi was an older, live-in maid who had worked for his family for over twenty years. "Won't Umm Hadi be surprised to see me with you?" I asked. "Or have you gotten her used to female visitors?" He seemed happy with my tacit acquiescence, finally. "I'm sure she'll be surprised to see you with me," he said. "Our only female visitors in the last few years have been older women, my sister's visitors. She'll think all sorts of things."

"Really? Wonderful. Let's go then!" I said.

My imagination scares me sometimes. The same curious imagination that led me to write my *A* journals, more than it did my *B* journals—or at least helped produce a combination of the two—makes me imagine things that turn out to be exactly as I've imagined them! The genie inside me plagues me with these extraordinary powers, whether I like it or not. How else can I explain the fact that as soon as I got past the doorstep, his house looked exactly as I had pictured it on the inside? Instantly I felt a shudder running through my body—frightening or pleasant, I'm not sure. "I know this house," I said as we stood in the entrance hall.

"You do?" he asked, surprised.

"Yes, as well as I know you. Don't say a word. I'll describe what it looks like as we stand right here. This has to be your library, and here the living room, right? The dining room is over there and right there is the kitchen, with its white and light blue cabinets. That room with the door shut is your bedroom. No one's using the bedroom next to it—a guest bedroom, maybe? And these stairs lead up to your sister's bedroom, and Ghassan's, right?"

"Unbelievable! You must have visited me in a dream! Was it your dream or mine? But the real question is: What's inside the rooms?"

"What can a library have other than a desk and bookshelves? And maybe two or three paintings, one of them big. I don't even need to describe it. But I'll tell you what's in the living room, more or less, of course. The furniture is mostly blue, right?"

"Easy guess. You know I like blue."

"Okay. You've got at least five paintings on the walls, six of them actually, and one is mostly blue."

"You're beginning to scare me. What else?"

"In the same room there's also a bronze sculpture, probably on the larger side. And abstract? Ah, in the living room there are more bookshelves, and you also have two large Czech crystal vases. Have I passed the test?"

"With honors! Come see for yourself."

I thought he was joking and that the living room wouldn't look at all as I had described it. But no, it fit my description exactly! I was stunned as I stood in front of the large blue painting I had described in previous journals.

As I had also imagined in my journals, Nael stood behind me while I gazed at the painting. He held my arms and buried his face in my hair, his lips searching between its locks for the nape of my neck, and then he started kissing me from the back of my ears down to my shoulders. For an instant I felt I was about to faint, like the heroine in one of those century-old romances, fainting when the hero kisses her for the first time. I felt my knees giving way. I would have collapsed unto the floor if I hadn't leaned my body against his chest while he embraced me. But I shook off my anxiety and pulled myself together with whatever strength I had left before he could realize what had happened to me, and he whispered, "Oh enchantress, fortuneteller, reader of streams of rain, seer of things visible and invisible—there's but one secret you'll never know."

"In your past?" I whispered.

"No, no, in my present, Sarab. Can you tell me what's inside the closed chamber of my heart?"

I turned around, holding his face in my palms as he usually did to me, and I gazed into his eyes. "Your heart is not a chamber. Your heart is a labyrinth of crisscrossing passageways. I see a woman who went in and can't get out. Or does she not want to get out?"

"How can she when exit is forbidden?"

As he leaned over to kiss me, I noticed an oil portrait behind him of a beautiful woman staring at me. I had to close my eyes, guessing that it was his wife Siham. So I pulled him along slowly out of the room, our lips pressed together. "I hear Umm Hadi scurrying over from the kitchen, perhaps to ask if we'd like coffee or refreshments," he mumbled.

He raced toward her, shouting, "Umm Hadi, two cups of coffee, please. But take care, not too sweet! Your best!"

He took me to his library while we waited for the coffee. I browsed through the books on the shelves as he pointed out some titles, his arm around my shoulders. Umm Hadi came in, set the coffee tray on a table, and went back out, the sound of her footsteps fading away until we could no longer hear them.

Then what happened? Ah, Randa, my dear counselor Randa, tell me why you let the ink flow so faithfully to the tides of sadness and pain, but when the waves of happiness—of insane joy—rise up so far that they touch the sky, then all you do is put my pen to silence, the silence of envy and conspiracy! Or do you, like me, find it impossible to describe a turbulent sea when its waves reach up so high to try to knock the sun away from the sky, but before they reach far enough the sun explodes, its blazing slivers plunging into the depths of the sea?

◆   ◆   ◆

Every day that goes by without seeing him I pour some of my burdens onto the pages. I dare show him only fragments of my writing, although he insists on seeing it all. Maybe I will show it to him one day, just maybe. I will show him all the journals I wrote before we met. But then again, maybe not. I must keep this crazy game a secret until I have nothing more to give the man I love. But there's still so much more to share during our moments together, and each day brings more.

Today I showed him what I wrote yesterday afternoon. I wanted to see how much I could communicate of what I had thought impossible to communicate. The title, *The Curse of Inner Fragmentation*, came to me spontaneously, and so did the lines that followed:

Numbers are symbols that vary according to the material objects they symbolize and the space these objects occupy within the universe.

And for us numbers symbolize a curse that pounced upon us from an invisible corner and occupied the human body, causing a split in the symbol itself, that symbol the mind calls for and is then given direction by the sticky, thick circumstances that surround us.

And then fragmentation between the self, the soul, and the mind begins, and each winds up in a number of singular formations, at which time the fragmented body experiences the moment of true confrontation with another person's body, which in turn finds itself laboring to produce its own finite configurations, each with its own unique number.

Then comes the stage of comparison in order to determine how and which to use and which is most appropriate for that particular moment of confrontation, resulting in the best possible material yield.

Therein lies the secret behind the instinctual, never-ending search for truth, that truth confined between the self and the other, lost among the numbers.

Inner fusion can be attained only through the affirmation of a final, intimate silence free of numbers.

And between fragmentation and fusion, time flows—a river of ashes[2]—my apologies to our great poet Khalil Hawi.

He scratched his head emphatically, confused with what he had just read, and before he could ask for an explanation, I shoved another page I'd written that afternoon in front of him. "Here, this might hold the key to what I wrote, but maybe not!"

He shook his head, still confused, and then laughed a desperate laugh at me and my ravings. "Your key will be no easier to figure out than your locks!" He went on reading:

The condition of living in a society of uncertainties . . .

A society fenced in by fear and stagnation. Pseudo-human forms squabbling over a handful of superficial utterances. The language of human understanding is doomed, and the life force is generated only in the innermost cores, and as soon as it comes out to take human form and character, it is doomed to spiritual and intellectual closedness.

The same ferocious cycle is renewed every day, and it gives the impression that it is constantly changing, causing an ever-growing weakness that advances gradually, destroying as it proceeds everything that tries to get in its

2. *river of ashes:* the title of a collection of poetry (Nahr al-Ramad) by the Lebanese poet Khalil Hawi (1925–1982).

way, robbing all human movement from its humanity and turning it into empty, mechanical motion.

And finally the hormone of feeling begins to dissipate little by little, disappearing down an ever-steepening slope, to the bottom of the swamps, the swamps of slavery.

He placed the two pages in front of him. I can remember only a little of what he said, but I do remember the beauty of the words he uttered as I studied his face, eyes and lips, moved to the core. He said I was bitter, rebellious, tormented, full of a love he couldn't describe. He said I was delusional, hallucinatory, passionate, resentful of all of life's hatred and cruelty. He said that nothing would satisfy me, and that I was intent on going outside the narrow, conventional margins and into that scary, tumultuous realm which entices me with all its voices and promises of freedom. Those who bear hatred, he said, philosophize it by turning it into laws, canons, and principles that the devil uses as a disguise, appearing in the wings of an angel ready to battle God in his lofty heights, shielding the light of love with the smoke of hellfire. With my background in theater and acting, I imagined this a drama unfolding on a wide stage before my eyes and me thrusting my words into it whether the audience could hear me or not. I said to him once again, for the thousandth time, "I don't like you . . . I am in love with you." And every pore in my body burned for him.

◆　　◆　　◆

Today Nael was in a special poetic mood that inspired him with beautiful images, ones he might use in future writings. But no, a true writer improvises from the inspiration of the moment and does not depend on the memory store—as important as it is—as much as he does on the gradual onset of haphazard impulses in his unconscious and semiconscious mind. But to me what matters is that he sees in me, as he said today, the genie who shatters his locks and turns loose to the winds all that lies trapped inside his thoughts.

In my usual spontaneous way, I read to him the last passage I wrote yesterday at the office. He took it from me and read it again. I could see his love as he resorted to words and metaphors more suited to an impassioned poet than a lawyer-novelist. Am I flattering myself to think that I have such a "genie-like" effect on him, as he claims I do? Listen to me, Randa, and quit your criticism, your suspicion and ridicule. As he gazed into my eyes during those moments, he seemed strangely beautiful and strong. He said I was as pure as sunshine on a day drenched with rain, as invigorating as the waters falling from the rocky heights into the deep valley. The image of the waterfall keeps coming back to him, as it does to me. Is there some mystical meaning to this puzzling symbol? He stroked his fingers through my hair, starting at the top of my head down to my shoulders and back, and he said, his lips on my cheeks, that whenever I turn my head around and let my flowing hair sweep across my shoulders and breasts, he imagines a wind ruffling the tree branches as though announcing a love that would overtake the world in a storm. The storm is another idea that preoccupies him, as it preoccupies me. I keep seeing it in his writings in different forms and with various names. When his passions for me are stirred up he asks, "Are you the tempest or am I?" And I say, "We're the meeting point of tempests. That's the scary part!" Can I deny the vanity I felt when he said that my lips tasted like the fruit of hills full of sunshine and rain, the fruit he caught with his ready lips when the wind shook it off its branches, even though his hunger and thirst became stronger every time he ate and drank from my lips.

◆   ◆   ◆

I talked to him about a strange inconsistency I saw in the way he constructed his stories. Sometimes he would mention the time of events without the place, and at other times he would do the opposite, indicating the place but not the time.

" 'Some day or year in the past' is what you seem to be saying when someone asks you about the time of your story," I said.

"You might think I'm being general, or misleading" he said, "but only when it comes to time. Everything else is precise and clear. I always try to take the experience out of its boundaries in time so I can put it in the absolute. But the absolute also needs to be anchored, and so the place becomes that which holds the experience by its loose ends and brings it together, helping to reveal its essence."

But on a different occasion or context he would say the opposite, "somewhere, in some city," and would mention the time during which his story takes place, if not the exact day or month, then at least the year. And he would say, "The events of our day can take place anywhere, especially those taking place in the Arab world. But the time must be specified, since it is in constant, insane flux. Only then can it give shape to the experience because time, regardless of the place, is what casts the lights and shadows, reveals and conceals, sometimes bringing out the truth and deceiving at others, in its attempt to shed light upon life's forces of advancement and progress, but also upon the forces of decline and emaciation."

When I asked him why he was not content to specify both time and place, like most writers ordinarily did, especially since he was capable of doing so, he replied saying, "As soon as you allow time and space to interfere with each other, you lose sight of the absolute and risk reducing the image and idea to a level of detail empty of larger meanings, not to mention the stifling, irresponsible results that such reductionism might bring about, in one form or another. People tend to rely on the particular—assuming they have the talent to convey it in writing—because they don't want to and cannot break free of their own personal limitations that are the products of the dialectic of space and time. But even so, most of them generalize from the specific, thinking that would bring them closer to the absolute. But the absolute is the real, hard-to-reach summation of things. It is poetry itself, that which bears out the human essence in all its virtues and vices, in all its greatness and lowliness. Think back on what you studied in school, the tragedies of Shakespeare, for example, which carry us beyond time and space to all time and space. Think back on most of the tales of *A Thousand and One Nights*. The absolute is what finally eludes the jailer and executioner. Maybe this absolute, after all, is nothing but the attempt to understand life as an expression of eternal being, of God. And it often seems to me that the human condition, with all its contradictions and ordeals, is only part of that expression of eternal being. We're only a small part in the comedy of the gods, where hell is a thousand times bigger than paradise, even though we might sometimes get a glimpse of paradise, even enter it once, only to be cast back into hell. Such is our eternal exile outside time and space."

After a brief silence he added, "Of course, this does not apply to all people, but it could apply to me, and you. Forgive me if I sound condescending, but I see that special sign in your eyes, in your voice, in every word you say or write, despite your age. We bear a sign that only those like us can see, those promised to eternal exile. I should perhaps correct what I said earlier about abandoning time or space and say instead that we, the outsiders, weave time and space together according to our own understanding in a way different from anyone else's, and so we create this fabric into which all things are woven—all symbols and signs, all forms of historical awareness whether lost or still remembered—and through it we relive old myths with all the violence of passion, death, stubbornness, and the treachery of being hurled into the pits of hell, and we create new myths for ourselves, always asserting that we're part of the grand cosmic movement with all its complexity, with all its celestial bodies, stars, planets, nebulas . . ."

I cried out, and I'm not sure if I did it in response to his amazing words, his sweet kisses, or to the music coming from the speakers—Beethoven's Piano Sonata No. 23, the *Appassionata*—which brought together the now and the forever, exciting my mind and turning my body into a thirsty cave that couldn't get enough of the flood of love and ecstasy gushing through it—I cried out, imagining myself spiraling among the planets of the universe for no reason I could comprehend. "But for a brief time only," I said. "For a few violent, stinging moments that soon retreat, and time and space appear as two monsters feasting on me, and nothing remains of Sarab except the woman I refuse to accept, who insists on being me, me among my family, among people. But when I'm with you or when I'm writing, I take off into space, and there I make my own myths. Do you remember that evening at Ansam when I told you how I like to go swimming in freshwater springs even when it's cold, and you told me about Jupiter as he watched the nymph who, consumed with love, ran out naked in the cold to bathe in the spring waters, and how he wooed her by throwing fireballs all around her? The image stuck in my mind. And I remembered that Leda swam naked in the river, and Jupiter saw how beautiful she was and fell in love with her at once, in his own way. And in order to get closer to her without scaring her, he turned himself into a white swan and floated on the water toward her, like a white dream drawing near. And Leda took the swan in her arms—that snow-white, seductive beauty—and she surrendered herself to it with ecstatic shudders. It was then she realized that the king of the gods had come to her in that delightful form of a swan. Does that make me Leda, and you the swan?"

He gave out a bizarre laugh and whispered into my ear as he fondled my hair. "The fruit of that surrender, do you remember what it was?"

"No," I said.

"Helen, the most beautiful woman in memory, and because of her the Trojan War was fought for ten long years, cities burned, and the course of history forever changed."

"The precious moments of love must have their price, and they are worth it," I said.

◆   ◆   ◆

We met this evening at Ansam. All the waiters had come to know us there, although they had known Nael before me—his name, his novels, his fame. Two weeks ago, one of the waiters, Diab, came running up to Nael and asked him for a copy of his novel *Salamander Island* and told him that he had looked for it in bookstores all around the city but could not find a copy. Nael didn't forget to bring him a copy today. After he got his copy signed, Diab ran elated to the back of the café and, to our surprise, returned moments later with a letter addressed to "the outstanding artist and writer Nael Imran" in which he expressed his admiration for Nael's work in a fine literary style that amazed us both. He admitted to Nael later that for some years he had been trying to write but that the long, grinding hours at work had kept him from pursuing his intellectual interests.

We had other similar experiences. Often a waiter would come up to him with three or four of his novels to sign. At first I used to wish we could go unnoticed, but soon I began taking pride in being the woman who, unknown as she might have been, was always in the company of this man who never failed to excite so much interest. And perhaps people were spreading rumors about her, but all she had to do was flick her little finger and they would come rushing to her service. On his account, of course.

We had an amusing experience a few days ago when we were in Nael's car on our way to a government office where he had some quick business to finish. We stopped at a town bakery to buy five loaves of bread that Salima needed for a dish she was preparing. We were met by a young man covered with flour from head to toe who was shoveling dough into the open oven. As soon as he finished counting out the five loaves, he looked at Nael and cried out joyfully, "Aren't you Nael Imran? Or am I imagining?" When Nael replied yes, the baker said, "I swear I won't accept one penny from you!" I looked on, amused, as they talked.

"No, you must take the money!"

"No, I've sworn to it."

"Why won't you? It's money you've earned."

"Because you're one of my favorite writers."

"And who are your other favorites?"

"Other than Nael Imran? Agatha Christie[3] and Taha Hussein. How would you feel if they came in here to buy bread and I took their money? Mr. Nael, allow me to say this, but your novels are my bread when I find myself exhausted and ailing from spiritual hunger."

As we left the bakery carrying the hot loaves, we laughed about the bizarre combination of writers our cultured baker admired, and had every reason to!

I'll never forget, when we first started seeing each other, the day we

---

3. According to his memoir, *Princesses' Street,* Jabra Ibrahim Jabra met Agatha Christie and her husband, the archaeologist Max Mallowan, in Iraq and became friends with them.

stopped at a pharmacy to get some medicine on our way back from the café, and a young woman no more than twenty followed us in, panting, and spoke to him with mixed boldness and courtesy. "You're Mr. Nael Imran, aren't you?" Even though I was talking to the pharmacist, I could still hear the young woman saying breathlessly, "Excuse me, but I ran so I wouldn't lose you, to tell you how much I admire you."

"You mean, admire my work," he said jokingly, as he usually did in such situations.

"Your work, and you personally," she insisted. He thanked her in his gentle way. "Your name?" he asked. She told him her name. I forget what it was. By then I had paid for the medicine, and I turned to Nael and grabbed him by the arm. "Come on Nael, let's go," I said, and I cast his breathless admirer with a severe glance that meant their "meeting" was over. I remembered the day I met him for the first time, how I too had run behind him panting and almost fell flat on my face when I caught up with him at the elevator.

Sometimes at Ansam the employees played Arabic or Western songs but always kept the volume down at the instruction of the manager to avoid bothering the customers. Tonight, one of the workers surprised us by playing an old French song, "Plaisir d'Amour," perhaps for the first time at that café. I called Diab as soon as the song came on and said, "Please, would you play this last song again, and would you turn it up a little?"

"I swear I brought the tape with me just for the two of you," he said mischievously. He went back and played it again, louder this time. "You understand French well?" asked Nael as he listened to the song.

"Enough to understand the words to this song."

"The joys of love, how quickly they go away, but the sorrows of love, how long they stay . . ."

I was completely lost in the song, between the joys and sorrows of love. Nael said he wished the scales would tip in our favor, letting the joys abound and lessening the sorrows. I told him that if sorrow was inevitable, then we must learn to find joy even in love's sorrows. I remembered a thought I had never had the chance to share with him. "I discovered that one of the wives of Uthman Ibn Affan[4] was called Naela.[5] If by chance I turned out to be an Affan, perhaps it's no coincidence for me to notice that your name is Nael. This Naela, my dear—just in case you've forgotten your history—was the faithful wife of the *khalifa* Uthman Ibn Affan. She came to his rescue when he was attacked by swordsmen in his bedroom, and as she tried to shield him with her body, one of the swords struck her, chopping off her fingers. I also found out that she was a beautiful woman still in her prime when he married her at seventy-seven. She was so grief-stricken with the death of her eighty-four-year-old husband that she said, if I remember correctly, 'I see how my sadness over Uthman is withering away like an old garb, and I dread the day when it would be completely gone from my heart.' Since she was among the most beautiful women of her time and looked even more exquisite when she smiled, Muawiya proposed to her. But the sorrows of love, how long they last. . . . You know what Naela did? She turned him down, broke off her own front teeth—known for their sparkling beauty—and she sent them to him saying, 'Am I still your future bride?' Nael, will you be forever faithful like your wonderful namesake was to her lover?"

He answered laughing, "Yes, even if the swords chop off my fingers! But, wait! I see you've turned the tables around on me."

"I'll go on loving you even if you live to be a hundred and eighty-four!" I said.

He turned pale all of a sudden, pain showing all over his face. He looked silently into my eyes, then he spoke slowly, reluctantly. "Sarab, you can't imagine what you're doing to my mind and feelings right now. You know that Siham is still important to me, and my grief over her loss . . ."

He fell silent.

"I'm sorry, Nael," I said, holding his hand. I remembered that her

4. *Uthman Ibn Affan:* the third caliph (khalifa), 'Uthman 'Ibn 'Affan, regarded as one of "The Four Righteous Caliphs" (r. 644–656).

5. *Naela:* the feminine of Nael.

bust was still in his bedroom. It was the last thing he saw every night, the first thing every morning. "You know? I'm jealous of her, even her marble bust," I confessed.

He threw his hands in the air in a strange, violent way. "No, no, Sarab, don't do this. She's the one who should be jealous of you always in my thoughts, in my entire being."

I wished at that moment that he would take me in his arms and I would bury my head in his chest, saying, "The sorrows of love, the joys of love, always . . ." I turned around and motioned to Diab. He came running. "Please Diab, would you play that French song again. Do you mind?"

"Not at all, not at all," he replied.

The melodies of love's joys filled the café, suggesting that even love's sorrows brought some of their own joys. "Is this love real?" I asked Nael. "Or is it all an illusion?"

He answered maliciously. "This is the love trance Ibn Hazm al-Andalusi[6] spoke of, the trance before madness. When I crush you in my arms, Sarab, don't you see how everything around us becomes an illusion, except for that which you speak of?"

I laughed. "God rest your soul, Ibn Hazm. Can't you see I lost my mind long ago?"

◆ ◆ ◆

"All in vain, in vain, in vain," he kept saying. "The struggle that never ends, the suffering, all the discord that crystallizes in words on the page. All in vain."

I didn't know exactly what was wrong with him the last few days. But today he was clearer. "What can we offer to the world, I and those

6. In his book *Tawq al-Hamama* (The Dove's Necklace), Ibn Hazm al-Andalusi (Abu Muhammad Ali Ibn Muhammad Ibn Said Ibn Hazm) offers a treatise on the phenomenon of the love relationship between the opposite sexes. In one chapter, "Bab al-Dhana" (Of Wasting Away), the author expounds on an "irrational" type of love that takes the form of obsession and leads to madness and loss of reason.

like me who in our constant struggles have reduced our relationship to existence to words and images?"

"You have everything to offer, everything," I said excitedly. "What would the world be like without you? Without color or flavor."

He shook his head. "We say we want to give people the dignity, the beauty, the freedom they deserve. But how much of this professed giving do we actually realize? Hopes, mere hopes, nothing but fantasies, while others do their best to keep people busy with the things that deny them their dignity, beauty, freedom. Don't you see, Sarab, that the creators of all the taboos and sanctions are the masters of our day—those who control all of life's means? What are we able to do with our rebellious visions to stand up to those watchdogs?"

I was firm. "Everything! Everything that's beautiful, everything worth living for, every wonderful emotion, everything that transcends the moment—it's all your work. In the end, salvation comes only through your visions."

His smile was mocking. "I wish I could agree. We all start out confident, then we find ourselves slowly giving in, disappointed, hopeless, and only the lucky recover, proceeding with firm steps toward their first conviction, against all odds. Countless artists have had to deal with feelings of guilt, that in their struggles against the hardships and sorrows of life they haven't measured up to what might be accomplished by a surgeon when he removes a malignant tumor or a plumber when he fixes a clogged drainpipe that was ruining the life of an entire family."

"No, Nael," I said, "I don't share your doubts. You've cut out a thousand malignant tumors from countless souls, you've given them unimaginable vitality, and with every passing day you open up another clogged drainpipe to wash down the stagnant waters, returning life to its unhampered movement. And there's no harm in having these feelings of guilt. All that it means is that your mind, your heart, your feelings, are sound, alive. In this jungle of watchdogs, every sentence you write sets another trap that will lure them all in one day, somehow . . ."

I held fast to my position as he went on expressing more guilt and pain. I told him—although it was obvious without me saying it—that I was an example of one of those souls he had healed and offered unimaginable capacities. I also told him that in the few weeks I had spent with him, after having known him for so long only in my imagination—that in those few weeks I had strengthened my belief in the things I had always been drawn to but had thought impractical, even impossible. I told him that falling in love with him was like falling into a well and then discovering that it led to seas of ecstasy—of paradise maybe—seas where I would sail to wherever my unruly imaginings took me. I told him he was urging me on a course that I knew I had to take, and in this way he would be my savior.

"I'm talking about what an artist does, while you're talking about love," he said.

"They're bound together. I can't imagine one without the other. The work of an artist in its broader meaning and love in its broader meaning, in your novels especially, are so closely connected, like cause and effect, like action and reaction. And both nudge me along in a way I can't stop or resist anymore."

After much argument and discussion he said, pressing his palms into mine, "I worry about you. I really worry about you."

I raised his palms to my mouth, kissing one, then the other. "Don't, please don't, my love. I will live for you only, no matter where I may go, no matter where you may go."

I looked into his deep eyes. They seemed to be welling up with tears. Was it just my imagination? He held my face in his palms, the way I liked, and he gave me a long kiss on the lips, followed by a longer one. "You interrupted my thoughts," I said as our lips mingled.

"You interrupted mine too," he said, and he kissed me again.

◆   ◆   ◆

Today Nael and I tried the impossible. We tried to analyze love, the way one person responds to the other, the joy one brings to the other, the attachment two lovers feel toward each other that speaks to them of the presence of a winged soul suddenly awakening after a deep slumber, its wings flapping as it tries to fly and soar to heights that in the past were only a fantasy, now an incredible reality.

But the body is a fundamental reality, as Nael says, backing his words with what he's read in *The Symposium* and *Phaedrus,* or at least with what he recalls of those two dialogues, saying that Plato speaks of erotic love as the true love one person has for another, because it is based on the other's character, his past, his entire being—a love that cannot be distinguished from intimate, unconditional friendship, just as true philosophy cannot be distinguished from what he calls "erotic madness." I did not quite understand this last point.

I hope I'm not distorting Nael's words, or Plato's, by simplifying the long conversation that kept us busy for hours. While the Greek philosopher speaks of the mind as the place where love resides, the mind as love's aspiration for a higher good, he also speaks of this love as a "madness" of love. Like the Arab poets, he links love to *junun,* madness, and he combines them in the concept of *janan,* the mind in the philosophical sense. Then he goes back to associate the body with the soul, which leads to the conclusion that the mind is but a part of this integral whole, the wings being attached to it in its totality, not just to one of its parts. In the same way, the outer contours and appearance of the body, when seen for the first time, point to an indivisible soul, a unified whole, with all that it represents of the person's character and world.

But the soul is in a state of drought until love germinates, satisfying the thirsty roots of the soul's aspirations, renewing its life. To this the soul responds with joy, reflecting on its own happy responses, as I am doing now, maybe? And when it does that, it brings back the person's identity out of the thick fog that surrounds it most of the time, so that the self's true goals can become clear . . .

I don't know if Nael and his teacher Plato are trying with their words to get to the root of my problem and understand it! One of them adds that this awakening of the soul and the rejuvenation that ends its drought take place as a continuous process, but with much unrest, violence, burning. And so the mind alone will never affect love one way or the other. What matters is all that happens in and around it—the interaction between aspiration and erotic desire, and the interaction of these two with the feelings of awe and intimacy toward the other person. These are the inevitable forces of love. Physical beauty, in the end, guides the soul as it soars toward the world of ideal forms, of whose shadows our lives are made . . .

I don't know how much I contributed to this discussion, but I do feel that I was its object, whether its conclusions were correct or not. And if I really was its object, then Nael had to be its other half, so closely bound that in a moment of clarity we would appear to each other as a single body, a single soul, and the only separation between them would be one sanctioned by the Creator, who set the one half moving toward the other and in their union caused a tremor of insane pleasure.

♦　　♦　　♦

After all the conversation yesterday about the body and the soul, I asked myself today, remembering the many things I'd heard and read about both, "Does every person I see, talk to, and deal with really have a soul with these same qualities, apart from the body that I see and the voice that I hear? Do my bosses at the office, Sharif al-Turk and Abd al-Rahman al-Mawla, bouncing like yoyos from one office to the other—do they too have souls that enjoy their own quiet moments, souls that throb, drink from the wellspring of experience, convulsing with invigorated shivers, fluttering their wings and soaring high? The people I see by the dozens every day, venturing into financial deals, chicken farms and hotels, dairy and chocolate production, putting up high-rise buildings—do all these people have souls that sometimes throb with a passion that stirs them into frenzy and fever, making them forget their immediate needs, losing them in labyrinths of confusion, or taking them up on heavenly roads where they see visions and dream of things they never saw in their night dreams and hear voices from other worlds that leave them unsettled in ways different from what the body is used to and instinct demands?"

Had Plato been too generous with humanity when he regarded the soul as God's gift to all who tread the earth? I will bring this subject up with Nael and tell him that I, in all modesty, see that this soul that suddenly becomes a ravaging fire is found only in those whom he describes as being promised to eternal suffering, estrangement, ecstasy, and creative genius—a minority chosen by God, by some wisdom of His, to be close to Him always in times of joy and sorrow, and whom he intended to set apart from others in their unique character and small numbers.

$$\cdot \quad \cdot \quad \cdot$$

A few days ago during the afternoon at the Holiday Inn, Nael introduced me to Abdullah al-Rami when the latter came to greet us upon spotting us at the restaurant, and Nael insisted that he sit down and join us for coffee. Nael had aroused my curiosity by talking to me about him several times before, and he was now saying how happy he was to have finally had the chance to introduce us to each other. Abdullah said he was staying at the hotel for a few days. He struck me as a pleasant man, sharp-witted and alert, but also one who listened closely to what you had to say, with a seriousness that gave him the appearance of frowning almost.

Yesterday, without informing Nael, I decided to call him. I slipped out around noon today and drove over to see him at the hotel café.

An incredible idea! But Abdullah did not want me to discuss it in any way with anyone. Things would become clearer once he came back the following month.

An incredible idea—but scary!

I would give it more time, more thought.

$$\cdot \quad \cdot \quad \cdot$$

Your name is beautiful,
but more beautiful yet
is your body.
You are a flower
lonely in the wilderness,
on the mountain slopes
and peaks,
where rain,
sun, and storm
allow only God's rarest creations
to grow—
like you!
Your body is a stone pillar:

Let your hair flow,
night springs
that sprinkle water across my face—
my lips on
your lips—
they too like a
wild rose,
redolent of perfume,
tasting of rain,
sun, and storm,
and the blackness of your hair
surrounds me
like night in the wilderness,
where only God
is present—
in your name,
your body,
your love.

He was gone for three days on a legal case in a city in the north. He couldn't call me because of bad phone lines, so he sent me this poem, which he said he had written on impulse and that it had kept him distracted during his evenings at the hotel among strangers. He said that he didn't usually write poetry; that was something he left to Talal Salih. He insisted on holding me so he could read it to me "sensually," as he put it. When he finished reciting it in his style, I said, "If your poem is your way of making up for not being here with me, then I've forgiven you. But don't count on me forgiving you every time you leave, no matter what poems you bring back. That said, go away if you like, and I'll be the one writing you poems. . . . You're laughing? Tomorrow, sometime, I'll bring you a poem I've been writing the last couple of days. You say I'm a flower lonesome in the wilderness? I am a wild horse bolting toward your far-flung shadows . . ."

◆   ◆   ◆

What a beautiful morning I had today! It was excruciatingly hot when I took a taxi to Janeen, where Nael was waiting for me as usual at the corner of the turn leading into his neighborhood. When I got out of the car, I felt as though the sun were pouncing on me, until I reached the other side of the street congested with people and wheels, where he sat watching me from his blue car. I felt like a sailor steering her ship through the rocky waters to safe shores—skillfully, cautiously. I felt a fire inside me when I sat next to him in the car, despite the cold air blowing from the air conditioner. His hand felt cold to the touch, and so did his cheek when I brushed it with a light kiss. "Your lips are so warm!" he said, "When a stone touches you it is touched with joy."[7]

"You mean, when a stone touches me it is touched with fire . . . I have enough to burn a whole city," I said.

"This is where poetry begins, where the fires begin to scorch," he said as we drove off.

We both left work early this morning without feeling a bit guilty. Even one day apart, let alone two, was enough to make us drop all our responsibilities. So many things would pile up—so many ideas, so many words, so many feelings—all bound to give rise to more ideas, words, and feelings. All the commercial offices could go to hell, and with them all the legal offices, government ministries, brokers, middlemen. . . . Nael parked the car in a shaded area of the parking lot around noon, and we got out into the heat and cut through it toward the entrance of the Holiday Inn. "Who set the sun's coals on fire today?" he asked.

"You and I. Who else?"

We walked toward the bar. The coolness of the dimly lit place made us forget the heat of the sun's coals. We went to our favorite table in the upper corner where three or four people we didn't know were sitting at a distance from each other, each clearly in his own lonely seclusion,

---

7. *When a stone touches you, it is touched with joy:* the line of poetry is from Abu Nuwas's *Da' 'anka Lawmi.* The English is from a translation of the poem (*To a Mutazilite Critic,* trans. Adnan Haydar and Michael Beard [Edebiyat 3.1 (1978): 45–46]).

drinking beer. I wasn't much of a drinker and usually ordered soda with a lot of ice, and Nael usually asked for the same. As soon as we sat down, I said, "I brought you my poem."

"At last, at last! And you're going to read it to me. But why do you have your hair up?"

"Because it's hot outside."

"You're reading your poem with your hair up? I don't think so! You will let it loose over your shoulders, then let the words flow with all the grace of God! Quickly, to the ladies' room."

"In that case, we'll have to drink wine, not soda."

"The finest wine."

"Only one glass, all right?"

I went to the ladies' room and let my hair down the way Nael liked it. I combed it and was back in a few minutes. He stared at me as I approached him, devouring me with his eyes. I sat down without saying a word. His eyes were still fixed on me. He was speechless, his mouth gaping. "As if you are seeing me for the first time!" I said.

He said slowly, puffing on his cigarette, "Every time I see you is like the first time."

I laughed, remembering Talal's poem. "Be quiet, stop exaggerating! Have you ordered the wine?"

"It's coming in a few minutes. Where's the poem?"

"What about the rituals, the pouring of red wine over the red sands?"

The waiter brought us the wine in two large glasses, each with a thin, delicate stem that seemed to hold the cup above it with arrogance and elegance, seductive even to the touch. I felt its lure flowing through my fingers to my arms and chest. The first sip I took, as I watched Nael sipping from his glass, heightened the pleasure flowing through my body, making me feel like a mythical character out of a Greek play. Randa al-Jouzy, you will never know this kind of delight, frightful to mind and body! I dare you to come in and spoil these moments with your needless logic and reason. I feel as if I'm not on earth in moments like these. Look at me and listen to my words, and his, and keep quiet forever!

I took the poem out of my bag and moved as close to him as I could, my hair hanging like a veil that separated us from everyone else. I took a big sip of wine and began reading, whispering or speaking loudly, I do not know, stopping every now and then to rescue myself with more wine.

I never sat on thrones or lived in palaces
I only had my head, and body,
and the promise of the day to come
bringing with it my dreams and treasures,
bringing a volcano of passion, which—if it erupts—
would bury all the love of the world in a pit
deep as anyone can imagine.

I came to you a wild horse bearing nature's tattoos,
on a path traced by the fingers of a Babylonian fortuneteller.

I found you crucified at the horizon of your visions,
your eyes two horseshoes nailed above your lips
like an amulet, ready to drive off evil!

What age have we entered together?
What sea?

My dreams are wandering ships,
gathering the foam of a love that floats in your shadows.
My love for you is an unfinished legend
lost on your isolated shores for a thousand years,
a legend that even your imaginary lines could not conclude,
while it waited.

The whistle was blown, in a moment
when the doors of captivity were still closed,
and only the faint flickers of light
could trickle in.

The escape began!
Time lost its contours, its boundaries,
and I sprang forth, a wild horse,

plowing the distances with her mad, giant leaps,
toward a rocky abyss where death is sweet,
if it means reaching you.

She neighs through a land of hot embers,
stumbling and tripping in the dark,
and rises again crying and soaring above the plains,
surpassing the clouds with dreams that
bleed dewdrops over the gardens of your awaited paradise!

In my heart the throbbing of the world
becomes an eternal waterfall of your love,
and the mad child in me exults
in warm sensations that mingle in the folds of your exile . . .

Love and the light of dawn mingled,
announcing their defiance,
and together they erased all traces
of a darkness that nested under the wings of your soul.

Defiance and struggle are the language of the distance between us.
My untamed love is always ahead of me.
Your open fields writhe like serpents,
wrapping around my feet in ever-growing circles,
and you are like a pendulum inside my head,
endlessly reflecting your image.

The fences around you multiply
and press together with the countdown,
only to recede into the distance,
becoming a prison camp and a finish line:
Two splendid choices for a painting
rimmed with the wreath of finality,
for a wild, tattooed horse . . .

"Wonderful, wonderful," he whispered, putting out his cigarette
and taking a big sip from the wine glass he had completely forgotten

about while I read. He took the pages from me and began reading again in a soft voice. My hair hung loosely like drapes in a breeze, separating us from the rest of the world. I listened to him and wondered, "Are those really my words? On his lips they take on meanings I hadn't thought of before."

"If this poem is really about me," he said, finally, "then no man has been loved like me before, and you are the greatest lover to have ever put some of her madness to words!"

We drank to those words and finished the rest of our wine.

We walked toward the dining hall for lunch. Could I but have welcomed the promise of more pleasure, even though I had exhausted it to the fullest and knew my parents would shower me with endless questions and reprimands for being late and not coming back home for lunch? As we crossed the bar and hallway leading to the restaurant, I felt like I was not only a tattooed horse neighing her way through the valleys and rocky abysses, but with him I was all the world's valleys and rocky abysses, all its cities. So keep quiet, Randa! This is an experience you'll never understand. And don't ask me where we sat and what we ate because, I swear to you, I don't remember. Nor do I remember how Nael and I crossed through the sun's burning coals to his car, by then no longer in the shade, and how we got inside and kissed in its infernal heat, and how finally around four o'clock he drove me back home where everyone was awaiting Sarab's return from another grueling day at work. My only way of avoiding my family's scrutiny was by running to the bathroom, quickly taking off my clothes, and standing naked under the shower, which despite its warmth refreshed and made me alert again. Then I went straight to bed and sank into a dark, deep slumber.

◆   ◆   ◆

How can I write about what happened? How can I write about an experience both painful and sickening, saddening and infuriating, an experience I was dragged into as though by the claws of a demon intent on tearing me apart at the peak of my happiness? I felt on top of the world with Nael yesterday. The heat. The cool, romantic dim light. The insane poetry. The wine, a glassful of which was enough to contain all of love's pleasures that transcend all experience. The words that mingled like the chants of dervishes, as Nael described them. Throughout our time together at the Holiday Inn restaurant we were completely oblivious to what we were eating and saying, our heads spinning with divine ecstasy.

I arrived at the office the next morning, still lost in my dream world. I could feel the clarity of everything around me, everything I came by, everything I heard—an incredible clarity that illuminated anything I looked at. I would see Nael at our appointed time tomorrow afternoon. I wanted to see him today, but sometimes his work schedule shows him no mercy. I was full of kindness toward an all-smiling Ismail as he brought me coffee, and toward Mr. Abd al-Rahman and the three auditors who came in. Even the documents I was working on passed through my hands like streams of crystal water. The first half of the day went by, and it was almost one o'clock when my boss left the office with Ismail. I told myself I would spend the next hour typing one or two pages, hoping to hold onto the last flames of a dying fire.

Right then, Mrs. Tala al-Turk walked in. I hadn't seen her in months, even though I had talked to her on the phone several times and she'd seemed very gentle and polite. I greeted her warmly, still overcome with the feeling of the pleasantness of people and things around me. She seemed beautiful in her mature femininity and the tasteful summer dress she had on. She wore thin earrings and an expensive necklace that sparkled against her throat and hung partly over her low-cut blue shirt, and she carried an elegant, blue handbag. The signs of the heat she had endured to come and visit me at that hour of a scorching hot day were clear on her face.

When she sat down, I offered to bring her cold refreshments or make her coffee, expecting her to respond with the same cheerfulness I was feeling. But she declined, giving me instead a piercing look—scrutinizing my face, my body, my hands, while I told her that her husband hadn't been to the office that day and that I was the only one there. I was getting ready to tell her about the new developments with the poultry farm, in which she owned the largest share. After some of the usual formalities, though, she surprised me by asking, "Sarab, where were you last night?"

I didn't understand. "I was here," I replied jokingly. "In this world."

Her features drew into a frown. "You skipped work yesterday, didn't you?"

"Ah, yes. I got busy."

"With what? With whom?"

"Excuse me? That's my private business, Mrs. Tala."

"Where did you go for lunch?"

I felt as though a tongue of fire had suddenly flared up inside me, but I controlled myself, thinking I was only imagining. "I see you're very concerned about me today?"

"You're not the one I'm concerned about, not in the least," she said coldly. "It's the man you were with. I saw you having lunch with Dr. Nael Imran at the Holiday Inn."

"Really? I didn't see you, nor did Nael. Were you there with someone?"

"That's none of your business."

"But it's your business to know where I was and who with?"

"Sarab, dear, listen, you're getting out of line."

"I don't think so. I was with a wonderful man, in a wonderful place, and the way we carried ourselves—should you want to know—was just as wonderful."

"Where did you meet him? Here?"

"No. He doesn't know I work here, for his friends."

"Then how did you meet him? I couldn't believe what I saw going on between the two of you yesterday. How did you start seeing each other? How could you even think of it? Did you know anything about him? He's older than your father and beyond anything you could ever wish for. Did you think you could take advantage of him? How could you imagine touching him, being next to him, talking to him the way you were, as if you were lovers?"

I looked at her in silence, shocked by her bad temper and hostility. I would have understood the reason for her anger and jealousy had she been Nael's wife, but I remembered him mentioning her only two or three times, and even then it was only in passing and in a way that hinted at feelings long gone. But it seemed her feelings for him hadn't completely gone away. I remembered the day I asked her about him and she said he had become a recluse. Maybe he was just avoiding her. And maybe she knew that her husband Sharif would be away from the office, and so she came to say what she wanted to say freely.

The tongue of fire inside me had become an inferno, but I kept quiet, waiting to see if she would stop her attack. My silence exasperated her even more. The color of her face changed from rose red, to deep red, to pale yellow, and had it not been for the thick layer of lipstick, her lips would have appeared blue and dry.

"They speak well of you here, not knowing what a disrespectful, irresponsible woman they're breeding. Perhaps you'd like to go as far as saying he's your fiancé, or husband? I called his sister Salima last night and found out everything. Listen, you'd better put an end to this relationship, today, right now. I won't hesitate to call your father, Dr. Ali Affan, and tell him everything."

I sprang to my feet in a fit of anger, shouting in her face. "Enough! Enough! Your jealousy, your lies, your attacks. They won't change a thing between me and Nael. You think because I work here you have the right to invade my privacy. I'll tell you what, why don't you take my place and run the office yourself? I'm going home, and none of you will ever see me here again. You can call me if you have any questions!"

Tala was stunned. She looked at me, speechless, as I scrambled about frantically for my belongings and took my personal papers out of the desk drawer and placed them inside several blue folders. I flung the cabinet keys across the desk and grabbed my bag, ignoring her, and slammed the door behind me as I left.

She ran behind me shouting as I rushed to the elevator. "Sarab, Sarab, listen to me, please . . ."

I didn't answer or look back. I was boiling inside. I got into the elevator, leaving her behind in the hallway.

I got into my car. My hands were still shaking when I grabbed the steering wheel. "What an incredible thing, jealousy!" I thought. "And how wonderful it is for me to love Nael and bring about this storm of jealousy in another woman!"

But suddenly I too became jealous. She and Nael must have had deeper feelings for each other than I thought, or why would Tala get so hysterical, especially when she was married and had kids? Or do the wounds of past love never heal, always quick to open up and bleed again? But what do I care? Nael, where are you? Where can I find you now?

I drove back home in a hurry. I tried calling him at his house, but he wasn't there. I tried him at the office. He wasn't there either. And now, I still can't reach him.

•   •   •

So I have a female rival, and maybe other ones I don't know about! And maybe there are spies and censors watching me while I, totally unaware of their presence, go about doing what I'm doing and writing what I'm writing.

The hours I spent waiting to see Nael since noon yesterday until I met him this afternoon were hell. I didn't tell my mother and father that I had quit my job, and since I couldn't reach Nael yesterday, I decided when I talked to him on the phone today to wait until I saw him to tell him about Tala.

Of course, I couldn't get a moment of sleep last night, but talking to Nael on the phone before he left for work early this morning made up for it. We had our usual brief conversation. He liked to hear my voice the first thing in the morning as much as I liked hearing his. We confirmed our plans to meet at Ansam, our favorite meeting place.

I got there before him. When he arrived, he hurried toward me and asked before Diab came to our table, "What's wrong? Didn't you get any sleep last night?"

I laughed for the first time since noon the day before. "Are you now the fortuneteller? Is it so easy for you to read my face?"

He looked intensely at my eyes and lips, as he usually did when he became emotional. "Do you really believe your face can hide anything that has to do with us? You sounded unusually shaken on the phone this morning."

Diab came to our table, and we ordered our cherished coffee. Soon afterward, "Plaisir d'Amour" was playing in the background. Ah, the joys of love, the sorrows of love . . . Then Nael said, before I could bring up the events of the previous day, "Sarab, honey, forget about Tala and what she said yesterday. Pretend it never happened."

I laughed again, though bitterly this time. "Did you read that on my face too?"

"Of course," he answered, smiling. "To tell you the truth, Tala called me at the office last night on my way out. I hadn't heard from her in a while. Everything she said was silly, unacceptable, and I let her know that. Sarab, you don't know what happened between us. It's an old story, and it's strange she doesn't want it to end. It's the same insane jealousy that's been eating away at her ever since I married her friend Siham instead of her. If you don't mind me asking, why didn't you tell me you worked for Sharif al-Turk? I could have put in a good word for you, even though you didn't need it. After Siham died, I purposely kept a distance from Tala and Sharif, although he was my friend too. I couldn't be around them because of how Tala was acting, especially the first two years."

"Is this what happens to the women who fall in love with you?" I asked.

"No, no, Tala has always had a hard time dealing with rejection and accepting what she can't change. She was born into a wealthy family that spoiled her early on, and she only got wealthier with time. She still acts like a spoiled kid who would stop at nothing to get what she wants. She was my student at the law school when I was a lecturer there twenty years ago. We got involved back then. That was before I met her friend Siham."

"In other words, she couldn't have you, and she hasn't gotten over it yet?"

"Yes, or why would she act the way she's acting? Please, Sarab, forget about her. Go back to your job."

"You want me to work for a woman who sees me as her competitor? There's no way I'll go back. I can get along well without the petty salary I was making. Anyway, I went against my father's advice in taking the job, just so I could keep busy and meet people perhaps."

"You'll have no problem finding a job if you want to, especially with your knowledge of English and French. How did you become so fluent in both?"

"I was taught by nuns, as you know. I finished most of elementary and middle school at the Sacred Heart, which is run by Catholic nuns. They stressed languages and music. Imagine, I had to take piano and ballet lessons twice a week, for years."

"And you spent two years in England?"

"Yes, we all moved there with my father so he could become a member of the Fellowship of the Royal College of Surgeons. My love for the theater grew stronger during my studies in London. I almost joined drama school, but we had to go back after my father got his membership, so I enrolled in the School of Fine Arts here. One day when we're alone, Nael, I'd like to play Ophelia from Hamlet for you. Ophelia after she goes crazy. My drama teacher Munzir Fadil, who was French-educated and whom I remember so fondly, used to like me especially as Andromaque in the play by Racine, the scene where she recalls anticipating the death of her husband Hector.

I was suddenly overcome by the tragic feeling that I was somehow a mixture of Ophelia and Andromaque, but without a prattling vizier[8] as a father and without a beloved husband[9] who would take on Achilles in a duel.

I told him how much I enjoyed playing Sonya in Dostoevsky's *Crime and Punishment*. I described to him that incredible heartrending moment when Raskolnikov falls down on his knees and kisses my feet—me, Sonya, the tuberculosis-ridden, destitute harlot—saying, "By kissing your feet, I am kissing the suffering humanity in you."[10] I felt as though I were really the epitome of a suffering humanity, the Arab

8. *prattling vizier:* presumably a reference to Ophelia's father Polonius from Shakespeare's *Hamlet*.

9. *beloved husband:* presumably a reference to Hector from Racine's *Andromaque*.

10. *"By kissing . . . suffering humanity in you":* a paraphrase from Dostoevsky's *Crime and Punishment*. In the English translation by Richard Pevear and Larissa Volokhonsky: "I was not bowing to you, I was bowing to all human suffering" (Fyodor Dostoevsky, *Crime and Punishment* [New York: Vintage Books, 1992], 322).

woman symbolizing the suffering and misery of people everywhere. "She is the most miserable creature on earth," I said.

"And her misery will only get worse unless she decides to pull herself together," said Nael.

We talked for a long time tonight and got onto many different subjects, thanks to Tala and her obsessive jealousy. Finally, Nael said, "Promise me, Sarab . . ."

"What?"

"Three things."

"The first one?"

"That you will play Ophelia in that scene for me, taking full advantage of your beautiful hair. I can just imagine Ophelia going mad, her hair flying everywhere."

"Yes, like her mind. And the second promise?"

"We're still on the first one. I also want you to act out the Sonya scene you just described, so I can be Raskolnikov, kissing your feet and the suffering humanity in you."

"Tomorrow, in your library."

"Second, you will promise to play a piano piece by Mozart. Don't you dare try to get out of it, or not play the piece well!"

"I'll start practicing right away. And the third promise?"

"That you'll go back to your job."

I almost screamed, "No, no way! I'll never go back to work for . . ." But I said instead, "Only if you'll let me be your secretary, without pay."

"With pay."

"How much?"

"Everything I make!"

"I warn you though, I'll confuse all your cases and make a mess of all your laws. And if some pretty woman asks you to take on her case, I'll cause you even greater suffering than Tala."

"By God, that's fine with me!"

During those impassioned moments, I couldn't bring myself to tell him about my plans to leave, which I'd been preparing for without him knowing. I was afraid from the start that he might succeed in stopping me somehow, especially when I too was still weak in my decision.

Suddenly, he said, "Sarab, leave your car where it is, and let's go eat dinner at the Holiday Inn. What do you say?"

"Great! And Tala can eat her heart out."

"What if you're a little late getting back home tonight?"

"We'll worry about that later. For now, let's put our trust in God, the God of all lovers."

And so it was. Our dinner at the Holiday Inn tonight was just as wonderful as lunch two days ago. When we looked around us this time, I hoped to see Tala watching us reproachfully, choking with jealousy, but she wasn't there.

God must have been watching over me because I got back shortly before eleven o'clock, and my family was still at the club. Now, shortly after midnight, I can hear them arriving in a cheerful clatter. They'll probably ask me why I didn't come to the club. They'll say they waited for me and played bingo and mom won a set of crystal glasses and fifty dinars on top of it!

I wish I could just say to them, "As for me, I won the whole universe!"

◆   ◆   ◆

Today, I was very careful in the way I told him about my decision to leave. First, I put it across as an idea that had occurred to me a while back but one that I hadn't given serious thought. So he assumed I was only toying with the idea—a fantasy. What, after all, could be more attractive than travel, no matter where? . . .

When he realized I was serious, he said, conceding, "Then let's travel together, for a month or two."

He was surprised when I told him I wanted to go away for years, maybe for good. He would not believe me, and suddenly he said, "Listen! Let's get married. We'll spend our honeymoon in Switzerland, or England."

He had clearly missed my point. "I can marry you tomorrow if that's what you want, and I'd be the happiest woman in the world," I said. "But what I've decided to do is so far from marriage. In fact, marriage would be its only obstacle. My decision to leave has to do with a deep desire I can't explain to you, because I love you, and I want to leave when our love is at its strongest."

He did not understand, refused to. I didn't have the courage to tell him my real reason for leaving. I was determined to give nothing away. At most, I'd make hints right before leaving. There were moments during which I feared that the idea of marriage would take stronger hold of me than my resolve to leave.

How easy it would be to go back on my decision if I were to choose the easy way for myself! Nael, how sweet is my love for you, and how hard it is to stay firm in my decision!

•   •   •

After much hesitation, doubt, and fear of rumor, I dropped all my worries yesterday and accepted Nael's invitation as the only female guest at a dinner party at his house that he was throwing for only "the dearest of his dear friends," Talal Salih and Abdullah al-Rami. I wondered if his sister Salima would join us, but she preferred to make all the dinner preparations with Umm Hadi's help and then withdraw to her room. Until now, I still don't know what she thinks of my relationship with Nael, and I've avoided asking him. She was either fond of me or thought I was immature to no limits. Either way, I didn't want to know.

It was an evening full of food, drink, and conversation. I recall only a little of what we talked about. I drank water only and ate a thin slice of meat with lots of salad and Palestinian green olives, which Nael usually brought with him on his way back through Amman. Toward the end of the evening, I was about to suggest making coffee for everyone—coffee had become a kind of ritual for me and Nael—but Umm Hadi beat me to it, first bringing us tea, and then coffee, which, thank God, she was very good at making.

Our conversations went smoothly from one subject to another. It was my first time with Nael in a group of other people. He made his arguments skillfully and displayed a breadth of knowledge and opinions every time he spoke. It became all the more evident to me that a conversationalist was only as good as his partner and that the surest way to stifle him would be to pair him off with a fool. I won't deny that, being with three of the best conversationalists, I felt a bit intimidated at first, but soon the ideas and words started coming to me in ways I hadn't thought myself capable of. Am I being vain? Perhaps. But I can tell the difference between a person who is just being "nice" and polite and not challenging anything I say, and someone who listens to every word I say and then confronts me, as he would anyone, with much analysis and scrutiny. And then comes the pleasure of agreeing or disagreeing.

I was the only woman there, but they treated me like one of them, addressing me like they did everyone else, or so I imagined. Every now and then I would start feeling intimidated again as I delved into unfamiliar subjects, and with whom of all people?! And even though the youngest among them was twice my age, all three of them—Nael, Talal, and Abdullah—were careful not to remind me of my age and lack of experience.

Talal was full of humor, all intended for me. His presence during my first moments with Nael won him a special place in my heart. The way he acted toward me seemed always to acknowledge that special connection we had, coupled with him admiring me for attracting someone like Nael. Early in the evening he said that when he found out I was coming he couldn't decide whether to bring me a rose or a poem. When I told him I was no longer holding him to his promise, since it was conditional on my visiting him in his office, he said the only condition was seeing me, wherever that might be! So I said, "If you haven't brought a rose, then where's the poem?"

"I didn't mean now," he said.

Abdullah yelled out, "Right now, before you finish drinking your first glass."

"And make it romantic," insisted Nael.

He took a sip out of his glass and kept holding it. He looked at me and began reciting, from memory this time:

The way you gracefully glide along,
I say: How beautiful it is,
I adore it.

And you say: Beware,
ask the mighty flood.
Was it not once
a peaceful stream
winding down its course?
The way you gracefully glide along,
I repeat: How beautiful it is,
how pure it is.
But then,
the flood lurks within.
You say:
You must fear it!
Fear it, you say,
when my greatest joy is drowning
for love of its waves?
In its outpour,
the universe flowers.
Limbs ripen with love
from savoring its might.
Dear God,
How malleable it is,
how violent,
how beautiful!

I loved the poem. I felt the urge to stand up and start dancing in the middle of the room to the ballet steps I had learned in elementary and secondary schools, but then Nael and Abdullah started yelling and shouting jubilantly as they all raised their glasses to drink to me, making me feel like a real princess. I stood up and curtsied like an aristocrat. Abdullah then said in his agreeable, exaggerated manner, "Hey, I swear as true Arabs we should all rip up our own shirts out of joy for what we've just heard and seen!"

"You remind me," said Nael laughing, "of the story by al-Jahiz about the man who drank so much wine and heard so much poetry that in his ecstasy he ripped up his shirt and said to a servant sitting next to him, 'You too, rip up your shirt!' "

"Did he rip up his shirt?", asked Abdullah.

"He must have not been a true Arab because he said, 'I swear I won't rip up my only shirt,' " replied Nael laughing.

" 'Go ahead, tear it man,' his master prodded him, 'and I'll give you a new shirt tomorrow!'

" 'Fine, then I'll rip it up tomorrow,' replied the servant.

" 'What's the point of doing it tomorrow? Get out!' said his master then went on shaking his head with joy and ripping up what was left of his own shirt."

Amidst our laughter, Abdullah said, "On the subject of tearing up shirts, have you heard the story of the man who was a complete failure at love, work, and marriage? When his friend saw him beating his chest one day and ripping up his shirt, from sadness this time, he asked him, 'What's the matter with you, man?'

" 'I just finished reading a chapter from this book about reincarnation,' replied the man, 'It confused—terrified—me, and the more I thought about it the more confused and terrified I got.'

" 'Why?' asked his friend.

" 'Why? Because I'm afraid that after I die and come back to the world, as this book says I will, I might come back as the same person I am now. Oh, what a tragedy that would be, what a tragedy!' And he went on beating on his chest and ripping up his shirt."

"Now listen to this true story," I began. "The taxi driver I rode with this morning was wearing a pair of dark sunglasses, unusual for taxi drivers around here. He looked at me in his rear-view mirror and said, 'Excuse me, ma'am. You see these dark glasses? Do you think I'm wearing them for medical reasons? They're only sunglasses, and I wear them because they make me look important. I can't do without them anymore. There's a story behind them. Two or three days after I started wearing these glasses, a taxi driver who lives in our neighborhood in a house right across the street from ours bought himself a pair just like mine and started wearing them every day. So I decided to take them off for a few days. He did the same. Then I put mine back on, and so did he. How strange! Before I had my old car, he didn't have a car either. When I bought a car, he bought one just like it. Some time passed, and I got a good offer on my car and sold it. Soon he sold his too. I was without work, and so was he. Finally, I bought this Toyota, the same make as my old car, and I went back to doing the same work. A few days later, he, too, bought a car and went back to doing the same work. But this time his car was an old, pathetic-looking Lada. I have no doubt he'll soon replace it with a Toyota. Right now I'm wearing dark glasses, and so is he. Is he my shadow? My double? What do you think, ma'am? What does this tell you about people?' "

Nael chuckled. "An amazing concept, I mean a person being another's shadow, his double, bearing not only his physical appearance, but his thoughts as well, until the shadow, on account of his match, gets into a fix he can't get out of because his match is off somewhere else. Do you remember Goethe's *The Magician's Apprentice*?"

Ah, Nael! How rare are the teacher-magicians, and how many are the apprentice-imitators!

Our conversations went on, ranging from the light to the serious. I wrote down the words to Talal's poem, and Abdullah talked about the new developments in the Palestinian cause as he saw them, and he promised to bring me Palestinian *zaatar*[11] "redolent with the fragrances of our mountains and rocks, in honor of the memory of your Jerusalemite grandmother." Right then I decided to ask to see him before his return to Copenhagen about the matter that had become so important for me to resolve, so I hinted at it secretly to him, and he acquiesced with a silent gesture.

Nael went into the bizarre details of the al-Saifi family court case and their struggles over inheritance—love affairs; legitimate and illegitimate children; marital ties extending between this country, Paris, and New York; competing claims to a huge inheritance tied up in several countries. And Nael's job was to sort out the legitimate from illegitimate heirs. Ah, love and all the troubles it brings! For an instant I imagined myself with an illegitimate child from Nael and us fighting over custody. What a frightening thought! "But why illegitimate?" I asked my-

---

11. *zaatar:* a spicy mix consisting mainly of dried, crushed thyme and sumac with roasted sesame seeds, usually eaten with olive oil and bread.

self. "Why not get married to him and get it over with? Or do love and marriage never mix, like East and West?"

For some reason, I started thinking about Siham's marble bust in Nael's bedroom and her oil portrait in the same room we were sitting in. Could she hear all our noise, laughter, and stories, excusing herself because she was dead and far away? Would she forgive all of that? It seemed to me at that moment that indeed she would forgive me for all the love and torment I was feeling, and perhaps she would become more understanding the more she realized how much of both I was suffering, especially the torment.

◆   ◆   ◆

I asked Abdullah al-Rami not to mention any of our plans to Nael, although he didn't need to be told that when he'd been the first to insist on keeping his involvement and my overseas movements a secret, even from my parents and the people closest to me. I was afraid that Nael might be supportive of the idea, only as an idea, but would still feel my staying here was more important and would argue his point in a hundred different ways. I was really touched by what he said to me two days ago about marriage—that he was well aware of our age difference and that he would no longer insist on marriage beyond what was appropriate, respecting my ability to look at the matter rationally. (Ah, those lawyers and all their logic!) And he went on to say that his love for me led him to believe—made him certain—that he would make me the happiest woman in the world, and that he therefore had the right to be insistent, but, out of his love for me, wanted me to give the matter all the "serious" thought it deserved. But perhaps that kind of "serious," rational thought wasn't possible amid all the feelings of love. I had no way of convincing him that marriage was never a concern of mine and that I was still firm in my old resolve to come out of the siege and fight for an organization that for the past ten years I had dreamt of joining, and with that affirm my all-out admiration for the heroism of those who defy the forces of oppression and darkness coming in from foreign places, while also affirming my own worth as a human being: another rock among the rocks of Jerusalem, another olive tree on the Mount of Olives, as my grandmother Khadija used to say.

* • •

The day we spent in the big orchard belonging to Nael and his siblings, thirty kilometers outside the city, was both beautiful and unexpected. There were orange and lemon trees and vines still ripe with grapes hanging in clusters, and apple, peach, and pear trees. We barbecued chicken on a wood fire and ate under the shady trees. The kindly fellah Abu Qazim showed up unexpectedly, and our romantic adventure got constantly interrupted for the rest of the day until sunset. I almost convinced myself to get married and settle down for good. A delectable, numbing languor overcame me. Ah, the love, the sunshine, the spacious skies. . . . Come to me, sweet slumber, and take me wherever you like . . .

* • •

Mona Issawi, why have you been so much on my mind in the last few days?

Her room had an ocean view. She'd been lucky with both its location and interior layout. She can sit for hours now in front of the wide window with its open glass panes and listen with her eyes closed to the crashing waves, to their roars and whispers. She surrenders herself to the strange images forever racing through her head, the result of years of reading, writing, and delving into the ancient folds of history. A multitude of imaginary characters weave their way into the web of her intermingling experiences until she can no longer distinguish between reality and fantasy during those moments of fatigue. She remembers events, but she can't be sure if they actually happened to her or whether they came out of the books she had read or written and had become engraved in her imagination. Is this a sign of illness? Aging? Ah, but in the past her life was wonderful. She knew adventure and danger. She knew love. She knew the extraordinary pain that comes before and after realizing the self in the midst of life's hardships. She had risen from the harshest poverty to unexpected peaks of fame. Important literati and admiring publishers flocked around her, and so did young lovers and carefree older men. How similar was all that to the ancient tales of the impossible! As soon as she settles into her chair in front of the window, gazing long at the sea stretching as far out as the eye can see, con-

stantly changing its colors, the shadows of foam endlessly ebbing and flowing, she asks herself, "Am I still the young woman I was forty years ago, lying in a comfortable chair next to a window in a hotel room overlooking the sea, a woman in whom fantasy and reality have mingled and become one, a woman for whom things no longer carry any meaning except for the sudden warmth they radiate every now and then from an inexplicable beauty?" Things no longer flow like water. Now they shrink on themselves, toss about, scatter, and she must wait, fully alert, for that instant that brings with it a sudden realization of beauty and gives things their shapes and meanings. At that moment she loses herself in the memory of a past event from long ago, and she sees a woman in her prime, in her early twenties, threading her way through throngs of people, her lips pursed and eyes focused, toward a train station where each passing train becomes a promise, a love, because the man she loves is waiting for her in a place only trains can reach, waiting to share exciting things and talk about exciting subjects that she can only wade through with vague conjectures. Then, when all is said and done, after all the blurry pictures have taken shape in a sensory, mental experience with its own contours and reflections, she goes back to her routine and work and writing, and the doubts come back: did all these things really happen, or did she create them in her imagination? Only the passage of time makes her certain they really happened, because the memory stays on, and because she will have to relive it at every chance she gets—the memory with all its lights and shadows, with all its sounds and pauses—before she is met with a dark finality without an image or a word to remember . . .

That's how Nael described Mona Issawi in her final days. I told him that she was occupying my thoughts lately as vividly as she had when I read *Entering the Mirrors* for the first time months ago. Was she the one causing me to do all the things I was doing?

Nael said it was as though I had turned the clock back on her forty years, recreating her as she had been in the prime of youth, in her every movement and gesture. I responded that in forty years I would find myself like her in a big room overlooking the ocean, perhaps in an Arabian Gulf city on a rainy day full of sunshine, and like her I would surrender myself to the roars of the waves and their whispers as strange images raced through my head, and reality and fantasy would mesh into one another and give me new life before the final sleep.

"But where's the train station in your life?"

"My train station is a sidewalk in Janeen. Did I ever tell you how I used to drive through the neighborhood on purpose on my way to the city and back, although it wasn't the shortest way home? That street, that turn, has become a symbol of all the promises of love."

"I thought only I did such foolish things!" said Nael, surprising me.

"You see? Now I have no choice but to leave."

"When will you quit saying this?"

"When I quit loving you."

It was hard enough explaining to him in any detail my plan to leave, not to mention my promise to be discreet, which with him was so difficult. I was worried that if I talked to him about my plan he would try to dissuade me somehow, as he did whenever I brought up the topic of marriage. He said he didn't understand that contradictory side of me, and then he added jokingly, "That, and a thousand other sides of you I don't understand. Will you keep me forever worshipping an unsolvable mystery? But then again, all the world religions began with the worship of unsolvable mysteries."

I laughed, amused by the thought. "Hush, don't exaggerate. Tell me, who is this Mona Issawi? And how many Monas have you turned into high priestesses whose mysteries remain hidden among your idolatries?"

His answer was evasive. "The priestess I'm with has abolished all my other idolatries, with only two words from her succulent lips."

◆　　◆　　◆

He asked me two days ago about Randa al-Jouzy. He said I no longer talked about her and asked me if being preoccupied with him had taken me away from her.

I agreed, claiming that because of him I no longer saw Randa as often to avoid arguing with her about my private affairs, but that I still considered her the closest person to me and saw her every once in a while or talked to her on the phone. I also told him that I'd ask Randa to call him the next evening, if he would be at home after ten o'clock. My old playfulness was coming back. Could I resist being playful with the one I loved? I wondered what Freud would have said about that kind of love intrigue?

So I called him last night. I was really afraid I wouldn't be able to pull it off on him this time, so I exaggerated my fake voice and accent. I imagined myself as the suffering woman in Cocteau's monodrama who talks to the telephone receiver. So come to my help, Stanislavski, with your convincing acting method, even if I am acting with my voice only.

He answered the phone. I began talking without saying who I was, until he asked. He didn't believe at first that I was Randa al-Jouzy, but neither did he say that my voice sounded like Sarab's although my ideas were Randa's.

"You've forgotten what I sound like, Mr. Nael," I said, "because we haven't talked in a long time. Sarab insisted that I call you today. Thanks for asking about me and sending me your regards, and without having met me yet."

Then he cajoled me by saying he felt close to anyone who was Sarab's friend, even if she was a voice without a face.

"But I'm also a face," I said.

"A happy or frowning face?" he asked. "Sarab tells me you look like a demon when you frown."

"Of course she'd say that, because her head is full of demons, and sometimes she likes seeing what a real one looks like. But we'll meet one day, and I'll let you be the judge. I don't understand Sarab these days."

"Since I started seeing her?"

"Yes, and frankly I pity her for what she's in sometimes."

"Why, Miss Randa?"

"I used to warn her against you before, and she'd make fun of me. And now I see her lost inside labyrinths I can't bring her back from anymore."

"Do you still warn her against me?"

"What's the use? You have no idea how complicated things have become between us. Since her grandmother Khadija died more than ten years ago, bless her soul, we agreed to be there for each other in times of crisis. If I ever thought she was starting to get reckless, I would stop and bring her back to her senses. And if I got too disimpassioned and removed, she would bring me down from my ivory towers to face the real problems of the world with the courage of brutes. And vice versa, of course. But with time we became opposites: one positive in her readiness to take on all of society if she had to—that's Sarab—and the other, meaning me, negative in her prudence and reason, always accounting for life's real and inescapable demands. And now I see she's decided to leave. I'm so worried by what she's about to get herself into. I warned her against you at the beginning, but now I'm the one urging her to stay with you and go on with this delusional craze she'll drive me mad talking about as long as she's with you, not to mention all the poems you keep writing each other. Mr. Nael, are you still there?"

"Yes, yes, and I commend you on your advice to her. That travel idea of hers, I respect her wishes and reasons for wanting to go on with it, if I'm correct in judging them that is, but for purely selfish reasons I still don't want her to go ahead with her plans. So keep firm in your position, Randa, and maybe together we can change her mind. Please don't tell her this, but I admit she's turned my life around in only a few months. I can't imagine being without her, even two days, let alone if she would leave for good! On a more personal note, why don't the two of us meet sometime?"

Here I had to fake my voice even more, like a bad actress with no control of her voice. "What did you say, Mr. Nael? What do you mean the two of us meet? What would I say to Sarab? What would you say to her?" I wondered how Hedda Gabler would have reacted, and with what tone of voice, if Ibsen had put her in a situation like mine!

But Nael, in all innocence, avoided the spark that could have lit the fuse, when he replied, "What I mean, Randa, is for you to join Sarab and me for coffee or dinner sometime."

"At the Holiday Inn?"

"There, or elsewhere. The important thing is to see more of you and talk."

"No, Mr. Nael. You don't know Sarab as well as I do. I think, I know, that she'd prefer me to stay in the background, a voice only."

"Are you married, Randa?"

Again, I answered with my exaggerated voice. "What do you care if I'm married or not?"

"Okay, I'm sorry. But let me ask you . . ."

"I have a question for you . . ."

"Go ahead."

"Do you really love Sarab? I mean, do you love her as much as she thinks you do? No, please don't answer. Between you and me, it doesn't matter what I think. I don't believe this woman thinks about anything or anyone, every day, every minute, as much as she does about you. Maybe it is best for her to leave."

"You're not going back to her logic and forgetting about yours, are you?"

"You do know that Sarab's grandmother Khadija on her father's side was a Palestinian from Jerusalem, from the al-Jabiri clan, which you may have heard of. This grandmother of hers was the one who brought her up during her adolescent years. Do you see how one's roots stay alive, how the blood runs deep? And there's a family secret she might not have revealed to you."

"A terrible secret? An insane grandfather?"

"No, no . . . It's a secret that Sarab is only too glad to share, but only when she chooses to. Her other grandmother, Yasmeen's mother, a Christian from the north, was called Marta Mikhail, and was wed unto her grandfather, Sheikh Ahmad Daleer, as a second wife in the early twenties when she was still sixteen and he over fifty. She was an orphan and lived under the protection of the family of Sheikh Ahmad. She was known for her pretty face and beautiful figure, and Sarab believes that she inherited her slender figure and dazzling, black hair with its long plaits. You see what a strange combination your friend the daughter of Ali Affan is?"

"This explains only partially the secret of . . . her magic, her many-sided personality."

"And that she wishes to come out of her siege."

Here he surprised me by saying, "I hear her voice in what you're saying!"

I feigned laughter to save the situation. "Ha, ha! Many people think our voices sound alike." Go on with your act, Randa!

But he answered innocently again. "I mean you remind me of the things she says, exactly. Next you're going to tell me that Gypsy blood runs in her veins!" (I said to myself, "Nael, my dear, why am I enjoying this crafty game with you?") Then he added, "And I must say you're just as confused as Sarab and me. Thank you for your kind call and your concern, or should I say your strange concern?"

"Don't mention it," I said. "I enjoy talking to you. I'm the one who should be thanking you. If the three of us ever get together, I'll remind you of this conversation."

"Soon?" he asked.

"Very soon. Good-bye."

Ah, Nael, we meet after tomorrow, and departure is drawing near.

4

NAEL IMRAN

In my years studying law, but more in my work on legal cases, some of which were very ambiguous and some contradictory in evidence, I would sometimes come across material that I found useful in constructing the events of my novels, as much as I claimed to distance my writing from my work. I did that in spite of my realization more than thirty years ago that on some level of one's experience, a clear line had to be drawn between reality and imagination, between the possible and impossible, between what is offered us by human relationships as we see them on the outside, with all their complexity, and the creative genius capable of imparting to these relationships its own magic, extracting what nature itself seems incapable of extracting. I often remembered Picasso's comment on his own art, that in distorting and recombining shapes, deforming and reconstructing them as he liked, he was creating what nature itself could not create, thus asserting his own superior talents and refusing to be under its control.

But with Sarab's sudden, unexplained departure, despite the hints she made in the last few days before she left, I was confronted with a mystery for which I had no real explanation except one that didn't satisfy me. I had talked to Sarab once about a method I used in explaining events that seemed ambiguous or impossible to explain. I would come up with three scenarios varying in detail but all equally plausible and, somehow, equally true, or put together came close to the truth, which in itself is highly complex and perhaps even self-contradictory. So I thought of several scenarios for what might have happened to her, but none satisfied me, leaving me no less confused with her absence and total silence.

I felt as though for six months I had lived a beautiful fantasy that had come masked in reality, drawing me inside its mirrors, as Sarab used to say, and then hurling me back to a place without fantasies or masks, where all I knew was that this woman had stormed into my life with a kind of love I had never known and had left me behind like a citadel fallen to a magnificent conqueror who had then abandoned it, gates flung open and terraces shattered, to the mercy of violent winds dallying freely in its desolate quarters. In my long experience practicing law, this was the first case where I was the central player and had no use for the evidence brought forth by investigators, let alone their rules and laws. Nature had brought what I had thought possible only in the imagination. But what pained me most for months was for that mystery to trap me inside the memory of a person I could no longer live without. I was reminded of a story I had written when I was younger and thought back then to be more symbolic than realistic. In it, the hero's lover disappears a few days after their wedding without leaving behind a clue as to where or why she went, and so he ponders a hundred different scenarios each making him reflect on his existence in ways he had never considered before. Sarab's disappearance was a total surprise. Had I foreseen way back then the bitterness and pain that I was now suffering?

I knew that Sarab's departure had to do with an Arab organization she'd been determined to join, hoping that she might one day find herself, as she had once said in her eloquent words, waking up under an olive tree on a Jerusalem hill and taking a deep breath to fill her lungs with the breezes of the city of her grandmother Khadija al-Jabiri and her chest "with sun rays that God could have created only on Mount Mukabbir." Only then would she realize her freedom, and after that, let there be what may.

But why her secretiveness, and why the agony that she was inflicting upon herself, not to mention my own agony? I was convinced that Abdullah al-Rami had a strong influence on her decision. He was working underground and expected those who worked for him to maintain total secrecy, even toward his closest friends. Was he training her through his organization for a secret commando mission that the Resistance might need her for one day—hijacking an airplane, storming military compounds, exposing a Zionist agent? Sarab had a wild imagination in more than one way. She felt bitter about the Arab predicament and always came out strongly against social decay and stagnation. It seemed that she could live only in the guises of dramatic characters whom she always took to tragic ends. This was part of the secret of her feeling besieged, of the avenues of salvation being closed to her and that she had to go back and try each one of them again to her best abilities with the hope of being saved. The same passion she brought into love she also brought into anything else she did, that fiery passion of a blazing forest on a pitch-dark night. I understood all that, but I couldn't understand how she could be in love with me and leave me when at the height of her love. My pride was my curse, for a long time blinding me to my own reality.

She said she would write to me from Rome. Days later she said she would probably write from Prague, and maybe from Stockholm. It occurred to me that she might be purposely misleading me. But was it me she was misleading or herself? Or did she not even know her final destination? She mentioned Copenhagen once, and right away I knew that Abdullah had to be involved somehow. When I persisted in asking her, she refused to give me clear answers, and she broke down in tears and fell on my chest, beating on it with her fists and saying, "I love you, I love you. But I must leave."

The next day, I called the hotel where Abdullah was staying and found out that he had left the country. After weeks not hearing from her, I thought about writing to Abdullah in Copenhagen but discovered that I didn't have his address, nor did Talal Salih, and both Talal and I were the closest people to him here. The overwhelming feeling set in that Sarab's absence would be as tragic as Siham's, an inevitable death that I would eventually have to accept. As the days went by, my fears grew stronger that Sarab might have died or been killed, or might have committed suicide, but I would also occasionally entertain the thought that she was on her way to attaining the heroism or martyrdom that would place her above the normal ranks of people. Each day I would think up a different scenario to explain what could have happened to her from the moment she left the city. I imagined her in European cities, in first- and tenth-class hotels. I saw her starving, thirsting, but always determined and never losing her will. I imagined her being pursued by men who wanted to attack and kill her. I saw her writing, fighting, inciting, risking her life, weeping, suffering, then writing and fighting again. But in all of that I found no real consolation or spiritual comfort.

I decided one day to call her sister Shaza. A woman answered the phone, most likely her mother, and told me that Shaza was overseas continuing her studies. She asked me who I was. "I'm Nael Imran," I said. "I just wanted to ask how Miss Sarab is doing." The woman was clearly shaken and broke down crying. "How can we tell you when we ourselves don't know? For the love of God, if you hear any news about her, even from afar, please let us know right away."

I waited in vain for a letter, a phone call. I remembered how much she used to enjoy our phone conversations. I kept remembering our last meeting. That day Sarab was full of sweetness, laughter, words. We began the afternoon with coffee at Ansam and ended it making love passionately in my library. Salima and Ghassan were away on their usual early summer vacation for several weeks at my brother Wael's. Sarab had brought me a palm-size seashell with a rough surface covered with delicate, sharp protrusions but smooth and shiny on the inside, tempting one to glide down into its depths. "This is from me," she had said. "Hold it to your ear, hear the sounds of the wind." So I held it to my ear and said, "I hear winds blowing over the oceans you will be cross- ing." The only gift she would accept from me was a recording of three of her favorite Beethoven piano sonatas that she played whenever we met at my place. I consoled myself by thinking she really wouldn't leave the next day, as she had said she would, and that in her own endearing way—which I loved her for—she was purposely playing on my suspi- cions and fears to make me love her even more, a female game she had mastered to the point of infuriating me sometimes.

I used to forget our age difference. She never made me feel older than thirty. She said to me once, "If we get married, I'll bear you ten children in ten years!"

And I replied, "If we get married, I'll make sure we never have children, so you wouldn't share even a tiny part of our love with them!"

Those were the kinds of words lovers would say.

"If I marry you, will your writing keep you away from me?" she asked.

"What would be left to write about after I marry you?" I said.

Feigning anger, she said, "Then I won't marry you! Your writing is a thousand times more important, as long as you continue to love me."

As I drove her back home on our last evening together, she leaned her head on my shoulder and wept most of the way. Then she sat up, wiping her tears and shaking off her grief, and she said to me for the last time, "I'll write to you as soon as I know my address. And you write to me, every day!" Her last kiss before getting out of the car tasted of desperation and madness, or so I imagined at that moment. But perhaps I was the one desperate and mad. Perhaps I was not able to appreciate her complicated, noble position, a position of both hardship and pride.

The first six months were very difficult on me. I opened my eyes every morning on Siham's marble face gazing at me with its large, sad eyes, as though pitying me. Or was she gloating at my misfortune? During those moments, I longed to hear the phone ring, even once, to hear Sarab's breaths as they used to come to me over the city phone lines, breaths that sounded more like sighs when she would whisper, "Hello."

The first six months were hellish, despite my busy work schedule and the late hours I kept at the office every day. When I got back home every night I would go to my library and hold the seashell in my hands, comforted by its firm, smooth touch. I would hold it to my ear and hear Sarab's long, endless sighs, and I would write her three or four lines of a letter that had no end. I realized to my surprise that I had never taken a picture of her, not one. So how would I have a bust made of her that I could place in my library, her favorite room of the house? But why have a bust made when images of her still crowded my head wherever I turned? One day Ghassan asked me as he turned the seashell in his hands, "Dad, where did you get this shell?"

"From a faraway shore, honey. Hold it to your ear and you'll hear the breaths of the sea. And sometimes you'll hear people's laments."

I visited Talal Salih in his office one evening near the end of the following winter. I realized suddenly that almost a year had gone by since I had met Sarab. Shortly into my visit, Talal said, "Have you heard from Sarab? How could you let her go like that?"

"So you can write a poem about her absence," I said bitterly. "The two poems you wrote evoke such a strong physical presence. Did you know that?"

I left his office and headed straight to Ansam. I sat purposely next to the glass window, wishing that the sky would share in my memories and pour some of its love the same way it had the evening we met. And who other than Diab would come to me during those sentimental moments, and whoever said that doctors of jurisprudence, as strong as they might be, never give in to their emotions? He greeted then reprimanded me for my long absence. "It's been over six months, Dr. Nael." Then he added, somewhat reluctantly and shyly, "The beautiful lady who used to come with you, what happened to her?"

"Sarab . . ."

"She had such a presence."

"Sarab, Sarab," I sighed. "Diab, do you remember how we liked our coffee? Would you make two? I'll drink both."

"Sure thing, and I swear they're on me!"

I made my decision that night. I resolved to forget. I had to forget. Would I let myself flounder again in the same swamps as I had for countless months after Siham's death? I would go back to my writing, and if I couldn't come up with a new idea for a novel, I would concentrate on two important papers I had to write on topics in my specialty area. The first was for a conference I had already agreed to participate in that coming summer in the Hague on the rights of private institutions to sue their governments in certain situations in Third World countries. I had to go back to my books and other sources to write it. The second paper was about a controversial issue that had preoccupied me for years. I entitled it "The Death Penalty and the Need to Abolish It in the Arab World."

And there were all the friends I had to get back in touch with. But more important were my responsibilities in looking after my son Ghassan and helping him in his studies in his final year of elementary school. I had placed too much of the responsibility on Salima in looking after him, especially during the evenings, which I now preferred to spend mostly at home. The al-Saifi family inheritance case was in its final stages, and our firm was awaiting the verdict, which finally came out in favor of my client and his family, and I ended up with the largest sum of money I had ever received from a single case. They say a person lucky in love is unlucky in card games, but it seems the opposite is true. After winning the case, I even toyed with the idea of writing a novel based on the subject of inheritance as I had experienced it: the conflicts, the characters, the victims and crooks. But my interest was short-lived. Such subjects failed to inspire me despite their immediate social relevance and their bizarre twists and quirks.

I don't think a day went by without Sarab coming to my mind one way or another. She had become as much a part of me as the blood in my veins, which I didn't have to see gushing out of my wrist to know was there. I missed having her around, especially since her favorite novel, *Entering the Mirrors,* had received widespread attention the last three years and all kinds of reviews and articles were written about it. Together we could have celebrated as some critics would prove her right in liking the novel while others would amaze us with their fresh insights, unraveling for us new meanings and interpretations. And together we could have laughed and cried—and would have been just as amazed—when more of those alleged critics screamed at each other with that persistent, blind ignorance at once laughable and sad, reminding us each time that even in our age of information and knowledge the voices of ignorance, thank God, were still relentless and loud everywhere. Every time I came up with an opinion, even legal or professional, I asked myself if Sarab would agree. I got used to her spiritual presence, to not having her physically next to me anymore, sadly of course, but also with a kind of resigned acceptance. What was important, I told myself, was for her not to have died or been killed, for her to be alive and well somewhere, and I'd be happy with the rest.

One Friday morning Sharif al-Turk and Tala surprised me with a visit at home. It was unusual for them not to call ahead of time. From my bedroom, I could hear Salima welcoming them into the living room, so I came out and joined them, and we exchanged greetings and the usual reprimands for not having visited or seen each other in a long time, not even in passing.

Tala was still as I had always known her, adorned and elegant. I noticed a large bouquet of yellow roses in the large crystal vase on a side table. When I asked, Salima was quick to inform me that Tala had brought them with her and had placed them in the vase right away. Salima ran to the kitchen with the vase and filled it up with water. When she returned, Tala took the roses from her and placed them on the center table, rearranging them with genuine pride. They were beautiful flowers, and they brightened up the room in a way I didn't expect. I thanked them for their gesture. Their flowers were the first to be brought into our house after our garden had been neglected for many months.

The coffee came, and our conversations went from one subject to the other. Tala was clearly avoiding any mention of her visit to my office months earlier when she had come to express her disapproval of my relationship with Sarab. She hadn't told her husband about her visit, nor had I told Sarab, to avoid provoking or upsetting her. I wouldn't have brought up the subject had Sharif not innocently expressed his disappointment again with me not coming to congratulate him on moving into his new office two years ago, prompting Tala to say to him jokingly, "Even when he had reason to come visit the office he didn't. You expect him to come now?"

Sharif laughed in a way that suggested his camaraderie with me. He looked at her, then me. "You mean Sarab Affan? She was an excellent secretary, but a bit strange, and very sensitive. She left us suddenly one day, for no apparent reason."

"You never found out why?" I asked.

"No, she refused to talk to me when I called. We had to send her last paycheck to her."

Then Tala came forth with her malicious question. "I wonder what's happened to her, where she might be working now?"

"She left the country," I answered tersely, determined to keep her curious, wondering.

I noticed Salima giving me a look of secret understanding because I had told her a few days before when she had inquired about Sarab's absence that she had decided to become a "freedom fighter." And so as a token of solidarity with me against Tala, my sister added, "What an intelligent young lady. I'm sure she'll be successful, wherever she is."

Tala appeared greatly relieved. I could imagine her saying to herself, "Thank God, she's gone!" But she said, "I wish her the best." Then her tone changed, and she spoke to me directly. "When are you going to get married Nael? It's been four years since Siham passed away, and I'm sure she'd approve of you getting married again, God rest her soul. What do you think, Salima?"

My sister laughed. "Convince him if you can! I'm with you all the way!"

"Perhaps he's still waiting for Sarab?"

"That's very possible."

"Have you nothing to say, Nael?"

What an amazing woman, Tala! "Say what? We've said all there is to be said." Then I continued, changing the subject, "Sharif, do you think I can buy stocks in one or more of your companies? I heard your poultry farm is one of the largest in the country."

"Of course. Come see us tomorrow."

After about an hour the two guests stood up, ready to leave. We walked out to the porch together, and while Salima and Sharif talked about his two sons as they continued to his car, Tala slowed me down on purpose. "Why won't you put my mind to rest?" she whispered. "Are you still in touch with her?"

"Of course," I replied.

"You're the biggest fool," she hissed. "I'll call you at the office."

"There's no need for that, no need at all," I said in a loud, cheerful voice. "Sharif, I'll be coming to see you at the office in the next two or three days."

I hurried to the car and held the door open for Tala as both Salima and I said good-bye.

When we got back to the living room, I pulled the roses out of the vase and carried them to the kitchen, water dripping from their stems, and threw them in the trash. Salima looked at me in disbelief. "Why? Why are you doing this?" she cried out.

"Because they're from a woman who doesn't like Sarab. I don't care if it is Tala."

My sister liked Sarab, although she had seen her only two or three times and seldom talked about her. She didn't know much about her or how serious our relationship was. Perhaps at first she had thought I was in a fleeting relationship with a woman, whoever that woman happened to be, and had forgiven me for it. But later she told me that she had come to realize that a woman who meant so much to her brother had to be extraordinary, even though she was worried that Sarab might be too young for me. "And what next?" she had asked. When she found out—I don't know how—that Sarab's father was the well-known surgeon Dr. Ali Affan, she went on expecting me at any moment to ask her to call Sarab's mother to begin planning for our engagement ceremony, and she sorted through the names of male friends and relatives I could take along with me to get her father's permission in marriage. Her only concern was that Sarab's parents might worry about their young daughter having to take care of a stepson, so she decided to free Sarab of that responsibility by keeping Ghassan in her care.

What a practical woman, my beloved sister Salima, and how traditional.

◆　　◆　　◆

Months went by. I finished writing my paper for the international conference, and I traveled to the Netherlands to present it in early September. I spent two enjoyable weeks in the Hague and Amsterdam and visited the museums of Rembrandt and Van Gogh. How misery and suffering bring out the creative energies of geniuses, so let me learn from it! I went back to my city excited about an idea for a new novel that had started taking shape in my head, only to discover a few days later that what at first had come to me like a torrent had completely dried up. I stalled. Weeks went by. Winter arrived, then spring, and I hadn't written more than fifty pages. But work kept me busier than any lawyer could expect to be, giving me the opportunity to travel to Cairo and Tunis in the summer. In the meantime I was invited to participate in a conference of the International League of Human Rights scheduled to convene early the following March. That gave me an excuse to get away from the pressures of writing and concentrate on finishing my paper about the importance of abolishing the death penalty.

Almost three years had passed since meeting Sarab for the first time. She had become a song playing itself over and over in my head, a beautiful song whose words I could no longer remember but that I would surrender to unconsciously, and it would die out, leaving me in a soft glow like that at dusk or dawn, I did not know. The seashell was still in the same place, full of sighs and sorrows, and the words that could have poured down like a torrent instead gathered up quietly in some corner of the soul, like water behind a fortified dam. In truth, I was afraid of letting them out, and by some trick of the mind I was able to keep them trapped inside me. It was as though the words were a ghost lurking inside a house, merciless toward those who disturbed its peace, and so I chose not to enter the house and to leave the ghost alone. I even stopped going to Ansam and went to the Holiday Inn only two or three times for work-related functions.

Before leaving for Paris to attend the conference on human rights, I was driving one day on the street just off of Janeen street where I used to meet Sarab whenever she took a taxi to see me, and I found myself going there and stopping like an idiot right at the entry to the neighborhood. Suddenly I had a frightening vision. I imagined a young woman with a beautiful body and long, flowing hair emerging from a crowd of pedestrians and coming up to me and saying, "Don't you remember me? Aren't you going to open the car door for me?" I panicked, shouting like a madman, "No! No!" And I sped off recklessly as though being chased by demons.

I got back home perspiring despite the February chill. I took out the manuscript of the novel I had neglected for months and began writing on a new page:

A street you enter from you know not where,
and there she is, springing to life,
tormenting your memory, bringing back
what forgetfulness had almost taken away,
what remains trapped inside,
hostage to silence, restless.
Can you possibly hold back the words
about the little that remains
and will not stop haunting you,
about morning trembling like dew drops
about night breathless for love like rain,
about the torments of the heart, devastating as a storm?

I left the page on my desk and said to myself angrily, "Yes! I will hold back the words. I will not write a word until I go to Paris. And after that, who knows?"

•   •   •

Like most conferences, the International League of Human Rights conference in Paris kept us busy for four days, from morning until midnight each day, between lectures, panels, meetings, and lunch and dinner invitations. I presented my paper, which I had written in French, on the afternoon of the last day. Both Arab and non-Arab lawyers and intellectuals contributed in important ways to the discussion that followed.

I found it particularly interesting that both the Arab and non-Arab participants agreed with me that the death penalty should be abolished because it keeps societies from respecting the sanctity of human life, thus hampering their efforts to modernize and become true democracies. But it was the non-Arab participants who expressed doubts as to whether Third World countries would abolish the death penalty in the near future, implying that unlike the real agents for social change—or social stagnation—intellectuals in those countries were marginal, a point that spurred on another debate of pros and cons until the meeting was finally called off with a closing statement by the panel moderator.

I was thrilled to see al-Tayyib al-Hadi in the audience when I sat down at the panel table to present my paper. I had called him the day before to tell him I was in Paris for a conference and inform him of the time of my presentation. He came up to me afterward as people were leaving the panel room. We hugged and made our way through the crowd and out to the street where we felt more at ease expressing our emotions with words, gestures, and laughter—in true Arab fashion. As we walked to a nearby café, al-Tayyib asked, "How long will you go on being a utopian, Nael?"

"Till death," I answered.

"The death of the hangman or the victim?" he asked, laughing.

I hadn't seen him since he had visited the city about three years earlier. The time went by quickly with all our banter and endless questions and answers. I had to attend the closing banquet for the conference participants that evening, so we agreed to meet the next morning, on Sunday.

He joined me for an after-breakfast coffee at nine the next morning at the hotel where the conference organizers had put me up, on a street near the Sorbonne. When we finished he said, "Put on your coat and let's go out. It's cold, but your Arab God still loves you. He turned off the rain last night."

We strolled down the Boulevard Saint-Germain. The shops were closed. We passed in front of an old church and heard an organ playing inside. Al-Tayyib suggested we go in and listen—I think it was Bach's *Toccata*—and so we did. The deep tones lifted us to a state of harmony that left us craving for more. When mass resumed, we slipped out quietly toward the door. "We can spend the entire morning going from church to church," said al-Tayyib. "From music to music."

"How about visiting Notre Dame? I haven't been there in years."

As we walked toward the Seine and Notre Dame, al-Tayyib said, "Remember Montaigne's words: to cure poverty of possessions is easy, but poverty of soul, impossible.[1] I thank God sometimes that ever since I learned the Quran by heart He's made me rich in spirit, at least in part, so that I've never had a poverty of soul—or at least I don't think so—but I've never been able to cure my poverty of possessions and money, contrary to what our great teacher claims . . ."

"Money? That filth on our hands," I said.

"Well, that's why I washed my hands of it and forgot it a long time ago. After Notre Dame, let's go to Centre Pompidou."

The Gothic cathedral was crowded with men and women—seated, standing, gathered around the altar and choir, or standing separately and scattered along the spacious, dimly lit outer aisles and among the columns—each in his own world. High above were the towering ceilings and the magnificent rose window, large and round, taking up the top portion of the wall, the sun pushing in through its stained, leaded glass into the dark spaces below that resounded with organ music and chanting voices.

Al-Tayyib and I were captivated in eye and heart, each for his own reasons. We were mystified, yearning for the trance of dervishes. "Are we in paradise?" I asked.

"Yes, and it would be so hard to leave!" he whispered.

Half an hour later, after leaving the exquisite sounds of music behind us and walking back out into the sunshine—bright despite the cold—al-Tayyib went on reciting Quranic verses in his deep voice, as we crossed the wide square teeming with people:

The Gardens of Eden they shall enter;
therein they shall be adorned
with bracelets of gold and with pearls,
and their apparel there shall be of silk.[2]

1. *To cure poverty of possessions is easy: poverty of soul, impossible:* the quote is from the translation of the original French into English of *Michel de Montaigne: The Complete Essays,* trans. M. A. Screech (New York: Penguin Books, 2003), book 3, chapter 10: 1141.

2. *The Gardens of Eden . . . of silk:* Quran 35.33 (al-Fatir), from *The Koran Interpreted,* A. J. Arberry (London: Allen and Unwin, 1955).

He paused for a moment, gazing off into the distance, then he added:

> See, the inhabitants of Paradise
> today are busy in their rejoicing,
> they and their spouses,
> reclining upon couches in the shade.[3]

He paused again, his silence emphasizing the music that was still playing in the background, and then he added:

> For them awaits a known provision,
> fruits—and they high-honored
> in the Gardens of Bliss
> upon couches, set face to face,
> a cup from a spring passed round to them,
> white, a delight to the drinkers,
> wherein no sickness is, neither intoxication;
> and with them wide-eyed maidens
> restraining their glances
> as if they were hidden pearls.[4]

I didn't want to spoil the heavenly mood that al-Tayyib had put me in with his breathtaking recitations, but then I said, "From one magic spell to another, Abu Muhammad? Still doing this to your friends?"

"Especially when I haven't seen them in years. Tell me, did you re-marry?"

"Remarry? Did I give you that impression last time?" I answered, surprised.

He laughed, nudging me in the waist with his elbow. "Abdullah

---

3. *See, the inhabitants of Paradise . . . the shade:* Quran 36.55–56 (Ya Sin), from A. J. Arberry's *The Koran Interpreted.*

4. *For them awaits a known provision . . . hidden pearls:* Quran 37.41–49 (al-Saffat), from A. J. Arberry's *The Koran Interpreted.*

al-Rami came through Paris more than two years ago. He said there was a beautiful young woman keeping you busy, or should I say you were keeping her busy? I hope I'm not giving away any secrets?"

"No, not at all."

"So?"

"She left the country. Disappeared. By the way, where is Abdullah these days?"

"God knows. As usual, he pops in and pops out."

"How about Umm Muhammad? Is she here?"

"Rabia, Muhammad, and Hassan—they're all back in Rabat. It looks like I'll be joining them soon. Paris has lost its charm for me. These days being a journalist here is more like trying to beat water out of rocks. No personal gratification, no nationalistic gain. Should we take a taxi to Centre Pompidou?"

"Taxi? In Paris? Who wants to be in a car in the middle of Paris? In such beautiful weather, it's a sin not to walk. And you're like me, a walker."

"You know, Nael, if I could write down all the thoughts that ebb and flow in my head when I'm walking down these streets, I'd have filled up entire volumes by now."

"So that explains your ebbing and flowing articles that read like endless philosophical meditations."

"That's been my life, a life spent on my feet, walking from the moment I opened my eyes on the Southern Desert."

"How about me and my escapades into the battlegrounds of mind and flesh, always at war with each other. As life changes and I get older, you'd think the battle would cease, but it only gets worse."

After a long walk, we reached Centre Pompidou, where all sorts of people—jugglers, magicians, fire-eaters, painters and caricaturists, lovers, quacks, hippies, drunks—mingled in broad daylight. And I, coming from a world of strict laws and rationing, full of the masks of uprightness and piety, felt that in the midst of that exciting chaos I was reconnecting with my true humanity. I wished that Sarab were with me during those moments. Finally, I gave up and told al-Tayyib about her—

conjured her up by describing her looks, her movements—until we entered Centre Pompidou and went up its clear plastic escalator tunnels among a crowd of people. We visited the art collections and exhibits on its many floors, wandering among the stunning sculptures and provocative paintings as though we were blessing those works for all that they offered and were still offering to humanity, broadening our thought and imagination, affirming our sensual desires and dreams, enriching our passions and creative madness, that madness so necessary for our well-being in the technological age.

Fatigue and hunger were wearing on us when we reached the self-service restaurant on the top floor of Centre Pompidou. We grabbed our trays and walked along the buffet line, choosing from among the meats, vegetables, soup, bread, butter, desserts, fruits, wine, and coffee. We carried our trays, heavy with food and steamy plates, to a table at the far end of the restaurant by a window from which we could see many men and women, mostly young, gathered on the open rooftop balcony overlooking the Paris domes and spires. Some took bagged sandwiches out of their coat pockets and ate and talked and laughed out there in the open.

I noticed a young man and woman, probably not even yet in their twenties, wandering on the rooftop then coming toward the window and looking at us through the glass, staring at the "banquet" that my friend and I had spread out on the table.

We smiled back, and they pointed to our food almost as if to say, "All this food!?" We waved back like a couple of Marcel Marceau for them to come in and share our meal.

The young woman untied the kerchief she had wrapped around her neck and let its two ends hang loose on her chest. Then she grabbed on to each end and started moving the kerchief up and down, rubbing it against her neck, while she made exaggerated gestures with her eyebrows and wide eyes and stared in jest at the food, moving her lips and nose as though she could smell the delicious, mouth-watering aromas. Her friend did likewise, making faces that would bring you to laugh and cry at the same time, as he pointed to imaginary tears flowing down his cheeks. Ah, Harlequin and Columbine![5] How beautiful they were, these two young people! And how real!

With an emphatic gesture, we repeated our invitation for them to join us. When they understood what we meant, Columbine pretended to be flying with joy, and she ran like a nimble ballerina (Ah, Sarab! Sarab!) toward the entrance, with Harlequin following right behind, bubbling with comic excitement.

They hurried toward us past the crowded tables. We invited them to sit, but they laughed and declined politely, silently. I offered the young woman a plate of meat, and again she shook her head no, and so did her friend when al-Tayyib offered him some of his food. We asked them again. "No, no," they both replied, and the young woman added, "Just this!" and with the lightness of angels she plucked the big apple off my tray. And the young man said, "Just this!" and with the same lightness picked up a piece of bread and cheese from al-Tayyib's tray. She bit into the apple with her white, sparkling teeth, making delightful sounds, and he took a bite of his bread and cheese. Gratitude showed on their beautiful faces, and they made grateful bows, the young woman still chomping on her apple. Then they waved to us in farewell, as though sailing off to some unknown continent!

I said to al-Tayyib, "Those two are paradise itself! The first paradise, not the paradise of those last days you described with your mystifying recitations this morning. What life! Gushing, pure as snow, radiant as fire!"

Al-Tayyib went on chuckling. "You're still a romantic, a lover of romantics! Will you ever grow up, Nael?"

"I swear if they'd agree to it I would go out and dance with them on the Paris rooftops and live only on bread and cheese and apples!"

"Then let's drink to them."

We poured ourselves some wine and drank to them and lovers everywhere. Then I said, "After all that I've written, do you know what

5. *Harlequin and Columbine:* in the Harlequinade, an eighteenth-century European variety of *commedia dell'arte,* the harlequin is the servant and then lover of Columbine, a beautiful woman.

story I'd like to write the most? A story about two people, just two, a man and woman. A love story. I'd isolate them from everything, the way you put a drop of blood on a microscope slide. If I could do that, I'd bring back paradise, the original paradise that God created for Adam and Eve, and no one else, when He blessed them with all the riches of the world. Then He caught them in that shattering moment of temptation, that moment when they discovered each other's overwhelming presence, each other's pleasant yet harsh powers of seduction that could not be pushed away. With this they discovered how the sap of life bursts forth, they discovered the secrets of creation in all its hidden meanings, and they discovered that their joy in having each other is the same joy that God experienced with creation. Perhaps the ancient serpent had profound wisdom and knowledge when it said what it said to Eve."

"Wonderful, wonderful," said al-Tayyib. He had stopped eating for a moment. "Go on, go on," he said, and he speared some food with his fork.

I ate some of my meat and vegetables and poured myself another glass of wine. "Our life is constant suffering. Our sorrows show us no mercy. History has never witnessed anything of such magnitude and severity as our ordeals. I think the Indians were right when they said that the ultimate goal to life is salvation."

"What's salvation got to do with the lovers you're writing about? Are you saying that love is salvation?"

"Not exactly, or at least not so simply. What's important about the Indian view is that salvation lies in uniting one's soul with that of the universe. This leads to the belief that when a man and a woman unite in the ecstasy of love, their feelings of separateness as individuals disappear. And the disappearance of that duality marks the beginning of freedom and salvation. The soul of the individual enters into communion with the soul of the universe through love. Or perhaps that communion is love itself, salvation itself."

"But we can't escape tragedy, and sorrow afflicts those who love and hate all the same. So where is salvation?"

"Salvation lies within the soul, in surpassing the ordeal, in rising above sorrow. Only then does your mind, your heart, your entire being become capable of overcoming the evil that bores through existence with the tenacity of worms. And perhaps people will know more goodness when they learn how to love."

"Nael, it amazes me how a woman who asked you for an apple could have unleashed all these thoughts from you, even as you eat! And you know very well that the capitals of the world have chosen debauchery over love, not leaving a dream for lovers to talk about."

"The poor capitals of the world! Whether they like it or not, they are always waiting for the innovations of the creators whose souls are one with the soul of the universe, who in that union alone experience salvation and the creative impulse itself. So no matter how much debauchery takes over love, the cities of the world will live and progress only by the dreams of their visionary lovers. Everything else is slavery in disguise, eternal death."

Al-Tayyib stared at me a long time, as if he couldn't believe what he'd just heard. He took a big sip of wine and said, "What has Sarab done to you?"

I laughed. Perhaps I had gotten too excited, too serious. "And I haven't even spoken about coming out of paradise."

"Ha! coming out of paradise, into the labyrinths of disappointment, evil, and suffering—that is the real source of inspiration. That is when art becomes necessary, the only way to salvation. And then, like you, I'll say that the cities of the world will live and progress only by the dreams of its suffering visionaries."

"Yes, yes, but it's still a coming out of paradise, meaning that paradise has to exist for those visionaries to leave it or be cast out, and then to look for a way that would give them the illusion of returning."

"No, no. You can't find a way back to the original paradise once you've left, no matter how hard you look. And it would be better for you to suffer, to be content with the colors, the sounds, the abstract ideas, the passage of the days, and to find in all of that the reason—or part of the reason—you need to go on being a law professor or a novelist always searching for a new story or a writer like me immersing himself in a sea of words to the point of choking, hoping in the end to bring back an oyster with a pearl, even a tiny one."

I held my cup of French coffee, examining its brown residue, and I took a sip. It was cold. Thoughts about the last painful months I had suffered, an outcast from paradise, came back to me. "My dear al-Tayyib, the day comes when all colors fade, when all sounds are muted, when your opinions seem irrelevant, just like the words you write. The day comes when all ideas are worthless, when nothing is enjoyable anymore, and you go on just existing, like a plant. Except that you keep on feeling disappointment and pain. As the poet al-Maarri[6] once said: 'We hope for the things we can't see and hear what we don't wish to hear.' The voices of friends fade away, their faces vanish deep into memory, life loses its luster, and there's nothing left that excites the eye, mind, or body. Everything becomes bitter, and even in the hot sun, darkness prevails at every hour. And the one fear is the fear of extinction, eternal silence."

"Man, you scare me," said al-Tayyib. He let out a strange laugh and shook his head. "The only thing you forgot to mention is a quote from your poet friend al-Maarri: 'Console me, for the light of hope has died, and time refuses to die.' I swear, if Paris doesn't pull these dark visions out of your head in the next few days, I'll keep you here until you confess that you don't mean what you're saying and promise me that you'll go back to your beautiful library back home, lock yourself inside, and write the story of the two lovers whose souls mingled with the soul of the universe until they realized the moment of salvation! And maybe in this way you too will be saved. Be honest. Tell me. How many times did you come out of this first paradise of yours, only to return again, even if it was only an illusion, and then leave again? I'll never forget that young Palestinian woman you were infatuated with in the mid-seventies in Beirut, when she would tell us about Ibn Arabi and his Sufi trance, when she herself was entranced by Nael Imran and tried to keep us all away from him so that she alone could enjoy his spiritual presence in her own first paradise. What was her name? Reem? Rasha? And

6. See chapter 2, note 1.

now you're telling me about Sarab, and only God knows how many Rashas entrapped you and how many Sarabs kept you thirsty during the years between the two. And did you notice that this Columbine, a rose that hasn't blossomed yet, was drawn to you from behind a glass window, through a different language, and she came to you running, dancing, so she could take an apple from you and bite into it with all those sexual innuendoes? What is it about you that makes them act that way, when they're still in their virgin spring? And after all that, you tell me, 'Everything is bitter, and the one fear is the fear of extinction and eternal silence.' "

Now I was the one to let out a strange laugh. "All I'm saying is that every few years I suffer yet another tragedy. Hasn't the same happened to you?"

"If not for tragedy, how do you think I'd find the strength to go on, as much as I love my dear Rabia?"

"But the years are catching up with us, Abu Muhammad."

"With you, maybe. Not me. I'd accept this kind of talk from anyone but you. Tell me, Nael, who among our friends hasn't gotten grayer, more hunched over, who hasn't lost his vitality in the last few years, except you and me? If we may put the subject of paradise aside for a moment, I have this theory that keeps making more and more sense to me the older I get. You and me, we're the type that never ages. Take it from me. Because the artist never gets old. That's just a fundamental rule. It doesn't matter if his hair turns gray, because that only makes him, as the songs say, all the more dignified and attractive. The artist lives from his wellspring of imagination and inspiration, and from nothing else. And this wellspring resides in that part of his body where his love energy is produced and constantly renewed—or you might even call it his sexual energy, which is really one's wellspring of youth that time does not seem to affect, as long as the wellspring keeps flowing with the imagination that gives it life. I mean, if you had only been Dr. Nael Imran the legal consultant and professor of law, you would have been a decrepit old man by now and your love energy—sexual energy—would have been consumed. And with it the energy to create anything new. But because you're an artist, and your imagination is therefore constantly at work by virtue of the force of that magical device inside you—the 'perpetual motion' device that inventors have been striving to invent and that the artists have beat them to—the years retreat away from you, vanquished, away from that mysterious youthfulness always flowing with the wellspring of love, vainglory, creativity, of physical and mental pleasure, you name it. Take it from me, Nael, this power lies in the two sacks hanging between your legs, where the true wellspring of every great achievement lies!"

I laughed heartily. "Whether or not what you're saying is true, I'm happy to believe it. Let's drink to this mighty power!"

We drank, and then I added, still laughing, "Ten years from now I'll remind you of what you said."

He poured out the rest of the wine into his glass. "And why not twenty years, man?"

The feeling that consumed us during those moments was wonderful, the feeling that even after we stood up and left Centre Pompidou, time eternal would be in our grasp.

                    ◆   ◆   ◆

On the afternoon of the next day there was the pleasant, refreshing drizzle, part rain and part snow, common to Paris in early March right before the coming of spring.

I left the hotel with a woolen scarf around my neck that protected me against the cold without denying me its pleasurable feeling. I strolled aimlessly down Rue des Écoles adjacent to the campus of the Sorbonne then took a side street that I knew led to the Pantheon square, which at that time of the afternoon, and because of the constant drizzle, was empty except for some young men and women going in and out of the entrance of a high building overlooking the square. I realized that it was the entrance to one of the university libraries.

I hadn't gotten too wet from the rain yet and wanted to enjoy more of the delightful breeze, gently brushing against my face, hair, and lips, bringing both rain and snow. I thought of all the other rains and the half-remembered tunes they usually evoked, much as music evokes vague memories of rainy days and strange rendezvous sparkling with beautiful fingers, delectable teeth, and smiling lips.

I stood near the gate, gazing at the Pantheon, that monument to great men and women who were raised by their nation to the ranks of gods for the love of their ideas and adoration of their art. I felt a sudden, deep urge to go inside the library. As I entered the hallway and began walking up the stairs, I felt as though I were in my own house despite the contrast in architecture. The air was stuffy from the humidity brought in by the students and researchers in their wet clothes that got mixed with the inside heat and the cigarette and pipe smoke of those who stood smoking near the ashtrays along the stairway because they weren't allowed to smoke inside the library. I walked past them and up the stairs, not feeling a stranger nor drawing any curious looks from people as I walked toward the main reading room.

At the entrance to the reading room, I saw a sign above the superintendent's desk that said: PLEASE PRESENT YOUR ID. I didn't have the proper identification to show the young superintendent. I almost turned back and left, but when I saw the big reading room and the tens of thousands of books stacked on shelves against its walls and the long rows of study tables crowded with students and researchers studying in a silence like that of shrines—I decided not to turn back because of an ID card. So I said to the kind-looking young man, "I'm a stranger here, and I love books. Would you let me in?"

Without hesitating, he replied, smiling, "Of course. Please go ahead."

I walked among the crowded tables toward the stacks. Young and old alike, men and women of all ages, pored over papers and books, reading, taking notes, some writing rapidly, others holding an open book while their eyes wandered off, thoughtfully or dreamily, toward the high ceiling. On such a cold night, I did not expect to see so many people gathered around those tables of knowledge, so many that I couldn't find an empty spot to squeeze into and read a book from one of the shelves.

I walked through the aisles among the tables, observing all the people studying around me—their papers, hands, pens, and sometimes their contemplative, focused faces appearing beautiful in their silence and total absorption in the mental absolutes in front of them. I imagined myself a Martian who had just landed on Earth to see humanity engaging in one of its greatest feats of love. The faces of the women—and there were many, most of them dressed in denim jackets or black woolen turtlenecks covering their long necks up to their chins—exuded a certain magic, which, at that moment, might have existed only in my imagination.

Walking slowly, I had almost reached the other end of the hall when I noticed the back of a woman's head, beautiful with long black hair that flowed abundantly over her back and partly over her shoulders. I stopped for a moment, my heart pounding in a way I had long forgotten. Although the room was full of black, blonde, and chestnut-haired women, she was the only one to captivate me, although I hadn't even seen her face and hands. I was overcome with a dreadful pleasure that made me reluctant to see her face.

I was mesmerized. Could it be her? Impossible! I better turn back while still reluctant to confirm what I've seen, I thought, and may this woman with the long hair forever remain a mystery that stirred me from the inside and I was scared of approaching, not because its magic would disappear if I did, but because it would cast me to a place far deeper and more dangerous.

In my confusion, I noticed that her hands were bare of jewelry. She was writing slowly, hesitantly, as though struggling for the right words, from right to left, in Arabic! I knew those delicate hands like my own. No, it couldn't be! Despite my reluctance, I moved around the table and into the aisle opposite her neighbor to assure myself that I had fallen to an illusion, that she was a stranger I had never seen before.

She was wearing black-rimmed glasses, her head bent over papers as she wrote in Arabic—words I couldn't make out. God! It was her, Sarab! She did not raise her head while I stood directly behind the balding man who was absorbed reading a huge book across the table from her. I leaned toward her over the man's shoulder, from between him and the person sitting next to him, and I said in a voice slightly above a whisper, "Hello! Sarab!"

All the faces next to her looked up at me with inquisitive, dissatisfied looks, except for her. She was completely absorbed in her writing. "Pardon me!" I whispered to the people next to her. Then I said, addressing her again, "Sarab!"

The woman sitting next to her gave her a nudge and pointed to me. She raised her eyes, and at once I recognized their blackness and long lashes behind the black frame of her glasses. She looked puzzled and spoke in French, "Oui, monsieur?"

"Sarab. Aren't you Sarab Affan?" I asked her, in Arabic.

She looked apologetically at the people around her then looked back at me, replying in Arabic, "Sarab Affan? I'm sorry. You must be imagining."

She went back to her papers as if to imply that the matter had been settled and there was nothing left to say.

I stood there dumbfounded. Was I that far-off in my imagination? But I was sure it was Sarab. Her voice, her intonations, everything about her seemed to confirm that she was Sarab herself. The time that had passed since I last saw her had done nothing to erase her image, still vivid in my head, as though each day that went by wiped the dust that had gathered from the day before. True, I had never seen her wearing glasses, but it didn't seem strange that she would need them for studying. Anyway, they had only added to her beauty, making her in the few seconds during which she looked at me appear more brilliant, more captivating, her eyes more piercing.

I stood there, at a loss. But I kept looking at her, hoping that she would look back. Right then she raised her head and looked at me, puzzled that I was still standing there, and she gestured with her hands, lips, and eyebrows as if to ask, "What? I'm not the person you're looking for."

There she was, Columbine of yesterday, Columbine without Harlequin, waiting for me to leave.

I started walking away through the aisles toward the bookshelves at the far end, but before I reached them I felt a strong urge to turn around and go back. Meanwhile, she had stood up and was walking in my direction with her papers, bag, and short coat. She was coming to me, no doubt! How beautifully she glided along! Now I knew, I was certain. I could swear it was her, Sarab Affan! No one else had her walk, somewhere between dancing and flying, between the swaying of gazelles and the flowing of waterfalls. Her height further emphasized the way she walked, and so did her wild, flowing hair. I thought to myself, "She's coming to tell me that she really is Sarab but that for some reason she had changed her name and buried her past, that she is no longer the same woman I knew." I remembered the "imagination-versus-reality" game she told me she had devised once and used in writing her journals day after day and how she had become an expert at mixing reality and imagination and having one take the place of the other until their boundaries were completely blurred.

I smiled as she came toward me, not a smile or the slightest expression of familiarity on her face, as though she had already forgotten who I was. I remembered how I used to wait for her in the usual place at the entrance to Janeen, sitting in my car behind the steering wheel while she emerged from a taxi and crossed the street toward me with that strange emptiness in her eyes, indifferent to the pedestrians all around her, until she would finally reach my car and swing around to the other door, which I would have unlocked for her, and she would get in and settle into the seat next to me, immediately switching into a cheerful, playful mood—laughing, greeting, giving me her lips, stroking my hair, until I'd start the car and we'd drive off amid our pleasant commotion.

But this time, when she had almost reached me, she swung past in another direction between the crowded tables and toward the door, without even looking at me again. I followed quickly. I was sure it was her, Sarab, with all the pretense to not knowing me. We met again at the security desk. She held her denim bag open for the man at the desk. I noticed a large "S" printed in black in an upper corner of her bag. I was now certain. I followed her as she exited. "Sarab!"

She laughed this time, as though expecting me to follow her. She answered without seeming exasperated or annoyed, in Arabic. "You seem convinced that I'm Sarab. Should I tell you my real name?"

"No, please. You are Sarab Affan. I don't care what other name you might be using. The 'S' on your bag proves it."

"Very well. I'm Sarab. Who are you?"

We stood among a group of students who were talking and smoking in the hallway leading to the stairs. Sarab—could I refer to her by any other name, as much as she tried to deny it?—took out a cigarette, which I promptly lit for her without answering her question.

"You haven't told me your name yet," she said, puffing on her cigarette.

"You know my name. You know it very well."

She laughed again. "Okay. So what is it you wanted to say to this Sarab?"

"Many things, so many things. Listen, do you mind if we go somewhere else?"

I held her arm gently, leading her to the stairs. She didn't mind and even had me hold her bag and papers while she put on her coat and took a large headscarf and wrapped it around her head, tying it in a knot under her chin. She took her belongings back from me, and we walked down the stairs and out of the building unto the Pantheon square. I was even more convinced she was the woman I knew. Even the way she clung to me lightly, my face almost brushing against her hair as I held her arm, was so much like her. Her mild, pleasant perfume seemed hers only, even in Paris, goddess of perfumes.

I was overcome by the desire to say many things to her, things that had occupied my thoughts for months, years, before and during the time I'd known her and after she'd left. I felt that she had come back to me, or rather that I had come back to her, discovered her anew, so that I could release some of the emotions that had built up inside me and couldn't talk to anyone about during all those futile months.

Our first conversations had begun with the last rains that usher in spring, and they lasted well into the burning July days. Could I ever forget the pages she would write and bring to me the next day at the Holiday Inn bar, where she would take refuge in a secluded corner away from the scrutiny of those who knew us, and how she came to me one day with those four pages that she read in a voice slightly above a whisper, a voice of sadness and longing, of desperation and rapture that seemed constantly threatened by a strange, mysterious, impending death. "I came to you a wild horse," she had read, her jet-black hair a veil separating us from the rest of the world so that we could see no one nor they see us, nor would they know what love, anguish, held us under its spell. Everything around us became an illusion, everyone a hallucination, because her face, her lips, had become the only reality, and her voice gave life to lines of poetry that bolted past like a wild horse leaping into a rocky abyss where death is sweet. Her lines told of palisades she had invaded, dark places where she had stumbled and tripped, burning coals she had walked on, screams that had filled her ears and were echoed back by ravines. That day, as her dark eyes welled up with tears, we talked about things I had talked to no one about before, but time ran out, the days ran out, and I kept most of what I had to say trapped inside my chest, unable to let it out except in her presence, to her. No one deserved to hear what I had to say except her, not because it was about her or related to her, although much of it was, but because to other ears the words would have gone to waste, without meaning, words more precious than to be scattered like dust in the wind.

It all came back to me that night, like lava that had for ages rumbled quietly inside a volcano and was now on the verge of eruption. I wasn't troubled by her denials because I didn't for once doubt that she was my crazy runaway mare whom the rocky abyss had almost torn apart but from which she had emerged unscathed, beautiful, even in a foreign land, in a city where she never thought she would be.

As the snow fell on us, she said, "I am Salwa. Salwa Ali Abd al-Rahman, as you could tell from the 'S' on my bag. You say I'm Sarab, whom you knew long ago, in another city. But the woman you see here, in this foreign city, you're seeing for the first time. I am Salwa, born in a Palestinian refugee camp in Jericho, in the Aqabat Jabr refugee camp. Even that miserable camp they thought too good for us, and so in 1967 when I was yet a child, they forced us to leave, pushing us from one hellish place to another. Our fate took us first to a camp in al-Zarqa, and from it we moved to Ayn al-Hilweh in Lebanon. I grew up in the camp and went to school there. The PLO[7] offered me a scholarship to continue my studies in Beirut, then America. I came back with a bachelor's degree from Syracuse University, and I refused to get married there because I wanted to go back to Amman to be as close as I could to Palestine. I've never been to your city. And here I am now, in Paris, in school again. Would you like to know how I ended up in Paris?"

I noticed that she'd been speaking with an authentic Palestinian accent all along, so I thought she was just being playful or acting silly, especially after having mixed with Palestinians for so long. But despite all that I tried to convince myself that her accent was not purely Palestinian, perhaps because I was determined to believe that she was the woman I knew. But I wouldn't let it worry me. If she insisted on playing games for whatever reason, because of a situation she was in or because of some strange affectation, then let her. There was so much I wanted to say to her. We'd have to spend the whole evening together, if I could convince her.

When I started doubting, even for a trifle, and fearing that she might really be the Salwa she claimed to be, I said to myself, "If she agrees to stay with me, she has to be Sarab." But she had to be Sarab whether she agreed or not. I was sure she would agree. During those few months in which our moments together were all that we lived for, our one wish had always been to stay up talking one whole night till sunrise, but it never happened. Now that we were in Paris—Paris of strangers—perhaps we could finally do the impossible, if only once.

Under the gentle, steady snow drizzle, we walked as though in a daze—my daze at least—first to the Pantheon. As we circled around it, lights mixed with the darkness in the distance ahead, adding to the feeling that I was walking with Sarab inside a dream. I was left with enough sense to be able to lead us back to the sloping street where I had started

7. *PLO:* Palestine Liberation Organization, a coordinating council of Palestinian nationalist organizations founded in 1964 by the leadership of Egypt and the Arab League. Initially controlled by the Egyptian government, the PLO soon came to be dominated by Fatah leader Yasir Arafat.

my walk, and I said to her, "I'll prove to you I'm not imagining as soon as we sit somewhere inside and talk. Please don't say you can't."

"Okay, where should we go? But I love being out in the snow. Look at it, so soft, so unreal, melting as if it never was."

"We'll walk until our shoulders turn white. There's an Italian restaurant near my hotel. I've gotten to know the owner. We'll have dinner there. What do you say?"

"I can't stay out very late. My roommate is waiting for me."

"Sarab, forget about her. I'll remind you of your poems, and you'll forget about everything else, even your friend."

"My poems? Ha! You've made me into a poet too! Let's get it straight, I'm not Salwa Ali Abd al-Rahman from Palestine, but Sarab. Sarab who? Sarab Hassan?"

In all seriousness, I corrected her. "Sarab Affan."

"Okay. So I'm Sarab Affan, a poet. And you're not a stranger. And you won't tell me your name because, of course, I know it very well. Tell me, did you love this Sarab?"

"Make fun as you like, my runaway, bolting mare . . ."

She stopped and stood facing me in the darkness mixed with snow, staring into my eyes for the first time. My God! It was her! That was her way of making sure. But then she said, slowly, "You're either a little crazy, or you're making all this up to make me stay, and God knows why I've come along with you this far."

I held her arms, dusting the snowflakes off her sleeves. "Because you know you're Sarab, as much as you try to deny it. You're just putting on an act to tease me."

She burst out laughing, shaking her head with the headscarf wrapped around it and pushing my hands away from hers. "Fine, fine. Where's your Italian restaurant?"

"It's very close, a stone's throw away."

"I want to go somewhere farther away."

"We'll walk till you get tired, Sarab . . ."

"Salwa, please."

This time I stopped and stood facing her, looking her in the eyes. "Please, would you take off your glasses."

Gracefully, she held her glasses between her fingers and took them off, saying, "You won't see much of me in this light."

At that moment I lost my mind. All that had built up inside me after months of waiting, confusion, and lovesickness erupted all at once, and I grabbed her with the force of lightning before she could resist, and I kissed her on the lips. Sarab! Could I ever forget these lips?

She didn't resist at first but then pushed me away with unconvincing anger. "What right, what right do you have to do this?" she said and put her glasses back on.

"I have no right, except . . ."

"Fine, fine."

She pulled me by my arm and quickened her pace, leading me down the street to Rue des Écoles.

I was afraid she would leave me there, but despite her silence as I spoke, as I rambled on senselessly, she kept listening to me, clinging unto me as the snow caressed our faces, until we reached the small restaurant and were greeted by its owner, who seated us at a table close to the heat coming from the open oven used for baking pizza.

Sarab took her coat off and set it on a chair next to her with the rest of her belongings. She took off her glasses and said jokingly, bringing her face closer to mine, "Now, take a closer look. Am I Sarab?"

I shrieked, then quickly lowered my voice as I became aware of my sudden outburst. "God! You're none other!"

She shook her head while loosening her wet scarf and let her hair down across her face and shoulders. "How about the way I talk, my accent, my being Palestinian?"

"Whether you're Palestinian, a rock in Jerusalem, an olive tree in Nablus, you're still Sarab Affan. Do you understand?"

The waiter came, and we ordered pizza and red wine. He wasted no time bringing the wine.

And then she said, "Why don't we change the subject, please? Would you like to hear about my studies? But first, tell me what you do. Talk to me about anything you like. Salwa Ali Abd al-Rahman is all ears."

I poured us both some wine and remembered the words to the

poem she had stirred my emotions with one day about three years ago. I gazed into her wide eyes, reciting, "I came to you a wild horse bearing nature's tattoos, on a path traced by the fingers of a Babylonian fortuneteller. . . . What age have we entered together? What sea?"

Her eyes welled up with tears, and she threw her hands up in the air between us. "Please, enough, enough," she said in an agonized whisper, choking on her sobs.

I was silent.

I reached for my glass and said, "Let's drink to . . . the Paris snow."

We talked about everything, except for what we were both in.

•   •   •

She asked me after dinner, "How long are you staying here?"

"Three or four days," I said. "May I have your phone number?"

"Write it down," she said.

I gave her a card with my hotel address and phone number, and I jotted down the number she gave me in my pocket book. She told me she was sharing a phone with a friend and a Moroccan family from whom they were renting their apartment, located on a street near the Gare du Nord, the North Station.

"Won't you stay with me tonight?" I ventured asking.

She wasn't surprised, but she replied as though the Sarab-Salwa mystery had been solved in her favor. "No, no. No way. How could I? Call me tomorrow. How about walking me to the Metro?"

"Would I be walking with Salwa or Sarab?"

"Whichever one you like!"

I gave up, imagining myself with a woman who was suffering from memory loss or split personality. I couldn't understand why she was making me suffer like that. I had nothing to say.

We walked toward the nearby Metro on Boulevard Saint-Germain. I accompanied her all the way down into the Metro tunnel, through the gates, and into the waiting area, where I hugged and kissed her with my old uncontrollable madness, overpowered by the feeling that I was embracing an illusion that had taken total hold of me and was only adding to my suffering every time it gave in to me for a few instants.

She withdrew from my arms gently, took a few steps back, then slipped through the revolving doors. My eyes followed her as she walked away in her usual style, a mixture of the swaying of gazelles and the flowing of waterfalls. She turned around one last time and waved to me, smiling in a way that ripped my heart in a thousand pieces from the joy and pain of having found and not found her at the same time.

She appeared from the distance to have tears in her eyes.

I went back to my room at the hotel. God only knows how I was able to find my way back. I tried to distract myself by watching television, to no avail. I tried reading, but I couldn't. Around midnight, I decided to call her, thinking she'd be back in her apartment by then.

I dialed the number she had given me. A man answered in French. I spoke in Arabic, knowing that the residents were Moroccan, "May I please speak with Miss Sar . . . Salwa Ali Abd al-Rahman?"

"Salwa? Salwa moved out more than two months ago."

I decided to try the impossible, so I asked, "Miss Sarab, is she there?"

"Sarab left with her too," he replied, not at all surprised.

"Sarab Affan?" I stressed.

"Yes, Sarab Affan."

"Did she leave a new phone number?"

"No, I'm sorry. I'm very sorry. It's a pity they had to leave. I think they moved to the Latin neighborhood, somewhere near the Sorbonne, because Sarab is getting her doctorate there."

I knew she was studying at the Sorbonne, but why for heaven's sake had she taken on her friend's identity? "Are you sure that Sarab is the one studying . . . ?" I asked insistently.

"I'm sure," he interrupted firmly. "We threw a graduation party for Salwa the Palestinian lady last year. But when Sarab got married . . ."

"You mean Salwa?"

"No, sir. Sarab. After she got married to Salwa's brother . . ."

I was thunderstruck. I couldn't concentrate on the rest of his jabber. I could hardly even hold the telephone receiver anymore. My hands—my whole body—were shaking. "Thank you, thank you," I interrupted somewhat rudely. "I'm sorry I disturbed you at such a late hour." But then I added, trying to control the tremors in my voice, "If you hear from Madame Sarab, please tell her I asked about her."

"Your name please?"

"She knows my name, very well."

I hung up.

The walls of my room seemed to be closing in on me, threatening to fall on top of my head. I put my coat and scarf back on, ran downstairs to the hotel lobby and handed my room keys to the receptionist. "It's cold tonight, very cold, sir," he said courteously.

I went outside. The snow was still falling lightly. I found myself walking toward the Seine. I crossed the bridge to the opposite bank, to the Théâtre du Châtelet, hoping that the loud noises coming from inside, which usually went on until morning, would drown the noises in my head. The night, the men, the women, all appeared like tattered rags scattered around me as far as my eyes could see.

◆   ◆   ◆

I got back to the hotel exhausted around five in the morning. The receptionist handed me my room keys and two written messages. "A lady called you twice. She didn't leave her name."

The first message said: *phone call at 2:15 A.M.,* and the second: *phone call at 3:05 A.M.*

Exhausted, I gave no importance to the messages despite their odd timing. Anyway, I wasn't in the mood to talk to anyone, lady or not. I took off my clothes and slipped under the bed covers, hoping to sink into a deep slumber that would last fifty years, or longer.

I woke up grumbling to the incessant, annoying rings of the telephone next to my head. I felt as though I'd slept no more than five minutes, but the sunlight had already seeped in through the cracks in the curtains, which I hadn't shut all the way. I looked at my watch. It was ten o'clock. I reached feebly for the receiver. "Hello, yes?" I said in a voice that sounded strange even to me, too ugly and gruff.

"Ah, back in your room finally!"

The voice stung me like a snake. I jumped out of bed in disbelief. "Who's speaking?"

"Who's the woman you'd like to be speaking to the most, first thing in the morning?"

"Oh, my God!"

"You're making me angry, Nael! Were two and a half years enough to make you forget my voice? I thought thirty years wouldn't be enough."

"Not even thirty times thirty! What got into you last night?"

"I called you twice after midnight but couldn't find you. I guess you were having fun in the Paris bars?"

"Fun? If only you knew!"

"I couldn't sleep all night."

"That serves you right! Listen, I have to see you today, if only for an hour. I have to. What were you thinking, giving me a useless number?"

"Useless?"

"Okay, I get it. You're married now. But I have to see you today anyway. I won't be in Paris much longer. Should I come and see you?"

"I'll be at the hotel in an hour. The address is on the card you gave me."

"We'll have our last coffee together?"

"Nael, please, don't make me feel bad."

In the brief silence that followed before she hung up, I thought I heard faint sobs.

I got out of bed and shaved hastily before taking a hot shower, which helped invigorate me and lift my spirit. I had just finished having coffee and a croissant when she arrived at the restaurant.

We walked out unto the steps of the hotel entrance. It was cold and sunny. I ran a little ahead of her then turned around, looking at her like a painter getting a full view of his subject so that in one glance and in the light of day I could absorb as much of Sarab as I could: her body; her presence; her face, which from the cold had acquired the same rosy color as her lips—she rarely rouged her lips, knowing that I loved their natural redness, like the petals of a rose freshly picked, still covered with morning dew; her hair, partially disheveled on purpose to give it a distinct look; her blue, buttonless coat, open all the way to reveal a black woolen turtleneck sweater emphasizing the roundedness of her breasts;

her dark indigo skirt, flowing around her knees; her black boots, reaching slightly above the ankles and revealing some of the white wool lining at the top, making her appear taller and adding to her delicate, beautiful balance. She was carrying a bag woven out of black wool.

She said in her typical way, laughing, "As if you are seeing me for the first time!"

And as usual, I replied, "Every time I see you is like the first time." We locked our arms together and shot forth to the street. "People will think I'm in the company of a famous movie star, not a freedom fighter ready to die for her nation," I said.

"You might change your mind if you saw me on a normal day. Anyway, disguise is necessary at all times, no matter how."

"I'm happy to go along, as long as you stay who you are, beautiful and . . ."

"Crazy?"

"Driving others crazy, more like it!"

I repeated my question. "What got into you yesterday?"

"I tried something I doubted I could pull off, and indeed I couldn't. How could I, with you?"

"You mean you were hoping to get rid of me?"

"As part of an old plan. I had already collected all my papers at the library and was about to get up and leave when I saw you talking to the man at the desk. During all my months of suffering, I kept reminding myself that I might some day run into you and that I'd be thunderstruck and would collapse, losing all self-control, and so I'd have to keep calm and run, somehow. But at that moment I was quick enough to find a chair where I could sit facing the other direction, hoping that you wouldn't find me among all the people, and all would be fine. I found a nearby chair and sat down right away, spreading my papers on the table. I was hoping you'd sit far enough not to see me. I didn't think you'd recognize me, one among a hundred other women."

"And in a place where the last person I expected to see was Sarab. But you were wrong. Don't you know that even if you'd been on the tenth floor of that building I would have found you without even intending to? What is it that drew me to the library in the first place, when

I never even expected you'd be in Paris? Although your act failed, you managed to convince me for a few moments that I was really talking to a stranger, and you did it with such shameless persistence."

"I failed because I got scared all of a sudden that you'd apologize and leave. I weakened. I felt a sudden urge to throw myself on your chest. At that moment I was happy to fail because with you failure is pleasant, honest."

"You failed on your terms, of course. What would your friend Randa al-Jouzy have said about you, once again abandoning reason and principle?"

"Randa? I'll tell her everything. When was the last time you talked to her?"

"Three or four days before you left. She never called me after that, not once, the traitor."

Sarab laughed. "Because she too came to Paris, and got me into all this."

"Got you into all this?"

"I mean, marriage, or more precisely, staying out of marriage."

"Back to your riddles?"

"My great writer, man of the mirrors, isn't life a series of riddles?"

We walked into a small café and sat at a table by the window. It was very warm inside. In her usual way, Sarab pulled her arms out of her coat sleeves and kept the coat hanging over her shoulders after sitting down. I observed her: the hair once again falling over her face and back; the shoulders and arms I was craving to hold; her breasts rising and falling with each breath under her tight sweater until they settled in what seemed like a position of defiance against a man intruding upon a woman who was married perhaps; and finally the hands, stretched out comfortably on the table, ready for the cigarette I would offer. As she puffed out on her cigarette with her luscious lips, and me still noticing her slightest sound and gesture, she started laughing. Surprised, I said to myself, "I thought she would cry, but she's laughing!" I noticed her sparkling teeth as she said in her cunning, tantalizing way, "What did Shakespeare say about life? Life is but a big stage, and we the actors, or something like that. Didn't he also say that life is one big paradox?"

"I don't know. You're the one who studied theater."

"And who is it that said the biggest of all paradoxes is that truth is uncovered by concealing it?"

The waiter came and we ordered two espressos. "Do you know what I'm writing my dissertation on?" said Sarab. "French drama and its influence on the Arab theater in the twentieth century."

"Wonderful. But let's go back to your little paradox, before we talk about life's greater paradoxes. Are you married or not?"

"Ask Randa al-Jouzy!"

"That man from the Moroccan home where you stayed, he told me. You made sure I called them to save yourself the pain of explaining?"

"I'm not married."

"You got married then divorced? So quickly?"

"Neither. It had to do with Yahya Abu Saad, not me."

"I don't understand."

"Yahya Abu Saad, the man we pretended was the brother of Salwa, my comrade in the organization and also my roommate at the Moroccan home."

"You misled that nice family too?"

"We were just trying to make it easier for Yahya to get around, and eventually escape. He's back in Jerusalem now. Salwa and I moved out, and we don't need to lie about marriage anymore."

"I don't see the reason for all these complications, perhaps they're a necessary part of the struggle in a foreign country. Anyway, what I want to know is, are you really?"

"Nael! Don't you believe me?"

"Am I not also a victim of this mysterious game of yours? Am I not being misled too?"

She pursed her lips and frowned, and she looked into my eyes, jestingly, seriously, reeling me along endlessly with her mind games, at once pleasant and teasing, while I waited for her reply. Then she said, "Me misleading you? I might mislead you a little, because I have to, perhaps to keep you in love with me or perhaps because I want you to be always searching for me or something that has to do with me, no matter what doubts you might have along the way, and this way I'll always be in your mind and thoughts. Am I being selfish? If I told you for example that Randa al-Jouzy is a fiction, would you be angry with me? Well, save yourself the guessing. I am Randa al-Jouzy, as much as I am Sarab Affan. By misleading you the way I did, I got to love you twice, once as Sarab, once as Randa—once as a lover, once as an intruder. Did it never cross your mind back then that every time Randa called you, she could have been me?"

I held her hands and started kissing her like a lunatic, in front of people in the café and passersby outside, kissing her fingers, her palms, the back of her palms. I felt a burning desire to squeeze her to my chest, and she laughed and laughed and said, "Nael, quit it. Quit it. There are people around . . ."

I felt that Sarab had at last come back to me, in body, in spirit, with all her contradictions. She had come back to the only man who understood her to the core, and yet didn't understand her, who loved her anyway. All the conversations, the arguments, the questions, the answers, the body gestures that followed, were but part of my endless Sufi trance. We went to a Greek restaurant on a street that branched off Boulevard Saint Michel. As we sat facing each other at a table in a dimly lit corner and ate barbecued meat and drank red wine, I felt as though we were having a meal in paradise. I mentioned al-Tayyib al-Hadi and our ruminations about the first paradise and the last. I also gave her his phone number in case she needed to call him one day, and I called him later to tell him that I had found her and that our conversation-filled "walks" would have to wait until another meeting. She was surprised when I asked her about her money situation. I was amazed how much more expensive Paris had become compared to only a few years back. I was relieved to know she had told her father about her situation and he had arranged to send her money regularly from a London account to cover her school and living expenses. "I never knew my father made so much money! You would have made more money as a surgeon, don't you think?" she said.

"Come back home with me, and you'll know."

"Some day," she said in her typical way, reeling me along craftily.

When I repeated the invitation, she said, "Do you want me to go back to compulsion, blindness, and this accursed individualism in everything, the affliction of all Arabs? I'm here in the heart of everything now, and living life the way I like. What I've committed myself to is my life now. I hold it sacred and cannot talk about it, to protect it and protect myself, even though it makes me abandon even the ones I love. You either have to stay underground or else get exposed and humiliated in two days. And in the end everything I'm doing pours into the Intifada[8] itself, the Revolution of Stones, the revolution that has baffled the world. Even the revolt of Spartacus does not measure up to it in courage, nobleness, and sacrifice. From this day on, no matter where a revolt takes place against oppression, the Revolution of Stones will be the example to be followed in fighting the oppressors. . . . Do you remember our conversations back then about the accursed siege and the search for salvation? Do you remember the writings I used to show you? Do you remember our adventures inside your mirrors? I am breaking the siege and setting myself free, every day. And I write. I write a lot, and I don't need to put the scissors today to what I wrote yesterday, as I used to do every day, fearing some ignorant, unknown reader. If only you knew about the pages upon pages of the journals I tore up, fearing that they might fall in the hands of other people, in the hands of ghouls lurking in every corner and in the entrance to every house."

"You have so much love to give, so much love, and that makes me love you even more," I said with pride and admiration, but also with sadness and defeat. "And of course, I am the only loser in all of this, because I have to live far from you. I'll go on worrying about you, every day, each moment. I'm worried that in this country you might sooner or later fall victim to a different kind of devastating siege that you might not be aware of right now."

"When it happens, will you still be there for me?"

I held her hand across the table and pressed on her fingers, replying

---

8. *Intifada:* the first of two Palestinian intifadas, or uprisings, aimed at ending Israeli military occupation. It began in 1987 and ended with the signing of the Oslo Accords in 1993. A common means of protest was rock throwing, and thus the references to "war of stones" and "revolution of stones."

the same way she usually did, "Who knows, who knows? I just hope that I won't have to spend all my money and that of Dr. Ali Affan trying to save you from the French police and courts, although I won't hesitate a minute."

Then she said, "My journals, my writings, you haven't read all of them yet. I'll show them to you one day, perhaps when I'm done with my studies here and carrying out two or three missions. Remember though, I don't want them published!"

"Your love journals, or your other journals?" I asked.

She laughed. "Am I any less important than Mona Issawi, your pagan sorceress? Any likeness that you might find between my language and yours is pure coincidence!"

That evening I talked to her about visions I could have only shared with her, because whether absent or present, she was the one who had inspired and shaped them. She poured her love on me, a torrent of thoughts and feelings, and kept saying she was trying to let out part of what had gathered up inside her—love, joy, death—gathered up in her head, her soul, defying words and explanation. "Don't you see what it means for me to love you this way and to go on being who I am and what I am at the same time, free of contradictions?

"In our sorrows and fears, our daily ordeals and tragic expectations, I'm like one searching for a lost melody, some hidden music that would reconcile me with our sorrows and tragedies. But how can we reconcile ourselves with pain unless we overcome it through action? I'm searching for that music of incredible, deafening proportions that transports us to a place where we still carry the burdens of the world yet by some miracle we're able to soar freely in space, free of any plan or goal, and all plans and goals can go to hell . . .

"Can't you see, Nael, I've decided I would only face death with my full volition, when I'm still fully in control of my mental and physical faculties?

"I wish the body were pure mental energy, unbounded, weightless, a thought that rises up like fireworks, then disappears, then comes back, then disappears again. . . . I wish existence would transform into pure motion like that of a cloud being pushed by high winds until it builds up with moisture and turns into rain, then builds up and dissipates into rain again. . . . And thus *being* and *nothingness* would become one, inseparable, somehow . . ."

She paused, moistening her lips with her tongue, feeling their succulence, then she asked, her eyes wandering, "What does it mean to *be*? Nael, to *be* is to be with your senses, your desires, as we *are* this moment. To *be* in our pain and struggles against death, against getting killed, as we *are* all the time. . . . To *be* inside a whirlwind of perpetual illusions in the heart of the moment, the moment with all its truths and painful demands. . . . To be inside a storm of thundering noises coming at you from every direction, noises that rise to a peak of violence then fall into a sudden silence of unconsciousness and death. . . . Oh, Nael, *being* and *nothingness* are forever inseparable, forever one, like the impossible . . ."

Our storm went on for three days and nights. I hoped time would stop right then because life would never again be as abundant with pleasure and the ardor of love. We finally took a taxi to Orly airport. There too we said many words, some we meant and others we didn't— explanations, promises, wishes. . . . And Sarab would at times shine like a faraway, unreachable star, and at others like a burning coal, but always slipping away like that quicksilver I'd become used to, taking pleasure in losing it and getting it back.

When we said our farewells, her tears flowed. The taste of salt from her rosy cheeks stayed on my lips. In the airplane, I fastened my seatbelt and refrained from smoking a cigarette I so much wanted to smoke, and I asked myself: will I ever see her in Paris again? Is the phone number she gave me without an address for real this time? Is she really a student at the Sorbonne? Is she really single? What is she really doing in an organization she refuses to discuss except through vague hints and allusions? I will know once I read the journals she promised me, if she makes good on her promise that is.

But none of that mattered anymore. All that mattered to me was knowing she was there—wherever, whenever. I would reach out to her with my arms, and if I could hold her, I'd be the happiest of lovers, and if she got away, I'd continue living in the hope of a next embrace as soothing as a waterfall on a cold morning, as hot as the midday sun on a July day, like the days of our first meeting.

And Siham goes on gazing at me with her marble bust when I wake up every morning and go to bed at night, smiling, questioning, grieving, waiting for an answer she can understand. But all I'm able to do is avoid her, apologizing, because the answer, any answer, would have to be long and difficult, full of excuses, and most likely in the end, unnecessary.

AFTERWORD

Ghassan Nasr

The opening lines of Sarab's journals suggest a very secular, almost desperate, struggle for survival. A strong sense of an abandoned, oppressive world abides—the world of the exile articulated by Jabra Ibrahim Jabra in his other writings, from his first novel *Hunters in a Narrow Street* (written in English, 1960)—a world that can be overcome only through mastering the skills of finding a "home in the running," which requires constant innovation, resourcefulness, and in which the only rule, as Sarab states, is that of "hit and run." It is a world in which the exile, the hostage, the refugee, must innovate, must employ his creative powers, at every turn must refine the instinct for identifying the enemy because when the thing being confronted "is not defined, and like the air all around us everywhere usually it is not, there is no other recourse but trickery, disguise, circumvention, no other recourse but to follow the rule of 'hit and run,' dodge, only to hit again" (chapter 1). Imitation carries the risk of being vanquished, squashed. One cannot help but feel that Jabra the artist is also speaking here: to become mired in any ideology, in any system of rhetoric, in any agenda, is to be "committed," to risk missing the opportunities and losing the struggle. With these powerful words, Sarab launches full force into the discourse on exile and salvation.

The last two novels Jabra Ibrahim Jabra published before his death (in 1994), *In Search of Walid Masoud* (1978, translation published by Syracuse University Press in 2000) and *The Journals of Sarab Affan* (1992), both employ the device of the vanishing character. Walid Masoud and Sarab Affan both disappear, and in both cases Jabra has elevated the drama of loss and the quest for salvation to new heights by playing on two competing forces. On one hand, the disappearance of the hero and the prospect in both cases that the disappearance has meant joining an underground movement for the liberation of Palestine offers a secular redemption. At the same time, considering that for Jabra's protagonists it is often a verbal presence that determines their identity, in a struggle against the threat of extinction through language, the hero's disappearance, even if it is cause of liberation, results in an absence, a defeat, on the stage of words. This is at the heart of dramatic tension in Jabra's last two novels, and both Walid Masoud and Sarab Affan offer fascinating variations on this theme.

Jabra was a flexible stylist with a variety of styles. His memoir, *Princesses' Street* (2005), is a model of sustained, conversational exposition of a single growing artistic perception. In his novels, however, Jabra privileges the multiple first-person narrative technique, which serves to heighten the drama of his characters' search for identity. Each character must speak, because words are action, and action is redemption. The multiple first-person narrative allows for a complex layering of voices. By giving each character his or her own narrative voice, Jabra not only creates a complex web of interacting voices but adds another layer of conversation, that between each character and the reader. The privileged character-to-reader relationship is used to its fullest in *The Journals*. Sarab Affan discloses to the reader part of her plan to join an underground Palestinian liberation movement while denying part of this knowledge to Nael Imran. In a narrative twist, Sarab disappears, as she has promised us, but she also disappears as a narrator, leaving the final narration to Nael Imran. In *The Journals,* the disappearance of the narrator, not only from the stage of the story but also from the stage of the narration, adds yet another level to the Palestinian drama of loss and redemption. *In Search of Walid Masoud* employs a different strategy: there the narration is truly circular. Although Walid Masoud has already disappeared at the beginning of the narration, never to return, the narrative begins and ends with the first-person voice of Jawad Husni, the archetypal chronicler of the events surrounding the mystery of the disappearance, a Sherlock Holmes, the assembler and organizer of all the verbal testaments concerning his life and tragedy.

The preoccupation in Jabra's novels with a quest for redemption in a fractured world, the world of the exile and the outcast, reaches a particular intensity in the character of Sarab in *The Journals.* The translator had to grapple, among other things, with the question of rendering two recurrent motifs suggested by the Arabic terms *khalas* and *hisar* that appear repeatedly and persistently in the novel, in their various syntactic and morphological variants, but always in association with Sarab, and always together as an inextricable pair within the same paragraph or page. In fact, the two words appear in the very first line of the journal, *kana la budda laha an takhlus bi-shaklin ma, fal-hisar yashtadd.* The sentence opens up various possibilities, each suggesting a subtle interpretation: (1) She had to be saved [*an takhlus*] somehow, for the siege [*al-hisar*] was tightening; (2) She would save herself, for the siege was tightening; (3) She must escape, for the siege was tightening; or (4) She must rescue herself, for the siege was tightening.

The pivotal word in the sentence is the intransitive Arabic verb *takhlus,* from *kh-l-s,* meaning "to be completed" or "to be saved." But *takhlus* is an active verb that does not take an object and can therefore have a passive sense. It belongs to a category of active verbs such as *da'a,* which means "to be lost" or "to become lost." The active and passive meanings are not always clearly distinguishable. The translator faces the task of reflecting that ambiguity when finding an English equivalent. The choice is between "be saved" and "save herself." The active meaning, "save herself," can also leave the translator with the choice of "escape" or "rescue herself." These two competing interpretations, the active and the passive forms, posit two potentially different kinds of salvation: One is voluntary and within her control (corresponding to "save herself," "escape"), while the other depends largely on external mediation (corresponding to "be saved"), which might present the translator with the possibility of a religious understanding of salvation involving divine agency.

Except for the opening line, "save" appears exclusively as its noun derivative *khalas,* or salvation, throughout the rest of the novel. But it is also observed, interestingly, that the words *salvation* and *siege* often appear together in the same passages, and sometimes in the same sentence. The two words become almost inextricable. Even when one appears without the other, a link has already been established between the two words in the opening line of the novel, whereby the attainment of salvation necessarily entails the breaking of the siege, and, conversely, the breaking of the siege is motivated by the yearning for a landscape beyond the circle of the siege, the place of salvation, whether imaginary or not. The two words come to form a sort of discourse, a poetics of exile and entrapment.

Jabra has set an intimidating example as a respected translator from English into Arabic (of Frazer's *Golden Bough,* Faulkner's *The Sound and the Fury,* or Shakespeare's *Hamlet, Coriolanus, Othello, Macbeth, King Lear,* and *The Tempest*).

> For to translate Shakespeare properly one cannot approach him merely with the skill of an interpreter or tenacity of a linguist. Only as a writer intent on a creative act, impelled by love or the passion of a humanist, or even the intensity of a man in agony, can one really get anywhere near him, round him. In the process one cannot help a secret empathy taking place, a tacit identification . . . (Jabra, *A Celebration of Life,* 148)

I would be pleased if something comparable had taken place in this version of *The Journals of Sarab Affan.*

References

Jabra, Jabra Ibrahim. *Princesses' Street: Baghdad Memories.* Trans. Issa Boullata. Fayetteville: University of Arkansas Press, 2005.

———. *Hunters in a Narrow Street.* Boulder: Lynne Rienner Publishers, 1997.

———. *The Ship.* Trans. Adnan Haydar and Roger Allen. Washington, D.C.: Three Continents Press, 1985.

———. *In Search of Walid Masoud.* Trans. Adnan Haydar and Roger Allen. Syracuse: Syracuse University Press, 2000.

———. *A Celebration of Life: Essays on Literature and Art.* Baghdad: Al-Ma'mun, 1988.

Said, Edward W. *Reflections on Exile and Other Essays.* Cambridge: Harvard University Press, 2001.